THE QUESTION OF DESIRE

"Joe. What if I said I don't want to? Not yet?" Tina asked him, even as she let him strip the bathing suit from her.

He lay against her, his tongue coming away from her nipple, his breath stirring on her skin, and his hand cupping her face as it had done before in the penthouse pool, when there had been such tenderness in his eyes that she'd been defenseless, the same tenderness that she could feel in his hand now. Was this the answer? She just had to say no, and he'd leave her alone, right?

Wrong.

He was a fully aroused male, hard against her. She knew that if she kept on saying no, he'd have to rape her, that was all. And even if she began screaming while he raped her, clawing at her and drawing blood and ripping into her in a frenzy of rage at her denial of him, no one would hear. No one who cared.

"Then we won't," he said.

∅

Great Reading from SIGNET

THE PENTHOUSE

ELLESTON TREVOR

Ⓢ

A SIGNET BOOK

NEW AMERICAN LIBRARY

TIMES MIRROR

Publisher's Note

This novel is a work of fiction. Names, characters, places, and incidents are either the product of the author's imagination or are used fictitiously, and any resemblance to actual persons, living or dead, events, or locales is entirely coincidental.

Copyright © 1983 by Trevor Enterprises, Inc.

SIGNET TRADEMARK REG. U.S. PAT. OFF. AND FOREIGN COUNTRIES
REGISTERED TRADEMARK—MARCA REGISTRADA
HECHO EN CHICAGO, U.S.A.

SIGNET, SIGNET CLASSICS, MENTOR, PLUME, MERIDIAN AND NAL BOOKS are published by The New American Library, Inc., 1633 Broadway, New York, New York 10019

First Printing, August, 1983

1 2 3 4 5 6 7 8 9

PRINTED IN THE UNITED STATES OF AMERICA

To
Rusty Hawkins

1

THERE WERE NINETEEN PEOPLE WAITING in the VIP lounge at Kennedy Airport when TWA Flight 343 came in from Rome, and four of them were there to meet the young woman with the camel-hair coat and dark glasses. One of them, her secretary, went forward and greeted her while the three men in their dark blue suits held back; then the whole party moved at a steady pace through the lobby towards the escalators, looking at no one.

A group of reporters was moving towards the doors of the lounge; one of them, catching sight of the young woman in the dark glasses, turned and trotted back towards the escalators and turned again, for an instant freezing the famous cheekbones and the long sensual mouth in the flash from his camera; as he shuffled backwards to correct the distance for another shot, two of the men in blue suits broke away from the party and made straight for him, but he saw them coming, and vanished among the crowd.

Outside, walking to the helicopter, Tina St. Clair stopped for a moment to look around at the lights glowing in the dusk; the sound of their polished shoes faded as the group halted, leaving only the rumble of the skycap's trolley as he kept on going.

"My God, it's good to be back in civilization."

Her secretary watched her, worried. "Was it very bad?"

"I was frightened to death."

"Do you want an appointment with Dr. Beinnen?"

"No. I don't need a shrink. I just need to be alone for a while, and play some music." She took Marlene's arm and they walked on again.

"You really think that's best?" It was what Tina had done three years ago, after her closest friend had hit a tree on the slopes at Aspen; as soon as the funeral was over she'd shut herself up in a mountain cabin with a stereo and a dozen albums, nothing but Brahms and Grieg, for two whole weeks. Dr. Beinnen had said it was a mistake. "You don't think you should see Dr. Beinnen?"

"No. Nobody."

The skycap was stowing the baggage on board the helicopter.

"You don't want me to tell anyone you're back?"

"Not anyone." She longed for privacy, and wished Marlene wouldn't fuss.

"We'll need to call—"

"How is everything with you, Marlene? Is your mother okay now?"

"She's fine. Everything's fine."

They climbed into the helicopter.

It was almost like an evening in summer, instead of late October; the air was perfectly still, and the noon temperature had been eighty-four degrees. As the limousine left the Midtown Heliport and turned north along First Avenue it passed joggers in shorts and T-shirts, and later, along Fifty-seventh Street, there were people window-shopping in the mild air, and children playing on the sidewalks, already in Halloween masks.

At Park Tower the three men got out of the limousine first, and the chauffeur helped them with the baggage as the doorman received the two women and escorted them along the carpet under the marquee.

"Did you get the instructions?" Marlene asked him.

"From Mr. Lindquist, yes. No one's to know that Miss St. Clair is here."

"Absolutely no one."

"That's perfectly understood." His tone was cool now; he'd had the instructions from the owner and resident of the fifty-third floor himself, and they didn't need repeating by the secretary of a guest. He left her to have a word with the security guard, then saw the baggage into the elevator and left Mr. Lindquist's chauffeur to take the party up.

This was at just after six o'clock. Ten minutes later, Tina St. Clair was alone in the penthouse at the top of the building, standing at a window with a drink in her hand and her green eyes reflecting the lights of Manhattan.

The young man with the pale hair dropped the eight-by-ten glossy onto his editor's desk.

"Who's this?" the editor asked. "Tina?"

"Right."

"Where did you take it?"

"Kennedy."

"Tonight?"

"Coming in from Rome."

"Surprise," the editor said. The last thing they'd got on the wire about St. Tina, three days ago, she'd got mixed up in some riots in Calcutta.

"From Rome, you said?"

"That's right."

"Anyone with her?"

"The usual riffraff."

"We might even print it."

"It's exclusive, for Christ's sake."

"And it's Tina. Could be you got a deal."

* * *

They weren't at their house in Connecticut, or at their suite at the Waldorf; she finally tracked them down in Dorado Beach.

"Mother?"

"Who is that?"

It was a terrible line; it had taken half an hour to get a connection.

"Wait a minute." She went across and turned down the stereo. "Mother, can you hear me all right? This is Tina."

"Tina! Where are you?"

"Back in New York."

"In New York!" Mother always repeated everything and then left a silence while she went to fetch Daddy. She waited patiently, feeling glad they were in Puerto Rico; if they'd been in New York she would have had a hard time making them understand that she didn't want to see anyone for a few days, even them. After what had happened in Calcutta she just felt drained, emptied by the terror that had gone through her as the mobs had flowed along the narrow streets, breaking like waves against the cars and the bullock carts and overturning them, while she'd tried to outrace them, plunging into the fetid alleyways and finding them blocked, turning back and facing the mainstream of the rioters and running for her life until she'd reached the shelter of the mosque. It would need Brahms and Grieg to drive out the memory.

"Sweetheart." Her father's voice came on the line, giving her immediate strength.

"Daddy-O!"

"Are you all right?"

"Of course! This trip I was in luck—I found fifty bales of raw silk for Marcus, and half a ton of hand-woven silver lamé for anyone who wants it—can you imagine?

And you should have seen the tapestries!'' She stopped suddenly: her voice had been too shrill, too false.

"Where are you, Tina?'' his quiet voice came.

"At Park Tower.''

"With Tom?''

"No, he's still in Hong Kong. I called him from Rome, and told him I needed to hide up somewhere. He sent his chauffeur to meet me, with the keys.''

"You're alone?''

"It's what I need, Daddy-O.'' She didn't have to explain; he wouldn't crowd her. But Mother would be a problem.

"She wants you to take the first plane,'' he said, as if she'd been thinking aloud.

"Tell her I'm fine. Don't let her worry.''

"I don't think I can fool her that easily.''

"But Daddy, I'm really okay. It was just—''

"Tina, darling!'' It was her mother again, on an extension. "We're catching the first plane to New York, of course. You must be—''

"Mother, please listen.'' It took ten minutes or more, and a lot of patience. Tina hated fuss, of any kind, from anyone; perhaps she learned to hate it as a child, when everyone had fussed, and been paid to fuss. "I'll get on a plane myself,'' she told her mother, "in a couple of days, and see you in Dorado.'' She even thought she might do that, as soon as her earth-mother city of New York had reclaimed her soul and given her peace again. As she went on talking persuasively, she was suddenly presented with the awesome sight of the moon's rim cutting an arc of light across the rectangular skyline in the east; and her voice became hushed, so that Mother asked at once what the matter was, and this too had to be explained.

Then at last it was over, and the concession made: she would fly out to see them for Halloween, in three days' time; and until then they would promise not to worry.

Lowering the telephone, she went across to turn the stereo up again, and with the sonorous tones of the *Song of Fate* filling the room she watched the huge disk of the moon break free of the city, to float unencumbered in the dome of night.

———— 2 ————

JOE HIT THE BUTTON ON the power climber and brought the stage down from the davits, stopping it at the windows and pulling the brush out of the bucket, the faint smell of the trisodium phosphate adrift on the morning air. The stage didn't have any sway to it; this building had mullion guides, and he hadn't even connected the gotcha to the safety rope: he liked feeling free to move around.

It was a fantastic building. All glass. It was the first time they'd got a contract for this one; they'd found Marvin hopping around the office ten days ago, a big white grin under his big black mustache—"Hey, fellers, ask me what we got?"

"What've we got?" they'd asked him.

"We got Park Tower!"

"On Fifty-sixth?"

"You're damn right, on Fifty-sixth! And we do it next, after the Mercury!"

They'd celebrated the same night, over at Mike's place. Park Tower was brand-new and fifty-three stories and all glass—a bonanza. They'd all gone home smashed.

Now he was here, fanning the squeegee on the east face, getting to know the building. They were all different; each had its own special character, and you had to learn how free the mullions ran, and what the wind did when it hit the face, and what kind of voice it had, depending on

13

whether the street below was full of traffic with an intersection or whether you found yourself over a park or a playground. It was like learning about a new woman.

"They have to be the highest-rental apartments in the whole of this fuckin' city," Marvin had told them. "You're goin' to see some things up there, you're goin' to see some people!"

But of course all the drapes were drawn. The management knew when you were coming, and the doorman was told to let every resident know, and the word went out: beware window cleaners! That was okay. Who the hell wanted to be a goldfish? Joe didn't want to look in at their private lives; he had one of his own. But sometimes in one of the West Side office buildings they'd wave to him, or say things in sign language—*Have a nice day*—and once a typist had come right up to the window and pressed her lips to the glass, and he'd pressed his own right over hers on the outside, and couldn't get rid of the taste of trisodium phosphate for a long time. That was okay too. You had to have fun.

He fanned the squeegee and holstered it and hit the button and dropped the stage and pulled the brush out of the bucket and swished it across the blue-tinted glass, wishing Sam was here with him, because this was a beautiful building; it felt as good as it looked. But Sam was off today. He'd checked in for work and then just taken off again.

"I don't feel like it," he'd told Marvin in front of Joe.

"Oh for Christ's sake! It's Park Tower, and all yours!"

"Marve," Sam had said in his quiet way, "I said I don't feel like it. Okay?"

There was nothing Marvin could do about that. When you didn't feel like it, you didn't feel like it. You'd wash a dozen buildings, twenty buildings in a row, dropping the stage and swinging over the parapet with the people down there looking like ants, and you'd work all day without even using the gotcha on the safety rope; then one day you'd wake up and drive to the job and suddenly go sour in your stomach, for no reason, no reason at all. Booze, late nights, a new girl—those things never made any difference; the job was the job and you could lose it if you didn't do it right. Then suddenly there was this feeling in you, a kind of warning, and you knew that if you went up there today you'd be taking a risk. Maybe it was just an accumulation of the stress over the weeks, over the months; every time the wind blew a gust, every time you looked down and saw how tiny the people were, every time the cables snagged and the drop was jerky, it got to you, somewhere inside, without you knowing it; then it all built up and one day you'd tell Marvin you didn't feel like it, and you'd go home.

Sam would be here tomorrow, no problem, and they'd work Park Tower together. It was a beauty.

He pressed the button and dropped to the bottom edge of the window, shuffling to the other end of the stage and starting over. The sun had come out an hour ago, and now the light was at the angle where bright reflection appeared, so that he wasn't washing the glass anymore, but the white curves and hollows of a billowing cumulus cloud as it floated in the ocean blue of the sky.

And in the cloud, the woman.

He stared at her.

She had opened the drapes, the silky, gossamer drapes, through which he hadn't been able to see; and she was standing there, three feet away from him, watching him through the glass, through the cloud. She was looking frightened, with her mouth open a little and her eyes wide. He couldn't do anything. He wanted to tell her, somehow, not to be frightened, but he couldn't do it, or do anything. He stood there with his lungs full of perfume, and a golden gong inside him beating, beating to the rhythm of his heart, beating softly until his whole body shook with it, while his eyes, watching her, tried to contain what they were seeing, tried not to be blinded by the face that looked back at him, by its radiance, by its breathtaking beauty.

The voice of the building had faded, as if all the traffic down there had stopped. The glass of the window had melted away, and all he could see was the billowing cumulus cloud, and the goddess in it. He knew that he was trembling, and couldn't stop himself; he sensed that his control, the control he had over his limbs, his breathing, his movements, was being compromised, perhaps to the point of endangering him; and the sense of this grew in him, somewhere, in his mind, in his head, and he felt himself surfacing, becoming conscious, until he reached out and put his hand on the rail of the stage, and steadied himself.

She was still looking frightened, and he couldn't bear that. Nobody must ever frighten her: he would kill them. He began lifting his arms and bringing them down, like wings, flapping them gently, looking up at the sky and down again, to mean he'd flown down here to see her; he folded his wings and smiled to her. She glanced upwards, then at his face again, no longer frightened-looking but with her eyes hard, and not understanding. Then she pulled the cord and the drapes drew together, leaving only the white cloud, and the shock of heartbreak.

"Did you know he was coming today?"

"Yes, Miss St. Clair. I forgot to warn you. I'm very—"

"Did you forget to warn everyone else in the building?"

"No, miss. Everyone was informed. But—"

"Then for God's sake, why leave me out?"

There was silence on the line, presumably while the doorman thought out some kind of excuse. The leaping

16

cadences of *Peer Gynt* filled the room, but failed to mollify her.

"Your arrival was unexpected, Miss St. Clair. I'd already warned the residents, and then clean forgot to tell you. The apartment was empty, you see, until you arrived. Mr. Lindquist was to be absent for—"

"The man scared me to death."

There was another pause. "Did he offend you, miss? I mean did he make any kind of—well—gestures?"

"He was waving his arms around. I pulled the curtains open and there he was. I mean, when you're completely alone on the top floor of a building you don't expect to see a man staring at you a few feet away." She reached for the gold Baccarat box near the telephone, but found only Egyptian cigarettes in it. There were some Bensons in her handbag. "It frightened me, that's all."

"I can quite understand that, Miss St. Clair. But if he actually made any offensive gestures, I'll report—"

"He didn't have to make any gestures. He was just *there* when I pulled the curtains. I wasn't expecting him, don't you understand? I could easily have been undressed."

"All I can say is that I'm extremely sorry, Miss St. Clair. I can assure you I shall take the utmost care in future."

"It's the least you can do for Mr. Lindquist's guests." She hung up and went to find her bag, lighting a cigarette and turning the volume up on the stereo.

He sat with his ham sandwich, looking through the rest of the paper, but not really seeing anything. The photograph was on page three, and he kept turning back to look at it again.

"How's it with Park Tower?" Marvin wanted to know.

Joe turned the page again, to the comic section. "It's a clean building. We can cover six frames with the thirty-foot stage and do it in nine drops, maybe ten at the most. Six-hour drops with Sam on board, but I'll be all day on three today, with overtime.''

"That's a long time you'll be up there, Joe.''

"I don't mind. I like the building. It's a beauty." He wished Marvin would go away and leave him alone. He still had this strange aching in him, the sense of having lost something precious, something he couldn't live without, in quite the same way. Normally he took his lunch on the stage, and a flask to pee in, using the stage as a home for the day, sometimes even taking a nap when the weather was hot in the summertime; he'd taken a hamburger up there this morning, but hadn't touched it. The office wasn't far away, a ten-minute drive, and he'd decided to come back here and eat a sandwich, because that meant he could power-climb past her windows and drop again after lunch to the lower floors, giving him a double chance of seeing her again. The drapes had been closed, on his way up. If they were still like that when he made the drop, he'd tap at the window, and maybe she'd open them and look at him without being frightened anymore. He wanted to see her smile. More than anything else in the world, he wanted that.

"You okay, Joe?''

"What?" He looked up. Marvin was still standing there, watching him with his big black shining head on one side. "Sure I'm okay.''

"So long as you're okay,'' Marvin said, and went and sat down behind his desk in the corner of the shed.

Joe turned the pages of the *Journal* again, to where her picture was. He wanted to tell Marvin—*You know who I saw today, up there? Tina St. Clair!* Yet at the same time he recoiled at the thought of telling Marvin, or anyone, even Sam. It'd be a kind of sacrilege, like writing her name on a wall.

THE PENTHOUSE

Safe home again in New York, the few lines said. *Tina St. Clair landed at Kennedy Airport last evening from Rome, to be greeted by friends who had been anxious for her during the past three days, after she was trapped in the streets of Calcutta by the political riots there.*

Poor Tina. She must have been scared stiff. When he dropped the stage after lunch, he'd spell out *Welcome Home!* in whitewash on one of her windows, and wash it off later.

No. That would be cheap, a cheap thing to do. There wouldn't have to be anything like that about them. He would have to learn how to treat her, how to behave with her, not to make her frightened, not to do anything cheap.

The perfume came back into his lungs when he thought of her, and the gold gong boomed softly inside him, like the beating of his heart. He sat there for a long time, drowned in the miracle that had happened to him today.

When at last he looked up, he saw Marvin watching him from the corner of the shed.

"Sam didn't feel like going up today," Marvin said with his head on one side. "If you don't feel like going up there again today, Joe, that's perfectly okay. We don't want any accidents or anything."

Joe crumpled the sandwich paper and dropped it into the waste bin, and went to the heater and poured himself some coffee. "Marvin, do you happen to know what your head is full of?"

"So long as you're okay, Joe."

He swung out across the parapet, six hundred and ninety feet above the street, and dropped onto the stage, hitting the power button and leaning his hands on the rail as the stage sank slowly, the whine of the gears adding a tone to the voice of the big glass building. There were no cumulus clouds floating in a blue sky now; there was a waste of

19

gray covering the city, in from the Atlantic, and the building no longer had the look of glass, but of cast metal.

The drapes were still drawn closed across the windows of the penthouse when the stage took Joe down there, and he stopped the motor and stared at his own reflection. After a while he found himself trying to see if she was there, behind the filmy folds of the drapes, and suddenly he came to his senses and remembered he was a window cleaner, not a regular visitor to her apartment. The idea, now, of actually tapping at the glass to get her attention embarrassed him acutely, and he started the motor and dropped the stage to the floor below, filled with relief that he hadn't made a fool of himself.

He was a window cleaner, and she was an heiress. It was like one of those dirty jokes: the Heiress and the Window Cleaner. He felt a flood of shame come into him. It wasn't going to be like that, with them. This wasn't the way to do things at all.

He worked until five o'clock, a little after. He dipped the long hogs-hair brush and washed the glass and fanned the squeegee and watched for runs and streaks and fanned them out with the steady movements of a robot, while he thought of the woman in the penthouse, vaguely aware of a sourness in his stomach, a shortness of breath, remembering with part of his mind the way Marvin had watched him at lunchtime, saying, *As long as you're okay, Joe,* like he didn't think he was okay at all. Marvin's head was full of shit. He felt like this because Sam wasn't up here with him, that was all. Tomorrow Sam would be here, and when they dropped the stage past the penthouse windows Joe wouldn't say a thing about who was inside. Sam wouldn't understand. To Sam, a woman was just a broad, and if he told Sam who was in the penthouse, Sam would start talking about her that way, like a fancy broad, and he would want to get Sam by the belt and fling him over the rail and watch him go six hundred and ninety feet down onto the street with his arms spread-eagled and his mouth in a silent O.

He didn't want to kill Sam.

Some more spots fell, and he holstered the squeegee. He'd intended to work overtime tonight, being single-handed, but if the rain was going to set in there was no point; he'd get soaked and in any case they might have to do the penthouse glass again tomorrow if the rain left drying soot.

Power-climbing past the fifty-third floor, he saw there were lights on behind the drapes, so that for a moment he glimpsed the furniture through the transparent fabric before he turned on the stage and stood with his back to the window, looking across the heights of the city, already glowing in the dusk. He must protect her privacy, from now on. He would be her guardian.

"Your name is George, isn't it?"

"Yes, Miss St. Clair."

"I remember you from my last visit. Look, I'm just calling to apologize, George. I was rather short with you about the window cleaner."

"I understand perfectly, miss. It was—"

"It was a shock, right. When I'm scared I get mad at people—I guess most people do. I appreciate your understanding."

"You're very welcome, miss."

"Is it going to rain?"

"It's started already, yes. I can see some umbrellas up."

"A good night to stay indoors. Thank you, George."

"It's my pleasure, Miss St. Clair."

* * *

George William Jarrat had been the doorman at Park Tower for more than a year, since the first resident had moved in. Going on fifty and with his gray sideburns whitened to make him appear distinguished instead of aging, he was quite a few pounds overweight, and he'd been advised by his doctor that if he could lose twenty of them inside the next six months he'd stand to add five years to his lifespan. This interested him, because he enjoyed life; on the other hand he'd have to cut down drastically on eggs and steak, both of which contributed a lot to the enjoyment. A man had to eat, after all, and doctors didn't necessarily know everything.

George watched the traffic splashing through the rain beyond the huge bronze doors of the lobby, and the drips falling from the scalloped fringes of the marquee. So far the evening had been quiet enough, with only three arrivals since six o'clock and flowers for ten and thirty-one. Rain always made a difference; cabs were hard to get, and people stayed home if they could.

"She apologized, at least," he said to the security man beside him. "She's a lady, at least. Called me up specially."

"I guess they need to act human. Or they wouldn't know where they stood. They need to touch base."

A limousine drew into the curb and George went forward, his big gold silk umbrella ready to cover the gap between the car and the marquee. The security guard stood watching, not the people getting out of the limo but the sidewalk. There was a new trick very popular nowadays, pulled mostly by fast young kids along the Upper East Side: they'd watch for the limos and jump anyone getting out, snatching a wallet or a purse before the driver or a doorman knew what was happening.

George Jarrat came back with his two arrivals and showed them into the elevator, then joined the security man again, enjoying the bouquet of Jean Patou the woman had left on the air. This was at 6:57 by the heavy bronze clock over the doors. The two men stood talking desultorily while drops from the furled umbrella made a rivulet across the marble floor.

"It's not the fats. It's the carbohydrates."

"It starts in the mind. You've got to think thin. That's how I stopped smoking. I kept thinking of what the inside of my lungs must look like. Disgusting."

Joe Dotson came through the doors at 7:03, carrying a bunch of roses. He was wearing a charcoal-gray suit, single-breasted, with rainspots darkening the shoulders, and a good pair of black brogue shoes with tongues on the uppers. These details were noted automatically by the security guard. The doorman's eyes were more on the man's face, though it took him a moment to recognize it. This man was the window cleaner who'd come down in the service elevator soon after the rain had started, earlier.

"I'm here to see Miss St. Clair."

George looked into the wide steady eyes of the man in front of him and picked the most logical explanation first: he'd realized he must have scared the woman on fifty-three, and was here to apologize—and handsomely; it would be the policy of the firm, where buildings like Park Tower were concerned. Working as he did for people to whom expense was no object, George was used to grand gestures, and saw roses brought in here every day.

"To see who?"

"Tina St. Clair." It was a youthful face, open and attentive, the eyes concentrating. "I'm here to see her."

"There's no one here of that name."

"She's in the penthouse." The man looked past George at the elevator, and George sensed a movement from the security man. "My name's Dotson. Joseph Dotson."

"There's no one here by the name of St. Clair." The

23

heavy perfume of the roses hung in the air between them. "You're the window cleaner, aren't you?"

"That's right."

George moved an inch towards Dotson, comforted by the feeling of his own weight; he was a difficult man to get past. "There's a lady in the penthouse who informed me you frightened her. I didn't pass this on to—"

"What? Yes. I frightened her. I've come to apologize." He lifted the bouquet of roses.

"That's not necessary, but I'll have them sent up, if you like. Is there a card?" His white-gloved hand fingered the foliage, until the man drew it away from him with a little jerk.

"I'm here to give them to her myself." He looked from George to the security man and back, and they heard the sudden note of tension in his voice.

"The lady's not seeing visitors," George told him brusquely, "and her name isn't St. Clair. You can give me the roses to send up, or you can take them away with you."

"Away?" The man backed off slightly, looking at both of them in turn with an expression that made George uneasy; there was nothing hostile in it; the man looked strange, out of his depth.

"You'll have to make up your mind," the security man told him. There'd be people coming through, anytime, and they wouldn't want to see any window cleaners around. He moved again, to block the man's path to the elevators.

"This is nothing to do with you." There was so much tension in the voice now that the security man moved towards him at once, taking his arm.

"Let's avoid any trouble, Mr. Dotson. We'll tell the lady you called here with the flowers. She'll really appreciate it." He was surprised to feel no resistance as he walked the man through the tall bronze doors. Dotson stood for a moment under the dripping marquee, looking at the marble walls of the ground floor as if he was trying to find another way in. Then suddenly he turned and walked into the rain.

At 7:09 a security-guard call was logged at the Eighteenth Precinct, Midtown North, of the New York Police Department. The complainant reported the visit of a window cleaner, Joseph Dotson, demanding to see a female occupant of Park Tower on Fifty-sixth Street. He offered no resistance when asked to leave, but by his manner he was suspected of being possibly on drugs. The name and address of the individual's workplace was given.

The rain fell steadily.

Standing in it, on the sidewalk, Joe stared upwards at the building. From here it seemed immeasurably high, a glass obelisk jeweled with light and rearing against the night, bearing aloft the goddess that once he had seen face to face in the curves and hollows of the cloud. But that had been almost in another world; there had been sunshine, and now it was dark; she had stood close to him, and now she was gone.

He was aware of traffic sounds, like the washing of an ocean against his feet; footsteps passed and voices spoke, but not to him. He was alone, and desolate. He had come to worship at the shrine of the goddess, but had been turned away.

These were not the words of his thoughts, but the color of them, the essence. They were the tears within his heart. At one time, as he stood there in the rain, he thought someone spoke to him, but by the time he looked down they must have gone; all he could see were black shining umbrellas; maybe someone had asked him the way, and then—*and then what?* Hadn't he looked all right? *So long as you're okay, Joe.*

Sure I'm okay.

He looked upwards again, with the rain flattening his hair and trickling down his face, soaking into his neat gray suit and chilling his skin, making his skin crawl as the sourness crept into his stomach and the cold came into his lungs and he began remembering, remembering, the things he must not remember.

He looked down suddenly, blinded by the rain and by the jeweled light of the building, and walked away from it; and after he had gone a little distance he opened his fingers, and the roses fell into the gutter along the curb, their reflection leaving rivulets red as blood.

3

SOON AFTER NINE O'CLOCK THE porter on duty at Park Tower had a call from the lady on fifty-third, asking him if he could possibly get her some Benson and Hedges. He told her he could do this right away: they would have some at the Tuileries Restaurant on the ground floor.

It was still raining, though the sky was beginning to clear in the east and the washed-out face of the almost full moon was showing through the clouds.

To protect the privacy of the residents, there was no entrance to the restaurant from the lobby, so that the porter had to trot for a few yards through the rain; the only person he saw on the sidewalk was a man whom he later described as an "odd-looking guy, soaking wet." Taking him for a bum or a junkie, the porter dismissed him from his mind right away; the Park Tower lobby was well guarded.

George Jarrat, the doorman, was at this time escorting a party of guests for the twenty-fourth floor to the elevator, so that the security guard was stationed alone in the main area of the lobby. He didn't recognize Joseph Dotson immediately when he turned in from the street, but realized he was the kind of person who shouldn't be coming in here, bareheaded and drenched with rain. He began moving forward to intercept him, and was within a few feet when he recognized the man as Joseph Dotson, his hair now clinging in dark streaks to his head, his eyes with a strange light in them. Behind the guard, the elevator doors were closing and George Jarrat was coming back in this direction.

Seven minutes later, the porter turned into the lobby from the street, with the two packs of cigarettes held under his uniform coat to protect them from the rain. Soon afterward, his face blanched and his voice almost unintelligible, he put a call through on 911, the city emergency code, and was asked to steady himself and repeat the information.

The SPRINT hookup computer threw a display on the radio dispatcher's screen within three seconds, indicating the precinct sector, the nearest available patrol car, the ambulance district and the relevant cross streets. A minute later Car 21 from the Eighteenth Precinct swung left onto Fifty-seventh Street from Madison Avenue and accelerated. Due to the nature of the call, three other vehicles, including an ambulance, began moving into the area, and the sound of sirens began filling the streets.

She opened the door to him, thinking he was the porter. Seeing the stranger, whose quiet face yet reminded her of someone, she thought immediately: *Telephone*. Something was obviously wrong: no one could reach this door without having telephoned, without being announced by the doorman in the lobby. At this level the elevator served only the penthouse, since it occupied the whole of the fifty-third floor.

"Who are you?"

She was moving backward, away from him and nearer a telephone; he followed her in, watching her as one would watch a revelation; in the wide-eyed stillness of his face there was a look of rapture. His voice, even though it was hushed, startled her in the quiet of the room.

"Oh my God, you're so beautiful . . ."

She stared back at him, unable to get anything straight, because nothing made sense: he shouldn't be here at all; it was impossible for him to be here; he was soaking wet, drowned-looking, his hair like weeds. And instead of saying he'd brought the cigarettes, he was saying she was beautiful. *Perhaps the porter had sent this man out to get—*

"Did you bring the cigarettes?" She said it with a sudden breathless laugh, because everything was so incongruous; but the alarm in her was strident along her nerves: she could feel her eyelids flickering, and a crawling sensation at the nape of her neck.

"Cigarettes?" He stood with water dripping from his fingers; it was gathering darkly at the ends of his sleeves and trickling onto his hands. Beyond him, through the open doorway, she could see the elevator across the hall. Its doors were slightly apart, and that was wrong, too; they always closed after you'd left it. But it was just something technical; if she could dodge past him and reach the elevator and press the button she would be safe. But surely things weren't that serious; her secretary dealt with a mass of what she called "admiration mail" every week—Marlene refused to use the term "fan mail," which was for film stars and footballers—and this was just a young man who'd somehow gotten past the doorman in the lobby and found his own way up. He'd only come to gawp.

"Please go," she said with her tone steadier. "This is a private residence."

In a moment he said quietly, "Tina St. Clair." It sounded as if he were saying grace. His light gray eyes never left her, and she drew the edges of her bathrobe closer together, though he wasn't looking down, but only at her face. On the air was the mushroom smell of his wet clothes, and in the silence she could now hear the wail of sirens from the streets below. "Tina St. Clair," he said again, in the tone

29

of a litany. Yes, this was just one of her admirers, bringing her a letter in person. She turned and went across to the house phone and called the lobby, keeping the man in sight.

He moved now, rubbing his hands together, saying ruefully, "It's cold. I was out in the rain." His smile was attractive, she thought; there was no harm in him. But the lobby wasn't answering; the ringing tone went on, together with the loudening note of the sirens in the street. She pressed the button for the porter and waited again, watching the young man and trying to think where she'd seen his face before.

"I'm Joe Dotson," he said, still rubbing his hands. "Joseph Dotson. I hope you'll just call me Joe."

The porter wasn't answering, either. Something had happened down there. They'd all left the lobby, and that was how this man had been able to reach the elevator. The sound of the sirens was very loud, and some of them were dying away to a moan, immediately below the building. She could feel the quickened beating of her heart now; there were things happening that didn't have any kind of logical explanation; there'd been an accident, some kind of accident.

The ringing tone went on. "Has there been an accident?" she asked the man. She musn't think of him as a sort of apparition, something she couldn't talk to.

"Don't call anyone," he said with a note of gentle pleading. "We don't want anyone here." He turned and shut the wide gold-paneled door, and locked it; and now she could feel the blood leaving her face as the first real fear came into her, filling her with cold. *Don't let him do anything to me.*

"Joe Dotson," he was saying, coming away from the door, moving with a certain catlike grace and measuring

30

his steps, "and Tina St. Clair. So we've met. We've come together. It had to happen. It was destined to happen."

The lightness of his gaze dwelt on her with such gentleness that she was warned again; adoration from a stranger suggested some kind of unreason. She cradled the house phone and had to look in the long gold-tinted mirror to locate the main telephone; she'd only used it once tonight, to call her parents. Watching the man, she lifted it, then had to look down to press the two buttons, repeating the second one. When she looked up again she saw the man moving towards her, light on his feet, the gentleness in his eyes changing to entreaty.

"Don't call anyone," he said. "You don't have to call anyone."

Watching him with her head moving back a little, she wondered whether it would be any use flinging the phone at him, at his face. How hard would she have to do it, to hurt him badly enough to—to what? Kill him? Stun him? Make him go away? His face was so gentle that it made the idea of hurting him irrational, uncivilized. It was his attitude that was so bewildering; if he came at her with a knife or something she'd know what to do, fight like a wildcat, scream, throw things at him. But he was just standing there with his hands spread open and his quiet voice pleading with her. "We don't want anyone up here, Tina."

The line opened.

"Police Emergency."

"Yes, I—" But she didn't know exactly what to say. Was there really an emergency? The sound of the young woman's voice on the phone should have reassured her, but it had scared her instead, confirming that, yes, there was indeed an emergency, and only the police could help her now.

"This is the police department. Can we assist you?"

"Yes. There's a man here. A stranger."

"Are you at home?"

"Yes. And I'm alone here."

"Is he threatening you?"

The man wasn't moving, just standing there with that strange look of entreaty. "Tina," he said, "just hang up. We don't want anyone here."

"No," she told the policewoman, "but he walked in here uninvited, and he won't leave. I—I'm afraid of him." She listened to the sound of another siren loudening from the street below, coming closer to the building. This was crazy: she was using the phone to call for the police and they were here already, downstairs.

"What's the address, please?" she heard the girl asking.

"The address? Park Tower, on Fifty-sixth Street. On Fifty-sixth and—"

"Fifth Avenue, okay, I have that. What apartment?"

The man was saying something again; she couldn't look away from him. Behind him, in the glass of the long windows, she saw light flickering, and thought at first there was a fire somewhere: she was ready to believe in anything disastrous; then she recognized the rhythm of emergency lights; she was watching their reflection in the windows of the building opposite.

"Tina," he was saying, "there's no point in calling them. They can't get up here. The elevators don't work. Don't be scared of me; I can't stand that."

She was warned again, but almost below conscious level. The elevators didn't work, and that was why the doors hadn't closed out there in the lobby. He must have done something to the elevators, so that the police couldn't come up here to help her. But this thought was half lost in the bewilderment, in the strangeness he'd brought in here like a waking dream, because he looked so gentle.

32

"Apartment Fifty-three," she said into the phone. "The penthouse."

"Apartment Five—three. Your name, please?"

"Tina St. Clair."

"Will you repeat that?" The woman sounded surprised; most people did, when she told them her name.

"Tina St. Clair." The man was taking a step toward her, and she tensed. *If he comes any closer, just one more step, throw the phone hard and—*

"We're sending a patrolman immediately, Miss St. Clair."

He stopped, shaking his head in frustration. "Please, Tina," he said, "please try and understand what I'm saying."

"There's a patrolman on his way, Miss St. Clair. Can you hear me okay?"

But there were patrolmen here already, and they couldn't reach her. He'd done something to the elevators.

"Tina, you'll have to understand. There's nothing anyone can do. Nothing at all."

4

THE CREW OF CAR 21 WALKED into the Park Tower lobby at 9:13, one minute after the call from the porter had hit the radio network; three other patrol cars and an ambulance were already slowing to a halt outside. The rain had eased to a drizzle as the edge of the cloudbank drew slowly across the city and the moon floated into a clearing sky.

Detective Sergeant Frank Paulino, who was cruising in the area when the first call came on the air, reached the crime scene at the same time as the ambulance and ducked under the dripping edge of the marquee to find six or seven patrolmen clustered in the lobby and a girl in a trench coat throwing up into one of the frescoed planters that lined the walls. Two of the officers were questioning a uniformed porter near the telephones while the rest were bent over someone lying on the floor with blood soaking into a big gold umbrella that had fallen across his chest. Paulino had already unhooked the walkie-talkie from his belt and was sending to base.

"We're going to need backup units as soon as you can get them here." He circled the white-faced girl and edged between the two policemen who had backed the porter against the wall. "For your information we have an ambulance here. There's a man down with a bullet in his head and— Hold it a minute." He turned to the nearest patrolman. "Who's that over there, is that another—?"

"The security guard. I think he's dead too."

"We could have two people dead," the sergeant said into his radio. "Did anyone call Homicide?" He got an affirmative. "Did anyone call Captain Eberhart yet?" There was so much noise from sirens approaching that he clapped a hand over one ear and held the radio close to the other. Eberhart was on his way, they told him. "Okay, I'm protecting the scene till he gets here." He swung round as he heard a metallic clatter from the street, but it was only the paramedics bringing a litter from the ambulance. He moved over to where the two patrolmen were talking to the porter. "Did he see anyone?"

"He thinks so."

"He *thinks* so?" The porter was an elderly guy, standing in a half-crouch with his back to the wall as if the two patrolmen had been punching him up. "Okay, take it easy, there's no rush." You tell people there's no rush and they'll relax and think faster for you. He swung round as the two paramedics put their litter onto the floor close to the big umbrella. "Hold everything, fellers. If those guys are still alive you can go to work, but otherwise don't touch anything." He looked back to the uniformed porter, wishing to Christ he'd get his head together because in actual fact there was one helluva rush on: he needed to know, above all else, whether the guy who'd shot these people was still inside this building or somewhere out there in the streets trying to find cover and ready to shoot again if anyone tried to stop him. "Paulino," he said into his radio. "We've got time to contain a close security perimeter in this area unless the suspect got away in a vehicle. I'd say between— Okay, Captain Eberhart's arrived on the scene, you got that?" He waited for an acknowledgment and kept the set open while he talked to Eberhart. "The man against the wall might have seen something but he's in shock right now, so we—"

"You've ordered backups, Frank?"

"You bet."

"This one's still alive," a paramedic called out, and the captain went across to where the doorman was lying. They'd lifted the big umbrella off his chest and loosened his collar. "He's been trying to say something."

Eberhart's tall frame collapsed into a squat as he put his ear close to the white drained face of the man on the floor. "You want to tell me anything, friend?"

The lips were moving, but there was no strength in the voice; it was hardly even a whisper. Eberhart found himself faced with a life-and-death decision to make, as he did every day of his working life, as they all did, every day of their working lives, without it ever getting any easier. He could keep this man here with the life draining out of him in the hope that he might give them a clue to work on, or he could tell the ambulance crew to get him to the hospital and an operating table without stopping to do anything else.

"Try again, friend." The bullet had smashed into the skull and taken away bone splinters and brain matter, and it didn't look like an operating table would be much use to him however fast they got him there. "Try again."

He gave it another minute, crouched over the heavyset man and smelling his blood, feeling the coldness creeping into him, getting to know him much too late, aiding and abetting in his imminent death and getting nothing for it but these two words, over and over, maybe two names, maybe *Hobson* and maybe *Sinclair*, with the consonants too slurred to be sure, and the strength of even this feeble whisper already dying.

"You can take him away," he said and straightened up, going back to Frank Paulino. " 'Hobson' mean anything to you? Or 'Sinclair'?"

"Nope. But this man says he saw a guy out there on the

sidewalk, skipper, maybe five or ten minutes before he got back in here and found the victims."

"Any description?"

The porter was coming out of his state of shock a little and finding his voice. "He was an odd-looking guy, with—"

"What was his age, would you say?" the captain asked him.

"Maybe thirty-five, forty. It was hard to—"

"What height?"

"Maybe five-ten. He—"

"Thin, fat?"

"Medium, I guess."

Eberhart told one of the men to send the description on his radio, possible suspect. "Clean-shaven?" he asked the porter.

"Yes."

"Color of hair?"

"It was dark, but that could've been because he was soaking wet, see."

Eberhart kept up his questions until he had everything the man could remember, and left him staring as the two paramedics shuffled past with the litter.

"Is he dead?"

"He's pretty bad."

One of the telephones was buzzing, and the captain picked it up. "Hello?"

"George, the elevator doesn't work, did you know?"

"This is the police. We'd like you to stay in your apartment in any case, ma'am, with the doors locked and secured. We'll let you know when it's safe to leave." He hung up before the lady could ask questions. A party of men in plain clothes was coming through the entrance doors and he recognized two among them: Williams and Bayez of Homicide. Two of them went over to where the security guard was lying, spoke to a patrolman there and began stretching their yellow tape from wall to wall around the body. The captain saw the thin stooped figure of Dr. Shaw, the civilian medical investigator, coming in from the street.

"Hi there, Doc."

"Hi, Charlie. I thought you were in Florida!"

"Got back last night."

"Should've stayed."

"Now he tells me." Eberhart turned as a young patrolman threw him a smart rookie salute. "Sir, we have a call about one of the residents here—there's an intruder in her apartment."

Eberhart's eyes snapped wide open. "What's the number?"

"Fifty-three, sir. The complainant's name is—"

But the captain was already four feet away, jerking the phone off its hook and dialing the number.

"Hello?"

It was a man's voice.

"Am I speaking to the resident?" Eberhart asked.

"Who are you?" The voice sounded quiet and reasonable; it didn't sound like an intruder's. The rookie had got the apartment number wrong.

"This is Police Captain Eberhart. Did you make a 911 call with reference to an intruder?"

There was a moment's hesitation, but the voice remained reasonable. "Look, we want privacy. We don't want anyone bothering us."

Eberhart said carefully: "The call was from a woman."

"Everything's okay now."

With nothing much else to help him, the captain found himself thinking solely from experience: family fight; exhusband has turned up; now they've settled their differences. But in a place like this?

"That's fine," he said into the phone. "But I'll just come up and make sure. We always have to make—"

"We don't want anyone up here."

Eberhart thought the tone was sharper, but couldn't be sure; the lobby was full of noise, and the howl of a siren was loudening in the street outside as one of the backup units arrived. The white-faced girl in the trench coat was waiting for him to hang up, so that she could speak to him: Pat Tolman, the police reporter from headquarters; he turned his shoulder toward her and concentrated on the voice he'd been listening to on the house phone.

"I need to know your name," he said, "and I need to know if there's a lady in Apartment Fifty-three who might have called the police about an intruder." He listened very carefully.

"You can forget about that. She didn't mean it. She's perfectly okay."

Eberhart was trying to match this voice, and what it was saying, to the kind of voice he'd expect to hear from the resident of a penthouse in what was probably the highest rent district in the entire world, and the kind of things he'd expect it to be saying; and they didn't fit.

"I'm asking you to give me your name," he said briefly, and looked around him for Detective Sergeant Paulino. He was talking to the Homicide team inside the yellow-taped areas, and Eberhart beckoned him over.

"I'm Joe Dotson," the voice said, and the captain reached across to the porter's desk, pulling open one of the drawers and finding the book he wanted. The list of residents' names was inside the front cover, and opposite the number 53 there was written *Thomas V. Lindquist*. There was no Dotson anywhere else on the list, but a faint bell was ringing in Eberhart's mind.

"How do you spell that?" he asked, not sure whether it

was Dotson, Dodgeson or Dockson, or even—what else?
The faint bell went on ringing.

"Look," the voice said, "if you're the police, you'd
better know one or two things."

Captain Eberhart reached for his radio, pushed the switch
to send, and brought it close to the earpiece of the phone.
Frank Paulino was standing beside him now, his head
leaning to catch the voice on the line.

"I'm listening," Eberhart said carefully.

"I don't want anyone up here, okay? I've fixed the
elevators so no one can use them. And I don't want any
more calls. This is a private residence."

Paulino jerked his head up to look into Eberhart's eyes,
and saw his own thoughts confirmed.

"Why did you have to fix the elevators, Mr. Dotson?
There's a doorman here to keep away visitors."

The silence on the line drew out, and both men waited,
watching each other. "It's simply that you have to understand what I'm saying. I don't want anyone up here, or
calling me on the phone. I don't want to be bothered."

The two detectives concentrated on the voice as it went
on speaking to them; their immediate environment was
being phased out as if someone had turned down a sensitiv-
ity control· the shuffling of feet as the policemen in the
lobby came and went, the distant sound of sirens, the flash
of emergency lights, the smell of rain, and wet clothing,
and cordite, and blood. Their senses had zoomed in on
ground zero: the voice in the phone.

"If anyone calls again, I'm going to get annoyed, you
understand me? I'm going to get very annoyed. And no
one had better make that happen."

Eberhart wiped away the trickle of sweat that had started
from his scalp, and tried to keep his tone absolutely normal.
"I quite appreciate your wish for privacy, Mr. Dotson, but
once an emergency call goes into the computer we have to

inquire into it and make a brief report. So let me just have a word with the lady who made that call, and we'll leave you in peace.''

There was a long silence again, and Eberhart used the time to think what had to be done. This conversation should be going straight into the network and onto the tape, and the radio dispatcher listening to it would open it up to everyone at headquarters, from the top brass down. But a radio was unpredictable inside a building with all the metal around, and he might not be sending a clear story. There was a standard telephone on the porter's desk, not far from Frank Paulino's hand. Frank was aware of it too.

"She doesn't want to talk to you," the voice came on the line. "We don't want to talk to anyone."

Quietly Eberhart said: "We think she's in some kind of danger, you see. All we want is her personal reassurance."

For the first time he heard the man's tone change to one of unequivocal menace. "I'm not going to take this from you anymore, you know that? Just how far do you figure on pushing me? I'm running out of patience, don't you understand me?"

The captain thought out the options; there weren't too many. "I think the best thing, Mr. Dotson, is for me to make a brief visit to the apartment, and we can wrap this whole thing up. I can use the stairs, and I'll be on my own, so you don't have to—"

"I've locked the door to the stairs and I've stacked forty pounds of explosive against it, and if you or anyone else tries breaking it open then you'll blow the top floor of this building right across the city."

Eberhart cupped the mouthpiece and jerked his head to the phone on the desk. *"Hit it, Frank."*

By ten P.M. the overall strategic and tactical situations had been established. The street outside the main entrance to Park Tower was closed to traffic and roped off; special police units were drafted in to evacuate bystanders and establish crowd control, and a containment perimeter was set up along each of the four streets that surrounded the building: Fifty-sixth and Fifty-seventh and Fifth and Sixth avenues. A temporary command post was set up in the fifty-first-floor lobby and the elevator doors on all floors from there to the ground were guarded by two police officers; the body of the security man had been removed from the ground-floor lobby and was now in the morgue at 520 First Avenue, and it had been noted that his gun was missing from its holster; a secondary command post was now established there to provide a physical liaison center between the fifty-first floor and the big headquarters van now standing in the street outside.

The police department had requested assistance from the fire department, medical services, paramedical services and the Medical Arts Center Hospital on Sixth Avenue, where beds would be made available in the event of an explosion on the fifty-third floor of the Park Tower building and subsequent injury to personnel. Chiefs and assistant chiefs of police had been called in, some of them from leave, and were now supervising the two command posts and the street-containment perimeter; a community-relations officer and a media-relations officer were brought in to deal with the tasks of evacuating the six apartments on the three floors immediately below the penthouse and of confronting the growing crowd of reporters, cameramen and TV crews that had begun closing in on the area since the first news flash had gone out from the pressroom at police headquarters.

The Emergency Services Division and the FBI had been called in, and flak-vested assault teams armed with Ithaca deerslaying shotguns were deployed inside and outside the Park Tower building; all task forces were netted into the standard police radio frequencies. The emergency number of the city engineer had located him at his home, and the command-post supervisors were now studying the plans of the building. A Bell 206-A Jetranger helicopter of the Police Aviation Unit had been placed on standby at Floyd Bennett Field, pending a decision to lower a two-man team of sharpshooters to the rooftop, where there was no space available for an actual helicopter landing.

The Hostage Negotiating Team had been called in, and arrangements were being made to set the negotiations in motion. This would be possible only if the man up there in Apartment 53 were ready to cooperate. It had to be assumed that his claim to have boobytrapped the staircase door was true unless it could be proved otherwise; a police dog trained to sniff out explosives was now on its way to the building. It was also assumed that the man in Apartment 53 had taken the security guard's gun after shooting him with it in a struggle, and still had it in his possession.

The residents of the six apartments on floors fifty to fifty-two were being escorted down the emergency staircase by police officers, carrying overnight baggage; they had been informed by the community-relations officer that temporary accommodation would be offered by the mayor of New York City in the guest suites at Gracie Mansion, unless they preferred to stay with friends or put up at a hotel at their own cost. The residents on all floors below fifty had been requested to stay in their apartments with the doors secured until further advice. They would be permitted to leave immediately if they wished, and would be escorted to the street or the underground garage; if they decided to stay, but wished to leave later, it would have to be because of vital necessity, since all traffic inside the building would be restricted to police and the FBI. Those choosing to remain in their apartments would be under constant police protection, and any essential supplies would be brought to their doors.

George William Jarrat, the doorman, died in the intensive-care unit at the Medical Arts Center Hospital at 11:34.

By midnight the Park Tower building was under conditions of siege.

5

TINA DIANE ST. CLAIR HAD been born twenty-nine years ago in New Orleans, in a white, columned mansion set among lawns and trees and ornamental lakes, which she assumed the rest of the world to be like until she was three years old, when she began taking an interest in the illustrated magazines that were always spilling across stools and tables, now within her reach; the picture of a half-naked child in a slum tenement— the subject of an appeal for charity—had shocked her deeply, and she had cried hrself to sleep for a long time, telling her nanny she was simply afraid of the dark, being quite unable to explain anything of what she really felt: that the child in the photograph must have run away from her home—which was of course a white, columned mansion—and had been seized by strangers and taken into that other world that must be on an island somewhere, or below the ground. The impact of the picture had left a kind of force in her, something akin to terror, and she couldn't talk about her feelings to anyone, not even Nanny, because not only did she lack the right words, but they couldn't just be spoken in an ordinary voice; she would have had to scream them.

Later, when she had learned that the name of the picture was poverty, and that it wasn't confined to some faraway island, she remained terrified of it, and begged her mother to ask children like that to tea, and spend the night with her in the nursery; she was discovered secretly asking one of the chauffeurs to drive her into the slums of the city, so that she could talk to the children there. Her answer to terror was to face it down.

She had always been beautiful, and this had troubled her until she'd learned to live with it, just as she'd learned to live with the idea that her father was so much richer than other men. But it was her looks that had brought the most misery, because they were personal to her and to her alone; they denied her something she valued more than most things, which was privacy. She didn't want to be chosen as the queen of the fairies at everyone's party; she didn't want, later, heads to turn whenever a young man caught sight of her; she didn't want, above all things, to be envied.

Her nannies had been English, her governesses French. She spent four years in a convent school, where she had learned to dislike God because he demanded blind obedience, and to masturbate for the first time as a means of showing her defiance: it was the wickedest thing one could possibly do, according to the ceaseless lectures on the subject by Sister Teresa, who seemed to think of nothing else. She spent most of her childhood and adolescence between the white mansion in New Orleans, a house in Paris and her grandfather's château in Provence, on the shores of the Mediterranean, where she had lain at death's door for three weeks after eating some wild mushrooms, and a year later had been deflowered by a fisherman's son in a back street of Nice during the carnival, where she'd got lost among the crowds; the event had been painful and frightening—he'd been like a dog on her, thrusting and grunting and pushing her spine against the cobblestones—and she'd been left with bruises, the reek of garlic, and a totally unanswerable question: how had she let such a thing happen? But sometimes in her childhood she'd had nightmares, in which there was usually some sort of cliff; and she'd always gone over it, however hard she'd struggled to keep back. The thing with the French boy had been a little like that.

As soon as she had been able to choose what she did with her life, she worked for three years in the slums of Naples, teaching the children English, caring for their sores, fending off the advances of their fathers and falling hopelessly in love with a young priest who was dying of tuberculosis, his divine face becoming hollowed month by month by the ravages of the disease and his dark eyes burning ever more hotly with his joy in the knowledge that in this way the Lord had chosen to punish him for his sins. She had loved him, she thought later, for his passions, even though they weren't for her. Her looks, he had often warned her, meant nothing to him; perhaps for this too she had loved him.

Her late twenties had been less rewarding: thrown several times from horses, rescued from a capsized yacht off Antibes with the mistral whipping the sea to a frenzy, trapped in the wreckage of an actor's Ferrari, she had been spared any meaningful experience—except that, for a time, she thought the facial scars of the car crash might leave her less beautiful and more interesting, until the plastic surgeon's skills had restored most of the order, so that the scars showed only when she used no makeup, or was very cold. Modeling, a minor film, fencing instruction, then six months in the Arctic Circle with a group of bearded Australians devoted to saving seals, with three fingertips lost from frostbite to show for it and every fur coat thrown out of her wardrobe the instant she was home.

Then that headlong and traumatizing marriage and divorce with Prince Vicente di Potenza that had delivered her body and soul to the tabloids and the women's magazines as the new Fairy Tale Princess the world had been waiting for. And finally the liberating privacy of travel abroad, hunting down textiles for the exclusive designers—mohair, brocades, tussah, wild silk, vicuña—and making a success of it as a business venture. But nothing real in her life had seemed ever to reach her; nothing had quite gotten through; she'd challenged herself a few times, and won out, but she'd never had to fight for anything she wanted. Tonight, watching this man's face in the mirror, with his wet hair flattened against his head and that strange light flickering in his eyes, it occurred to her that she was going to have to fight at last for something she wanted very much, which was life itself.

"Who are you?" she asked him.

"I told you. I'm Joe."

"Yes, I know. But where have I seen you before?"

He smiled secretively. "I flew down to see you, remember?" He waved his arms.

She jerked her head to the windows, remembering, perhaps thinking he might still be there outside, safely outside. But there was only the reflected flashing of the emergency lights.

"How did you get past the doorman?" she asked him, wishing her voice sounded steadier.

He looked down, hugging his body now and beginning to shiver; she couldn't see his eyes. "He's not there."

"But what about the porter? And the security guard?"

"We don't have to think about anybody else. There's just you and me now."

She went to the gold box and took a cigarette and lit it, her hands shaking. "What's happened down there? Why are all those police cars there?"

"They'll go away soon," he said.

"What did you do, Joe?" She knew what he was capable of doing; she'd heard what he'd said on the phone, about the explosives, about blowing this place across the city.

"We needn't think about anything down there." His face looked pinched and he was shivering all the time now, his wet clothes drying on him.

"Where are your shoes?" She'd only just noticed he wasn't wearing any.

He looked at his feet. "I don't need any shoes. I'm not going anywhere."

She drew smoke deep into her lungs, wanting to ask, not wanting to ask, having finally to ask: "Why did you come here?"

He looked at her again, for the first time since she'd asked him about the doorman. "To be with you. To be with you for the rest of my life."

She looked away. So it was as bad as that. He was a madman, not just one of her admirers who'd come here to gawp and go away again, to be sent away. . . . *George, would you come up here, please, and ask this person to leave?*

But George wasn't there anymore. *This man had killed him, and the others, and brought explosives up here with him, and if anyone tried to come up here he was going to blow this place—*

The phone started ringing and she cried out in shock.

He went over to it and took it off the hook and put it down on the gold-lacquered shelf, and she heard the voice coming from it, *Hello? Hello?*

"We won't answer them," the man said. "We don't want to talk to anyone."

She crushed out the half-smoked cigarette; it was leaving a foul taste in her mouth. She had to think what to do. There was something about this man, an undercurrent of appalling tension below the gentle voice and the quiet face, that warned her that if she said the wrong thing, he'd

49

blow up in some way, come for her, rape her, kill her blindly. That was why she hadn't dared ask him: *Did you kill the doorman?* It was why she didn't start running, right now, running through the other rooms and the servants' quarters and the kitchen to the back door and across the hall to one of the elevators in the hope that it would work if she pressed the button. She could run fast, and slam doors in his face, but she knew without any question that she wouldn't get away from him. You can never be as fast, or as strong, as a madman. There was a phrase for it: the strength of a madman.

Hello? Hello?

She looked at the telephone, and at last the voice stopped, and there was just the steady tone, bringing desolation.

Think what to do, what to say.

"Joe, how did you get so wet?"

"It was the rain."

"You'll catch a cold, like that. You should take a shower."

Once he was in the shower, she could run.

Life isn't so simple tonight, Tina.

"Sure. I'd like that. Hot water." He gave his attractive friendly laugh. "You know something? I'm soaked to the skin! I didn't think I'd walked that far." The box ottoman was heavy, teakwood bound with brass, but he moved it easily enough, dragging it across the pile carpet one corner at a time, like porters moved trunks, live porters, not dead ones, her heart missing a beat again. "We don't want them to get in here," he said, and she noticed he was hardly out of breath as he straightened up, with the box ottoman firmly across the door. "You know what they did? They tried to stop me getting up here." He just sounded surprised, as he'd sounded surprised about walking that far in the rain.

"So what did—?" but she stopped right there. She

wanted to know, terribly wanted to know, what had happened down there in the lobby; but she already knew, and what she really wanted was to hear him say it, and bring the reality home, so that she'd know where she stood, and could start facing the terror down. But he might go beyond just answering the question; it could trigger that hideous tension and blow everything up. Talking to Joe was like playing with matches near a gasoline tank.

"Take a shower, Joe. Or you'll catch your death of cold."

Just an expression, nothing significant. Nobody had ever died of a cold, you had to use a gun or hit them with— Must watch thoughts like that one getting out of hand or she'd start losing her reason. *How had he done it, down there? Why were there so many police cars still in the street?*

"Sure," he said, "I'd like that."

The pineapple plant was in a huge gold pot, ceramic, she supposed, and gilded in some way—everything in this room was gold and charcoal gray, gray carpet and gray silk walls and mostly gold furniture, lacquer and leaf and metal—but he managed to lift the plant pot and heave it on top of the ottoman against the door, its weight making the teakwood creak. Then he stood back a little and looked at it and dragged it a few inches sideways, standing back again until she felt a terrifying urge to laugh, because he'd killed someone down there and was going to blow the top of this building across the city, but not until he'd made sure the plant pot was exactly in the middle of the ottoman, so that it looked right.

Make a run for it now, while he's standing with his back—

He turned and she flinched. It wouldn't be any use anyway; with what she knew, knowing herself, to be unerring instinct, she was perfectly certain that he was in command here, and in full possession of the kind of wits that would give him a head start in anything she tried to do. He could let her stand here, braced against the edge of the long gold cabinet with her hands gripping it and her knuckles white as she watched him, and feel totally confident that if she tried to break for the doorway into the next room he would be faster, and catch her, and in his anger throw her down and rip her bathrobe off and, yes, she must watch thoughts like these, it wasn't the time for the imagination to run wild. *So no one has ever been raped and left for dead in New York City? What do you think he's here for—to rearrange the furniture?*

"That look okay?" he asked her.

He was standing there with his face innocent, his light gray eyes smiling, pleased with what he'd done, and hoping she would be pleased too. She found herself thinking for the first time about his mind, his actual brain, the living tissues inside the skull over there with the wet hair sticking to it; she had often stared into the eyes of a cat and wondered what was going on in its brain as it stared back at her. All this man was concerned with right now was the plant pot: whether it was exactly in the middle of the ottoman, and looked right; somehow his mind was capable of setting itself along a single track with only one destination, and as he went along it he was able to throw off all other things and people and considerations until they were lying behind him, becoming smaller and smaller, becoming lost and out of his way, out of his memory. Tunnel vision. Tunnel mind, or tunnel something. And at the end of the tunnel, the destination: *To be with you. To be with you for the rest of my life.* Her destination, too. To be with him.

Her tongue moved in her dry mouth. "It looks fine," she said. The plant pot. They had to concentrate on the plant pot, and forget all about the police cars and the doorman and . . .

Oh, Daddy-O, I need you now.

She would call him again, somehow. Couldn't you trick mad people easily enough? Or were they too bright? If they were bright, why were they mad? Big questions. Tonight is a time for big questions, Tina.

Another siren was wailing down there, and fading out; she went across to one of the huge tinted windows and looked down, seeing the reflected lights flashing in the windows of the building opposite, pressing her hands against the glass and looking right down into the street itself, seeing tiny men and toy vehicles moving, the wash of light as the beams of headlamps swept across them; and as she raised her eyes she saw Joe's reflection watching her, as he'd been yesterday, watching her through the window, but from the outside. He wasn't smiling anymore, now that her back was turned; from where he was, he might not see she was watching his reflection; she might be looking across at the building opposite. Did he only smile when she was facing him? He was just staring at her now, at her back. What was he thinking? How long would she be able to stay here, shut in a trap with someone who might be thinking of murdering her, whenever he stared at her back?

Stick to logic. She'd told the policewoman she was frightened at having a strange man in the apartment, and the woman had said a patrolman was on his way. Whatever had happened down there in the lobby, the police knew she could be in some kind of danger, and needed help. They'd be trying to reach her now.

"There's nothing they can do," he said, coming towards her. She turned quickly, ready for anything, feeling stupid when he simply stood there, with no intention of attacking her. "We're perfectly safe up here, Tina."

"I was just—" Then a phone began ringing, not here in

the living room but somewhere else. He turned and went through the arched doorway, and she heard him lift the phone and drop it back onto its cradle. He came back and stood between the fluted gold columns, looking smaller from this distance, less dangerous.

She took a deep breath. "Joe, do you mind if I call my parents?"

"Go ahead," he said, startling her. He'd sounded almost surprised at the question. She shouldn't have asked him; she should have just gone across to the phone and picked it up; he was a damned window cleaner, wasn't he, an intruder? She felt a kind of courage coming into her, even anger.

"Joe, I want you to get out of here now. I've been patient for long enough. I want you to get the hell out of this apartment while I call the police to say you're on your way down."

He was standing close to her without having seemed to move; he'd crossed the thick gray pile so fast that the movement had hypnotized her in some way. "You don't know what you're saying, Tina. You don't know who I am. But you mustn't ever call the police. You musn't ever do that."

And in his eyes, and the way he said it, and in the set of his whole body she heard the warning. If she ever called the police, or did anything he didn't want her to, he would have to kill her.

You know what they did? They tried to stop me getting up here.

The anger went out of her, and she was shivering.

"All right," she said.

A phone had started ringing again somewhere, and he stood listening contemplatively, as if he wasn't sure it was important enough this time to bother about. It had the sound of an echo: there were two or three phones ringing on one line.

"Is that in the next apartment?" he asked her.

"No." Abstractedly she wondered why he thought you could hear anything in the next apartment, in a place like this. "There are four or five guest suites." Then another phone started up, much closer, either in the main dining room or the library; its rhythm was out of synch with the other phones that were still ringing.

"My God," he gave a little explosive laugh, "just how many phones are there in—?" Then the one nearest him, on the gold shelf, began ringing, and he turned to watch it, in a moment taking her hand and leading her through the two gold columns and into the music room, past the piano and the enormous church organ and the wall filled with volumes of music and through the archway into the next room, her hand still in his as they reached a terrace and the swimming pool with its huge bronze dolphins and amethyst-striped canopies above the dressing rooms, with both the telephones—coral-handled and cradled in shells—ringing as they made their way through the arches at the far end of the terrace and came to a garden room with ferns and roses and white trellis and a fountain playing. "This *place*," he said in wonderment, shaking his head, "you mean you really *live* here—people *live* here?" They made their way through some of the guest suites, one with a pink satin decor, one with oak paneling and hunting rifles on the wall, one with mostly mirrors and Lalique glass—"I mean it's like something at Disney World, except that this is real *class*, I've just never *imagined*, you know, when you look at these buildings from the outside . . ."

She followed him with her hand ice cold in his, hardly seeing anything, hearing only the insistent ringing of the telephones wherever they went, like a kind of mad music.

─────── **6** ───────

BY THREE O'CLOCK IN THE morning the media were locked in at the scene. Following an emergency meeting with advisers from all police commands involved in the hostage situation, the deputy commissioner in charge of press relations drew up the necessary provisional regulations governing the presence and movements of reporters and camera crews in the cordoned areas surrounding the Park Tower building. Permission was given for a skeleton unit from each newspaper, radio and television station to observe the scene from within the four special areas set up for their containment on Fifth Avenue, Fifty-sixth Street, Fifty-seventh Street and on the roof of the building opposite Park Tower, where FBI and police-department sharpshooters were now permanently stationed around the water towers and elevator housings, together with a standby negotiating unit armed with searchlights, field glasses and bullhorns.

Sixteen police officers were in exclusive control of all representatives of the media, with strict orders to evict anyone who broke or even attempted to break the emergency regulations in force. In an informal address to a crowd of reporters who had besieged the officer in command of media relations in the field, Lieutenant Jim Sangster had told them: "You're not going to be allowed a lot of movement. For the most part you're going to be stuck there looking up at a skyscraper and developing a pain in the neck, and the only big moment you're liable to get is when that lunatic blows the top of the building off, and you'll be so busy running for cover that you won't even get any pictures.''

Soon after one A.M., Daisy, the police-department wolf-hound trained to sniff out explosives, had been escorted up the staircase to the fifty-third floor of Park Tower and had reacted immediately, backing away from the door and whimpering until her handler led her down the steps again. That Joseph Dotson had rigged a booby trap was no longer a cautious assumption; it was now assumed that since he had indeed placed explosives on the other side of the door, it was on the order of forty pounds, as he had claimed earlier. This was the reason for the sparse deployment of police officers and auxiliaries in the open streets, where debris could fall with the lethal effect of shrapnel if Dotson were provoked into blowing himself and his hostage off the face of the earth. ''We're trying to save a life,'' Captain Everett Mundy had told his field units, ''but we don't have to risk a hundred other lives to do it.'' The three officers at this time manning the top of the staircase were ordered down to the fiftieth floor, where they would no longer be in danger.

Since midnight, when the city media had picked up the name Tina St. Clair from the police radio dispatcher who had received her call for help, reporters and photographers from nearby states had been flying into Kennedy and La Guardia; by three in the morning the Canadian media forces were arriving, some of them in hastily chartered executive jets to beat the delays in waiting for the scheduled carrier flights, while top journalists and cameramen from the *Daily Mirror* and *Daily Express* of London were airborne over the Atlantic, together with an Air France flight bringing representatives of *Paris Match* and five

major newspapers covering more than eighty percent of the
French readership.

It was estimated that better than a hundred correspondents and photographers had arrived in New York City to
cover the scene at Park Tower, and this figure was expected to triple by morning. Soon after three o'clock the
contingent of media-relationship officers was increased to
twenty-five, to avoid what Captain Mundy had described
as "potential chaos."

The chief executives of the three major television networks had been wakened by telephone and had convened
summary conferences with their staff leaders. The situation
had caught everyone by surprise, and some difficult decisions had to be made: how much coverage should they
give to an incident involving the possible murder of only
one individual, taking into consideration the fact that
this one individual involuntarily supplied every popular
newspaper and magazine with copy in the form of tidbits,
rumors, gossip and blatant assumptions on the subject of
her day-to-day life? Tina St. Clair was news. As one
executive at NBC put it: "It's news when she changes her
brand of toothpaste, so what is it when she's up there in
that ivory tower being raped and possibly murdered?"

The networks' ratings and credibility would depend critically on the decisions these men were going to make,
against the increasing pressure of time and logistics. This
was a late-breaking story, and correspondents around the
world with material for U.S. eastern-time stations had filed
their reports on what tape or film was available; it wasn't a
question of how to get an exclusive: the spotlight was
already shining on Park Tower and nobody could hope for
sole coverage; it was a question of what would happen to
the ratings if a company failed to provide as much coverage as its competitors. When Elvis Presley died, CBS
opened their Cronkite broadcast with the news of the

endorsement of the Panama Canal treaties by President Ford. Millions of viewers, anxious to see the Presley coverage, switched immediately to one of the other networks, and the Cronkite show had its lowest rating in years. Tonight, at the hastily ordered conferences throughout the networks, news chiefs were being told to hold the lineup and open with the Tina St. Clair story, even though it would only amount to roving-cameraman scenes of the police units and still shots of the entrance to the Park Tower building and the highest row of windows, behind which the drama was being enacted. Unless of course Dotson decided to come out quietly or release the hostage or blow the penthouse into the street. For a worthwhile story, something would have to happen.

It wasn't much different for the newspapers. The New York *Times* had been put to bed at nine o'clock last night, and the *Daily News* even earlier; it was only the papers with a series of late editions that could hope to catch any kind of flash coverage in the event that anything happened; meanwhile all the editors could do in their offices was to sit with their scanners tuned to the police wavelength and pore over material pulled from the Tina St. Clair file, in case she'd ever come close to a similar experience that could point up the present situation and give it a little background.

Reporters on the graveyeard shift were meanwhile trying to make themselves comfortable in the street, the most enterprising among them having brought rugs, cushions or a director's chair. Pat Tolman of the *Eastside Chronicle*, who had been by sheer chance first on the scene of the shootings in the lobby, had volunteered to extend her shift and stay with it until something broke. At this moment she was curled up in an ancient quilt in a doorway of Bonwit Teller, gazing up at the one lighted window at the top of the Park Tower building, thinking—Okay, so you're an heiress, a girl so stinking rich that you probably never even heard of money, and so stunning to look at that even Warren Beatty's long since given up trying, and now you're up there in the sky all alone with someone like Son of Sam who's killed two men just so that he could get at you. And what does it feel like, little Miss Gucci Two-Shoes? Is he just screwing the insides out of you all over the floor, or is it more subtle than that, has he got you backed up against the wall with a knife at your throat while he tells you what kind of patterns he's going to make with it all over your body before he finally shoves it into your—

"Jesus," she said to the cop mounting guard on the doorway, "I wish you guys would *do* something."

A half hour ago she'd sneaked through the ropes and joined the press group inside the Park Tower lobby, but all they could think of asking the cops was, "Can they hear any screaming up there? Can we say she's screaming?" She'd left them and thrown up again into a garbage bin on her way back here. What else would that poor little bitch up there be doing, if she was still alive enough to do anything at all?

In a handout to the press shortly after three o'clock it was reported that New York Telephone had been asked to change the circuits in the Park Tower building, since complaints had been made by several of the residents still keeping to their apartments. The news-media staffs had been pulling their files on the ten thousand or so important people in the city and calling up those living at Park Tower to ask questions: How did they feel to be marooned like this? Were they scared? Could they hear anything from the top of the building? As soon as it was discovered that Apartment 53 belonged to Thomas Lindquist, they'd begun calling every one of the seven lines without letting up, hoping that sooner or later Dotson would decide to pick up a phone and say something, no matter what. They had the most dramatic standoff situation for years going on, but nothing they could print.

Around 4 A.M. the first of the garbage trucks moved into the area, the police making gaps in the cordons for them as they went from bin to bin removing the detritus of another day in the city's life, much of it newsprint. The street cleaners followed, scooping up the litter that had been gathered into the gutters by last night's rain: empty cigarette packs, cigar butts, paper bags, and near the intersection at Fifth Avenue and Fifty-sixth Street, the remains of a bunch of red roses.

Everett Jefford Mundy had left high school at sixteen, to drift around New York City, mostly Queens and Brooklyn, slinging hash, delivering papers, fixing bicycles and lawn mowers and getting into fights with the kids he ran into on the street and in the bars and game parlors and back-street cafés, until the message got through to them that if they didn't want any more smashed noses they'd have to leave him alone.

When his father died of cancer in 1950 and left a handicapped wife and three kids younger than Everett, he went straight to a trucking company and harassed the foreman into giving him a job on the local city runs. Two years later he got sick of carting trash around and joined up with a security service as night guard, partly because the pay was a fraction better and partly because he'd grown to like guns and wanted to wear one officially. But night guard was even less interesting than carting trash: it was like being an airline pilot, he said, one year's boredom interspersed with five minutes' stark terror when the air brakes failed. He had actually fired on three apprentice burglars and brought two of them to justice during his stint as a guard, but the periods in between were so uneventful that in 1953 he suffered from what he later described as a brainstorm and turned off the sidewalk into an NYPD recruiting office and five weeks later put on a uniform as a rookie under training. Soon afterwards, he was "bat swinging"—walking a beat in Laurel Hill, Queens, with a silver badge on his chest and a service revolver at his side, wondering why the hell he'd never thought of being a policeman before: at only twenty-one he owned the town. What he'd been hungering for, he realized, wasn't a gun on his hip but the silver badge, the symbol of authority.

He didn't want the authority to enable him to dominate others; he'd proved he could do that easily enough when he wanted to. He saw it as the means of putting across his ideas to people without having to waste too much time in argument. As he rose through the ranks and the silver badge was changed for a gold one in the Detective Division, he came to have more and more people under him, and less and less need to argue with anyone: when he wanted his ideas put into action he simply gave the order. And most of his ideas were sound; he developed a grasp of procedure and politics within the department that steered him upwards past other men who were so busy soaping the stairs for him that they failed to notice he was in the elevator, going up. By the time he gained his captaincy at the age of forty-two, he had gained also the mixed admiration and resentment that accompanies most successful men; to proclaim his reputation as someone on whom the sun always shone, his staff placed on his desk the first day he sat behind it as captain, a plaque reading IT NEVER RAINS ON MUNDY.

It was partly for this reason that he found himself in the fifty-first-floor lobby of the Park Tower building at four o'clock this morning with two members of the Emergency Services Division, two F8I sharpshooters and three hostage negotiators. He was in command of the entire field, including the two other posts and the mobile street units, but the real focus of operations was right here in the soft-lit hallway with its plush red carpeting and bronze-framed lamps and paneled walls. Yet they just weren't getting anywhere.

"This is no damned good," he said. "I've got to *see* the man."

They thought that would be a big help, but even Mundy didn't have X-ray eyes.

Nick Valenti spoke into the microphone again, his tone showing nothing of his frustration: he'd been sending this message every minute for three hours now and getting no response of any kind.

"Joe, we have some very interesting information for you. It's something you'd really like to hear. But we can't give it to you if you won't pick up a phone and talk to us. Pick up a phone, Joe, because it's really important you hear what we've got to tell you."

Nick had been ringing the changes with every attempt at contact, but this was the basic meaning: Joe Dotson was missing something if he didn't pick up a phone and listen. Three hours ago Mundy himself had climbed the steps to the fifty-third floor, quietly placing a loudspeaker outside the booby-trapped door, unwilling to detail anyone else to do it in case that stuff went off; it was the only way they could get Lieutenant Valenti's voice within earshot at least of the penthouse lobby: a bullhorn would only deafen them all and probably not reach the apartment through these heavily soundproofed walls and ceilings. If Dotson decided to pick up a phone and ask what information they had for him, the call would go straight into the hotline circuit and Nick would answer it himself.

Everything had been worked out. The content of the message had been designed and changed around a dozen times until it was refined and polished.

"He could be there to kill again," the police psychologist had said, "or he could be there simply for sex. He might have gone up there for both. He could kill her in a frenzy and smash all the mirrors and wreck all the furniture and then blow himself away with the building, or he could suddenly snap out of his psychosis and open the door and surrender—or a dozen or so variations of all those things. But what we *must* assume is that if we provoke him in any way, he'll kill her."

The psychologist, Lieutenant Keith McNeil, was down there now in the ground-floor lobby, waiting for the telephone to ring. The company had diverted every phone in the penthouse to a single line, so that the police had only one number to think of; conversely, every call made from the penthouse would go out to only one number: the outside phone at the ground-floor command post, where an amplifier would carry Dotson's voice to everyone there; it would also be automatically relayed to a dozen offices in headquarters at One Police Plaza, including that of the chief of detectives, who was in overall command of the operation.

Shortly before five A.M. Valenti lowered the microphone again and looked at the captain. "I don't think he can hear us. I think he would have responded by now. Or, you know"—he shrugged—"they're both dead."

Detective Lieutenant Nick Valenti had been brought into the Hostage Negotiating Team four years ago, getting his promotion at the same time. Now he was already nudging captain after seventeen major hostage and barricade situations, during which only two people had lost their lives, and those simply because the hostage takers had been too mentally disturbed to understand the meaning of the negotiations.

Nick, like Everett Mundy, had been a cop on the beat as a young man, though he'd started quite a few years later:

he was still only thirty-two, to Mundy's fifty-one. His work as a negotiator had begun officially at three o'clock one morning when he'd found a young black dangling his two-year-old kid over the parapet of Brooklyn Bridge, with his wife a few yards away pleading with him in desperation. The situation seemed simpler than it was: the girl had been threatening to leave her husband, and it had blown his mind. She was now saying she'd stay with him if he'd bring the kid to safety, telling him over and over that she'd stay if he didn't drop the kid; but he was still over there holding on to the kid's little wrists and swinging him to and fro a hundred feet over the black waters of the river. Officer Valenti was standing back and for the moment doing nothing and saying nothing, knowing instinctively that to do or say anything precipitate could bring tragedy. He thought at first that the guy just wouldn't believe his wife: she'd leave him the moment the kid was back in her arms again.

So Valenti said to the man: "She means what she's saying, don't you know that? She's going to stay with you, man, so bring the boy over here."

The kid still dangled, and to this day Nick could remember the huge eyes in the dark face full of terror, the two spindly legs swinging, one sock up and the other down, the gleam of the water under the lights of the shore, way down there below.

"She gonna leave me. She gonna leave me."

It was all the man could say. It was the one thought filling the whole of his head.

"She's changed her mind now," Nick told him. "She's going to stay. You've won out, can't you see that, man? She didn't know how much you loved her, and now she does." The sweat was running on Nick's body like he was under a shower, and his eyes were on the eyes of the kid in a kind of prayer going out silently while he kept on

65

talking. "You've made her see you love her so much you'd even do a thing like this if she went away. So it's okay now, you can bring him over and we'll all of us go and get a sandwich and a coffee down at Abe's place."

The kid could only watch Nick now, maybe hearing something in his tone that gave him comfort. But his father could only say one thing.

"She gonna leave me."

The girl wasn't answering him anymore; she was leaving it to the policeman now; she'd tried all she could. They were all leaving it to him, Nick thought, and somewhere beyond panic he found courage in himself. People tuned in to him easily, and he was going to trade on that.

"She gonna leave me," the black was saying—and suddenly Nick knew why he was saying it. He believed his wife, all right, but he wasn't done with her yet: she'd scared the hell out of him by telling him she was going away, and now she was going to get punished. And Nick Valenti changed his tactics at once.

"Listen, she's hurting pretty bad, man. You can see that. What you're doing to her is, well, Jesus, she's kind of dying. You can see that. She knows what you're telling her, see. You're just jumping mad at her, and she's going to get it, right? Well, she's getting it. She's like dying, you can see that. So now you can stop. She's real hurt, and she knows you did it, and she's never going to forget. That's why she'll stay with you now, and you'll watch your beautiful child grow up, and forget about all this."

The sweat running on him and the breath tight in his chest as he crept with infinite care through all the hundreds and thousands of words he could choose to say, safe ones and dangerous ones, each one working inside that poor sap's head and changing the chemistry there, while the fingers kept their grip on the miniature wrists and the spindly legs, one sock up and one down, swinging against the cold sooty parapet of the bridge. Creeping through a whole mine field of words, with only his instinct as a compass. "You know what I mean? Nothing's ever over, see, there's always tomorrow. And tomorrow you two are going to take in a movie or go down to the bowling alley while your Ma or someone looks after your fine little boy, okay? Tomorrow you're going to have yourselves a real nice day." The eyes of the black were looking at him now, as he began listening at last. "That's tomorrow, man, and it's going to be beautiful, so why the crap are you hanging around here playing games when we could all be down there in the warm at Abe's place—and I mean the chow's on me, you know, I'm not trying to con anybody, so just bring him over here and we'll wrap him up and make a fuss over him—you know that poor kid's scared out of his head? So c'mon now, man," holding his arms out but not daring to take a step closer, not yet, because that could blow the whole—

"You're not gonna leave me?" the man asked suddenly with his face turned to his wife.

"Of course not, honey, I'm gonna stay, *I'm gonna stay*—" and suddenly it all came together and the man was swinging the kid up into his arms and coming across to the girl and the girl was reaching out and they were both crying as Nick stood back and watched them come together in a big shaking kind of hug with the kid lost somewhere between them; and Nick didn't know if these guys were going to do the same thing tomorrow and the next day just for kicks or whether he'd just saved a kid's life and maybe a marriage; all he knew was that the slow black water down there was moving under the bridge with nothing breaking the surface, nothing making a splash, just the lights along the shoreline looking prettier than he'd ever seen them before.

"For Christ sake," he said, "isn't anyone hungry?"

That had been five years ago, a year before he was actually brought into the negotiating team. Since then he'd faced bank robbers, rapists, terrorists, kidnappers and psychopaths, but for the most part he'd faced ordinary people, usually men, who had gotten into a situation they couldn't get out of without a show of force on the spur of the moment; they'd been pushed to the brink and lost their marbles, that was all, but with a gun or a knife in their hand they were just as dangerous as a professional terrorist or a certified lunatic.

"There are professional nuts," he'd told the group he was teaching, "and there are amateur nuts. The pros can be dangerous all of the time; the amateurs are people like ourselves: most of their lives they pay the rent and do a job and raise the kids, only with a few of them something suddenly happens that blows the marbles clean out of their mind and—bingo! You've got a crisis on your hands, and it could be fatal. You talk them down, you lower their stress to the point where they can see reason again, and you've got it made, because most of us listen to reason. But with the pros—the psychotics, the psychopaths—you're on ice all the time, and it's thin, and the water's deep, because if they've lost their power of reasoning, you can't reason with them. They're the worst."

They'd got one tonight, one of the worst. As he lowered the mike for the umpteenth time and reached for another cigarette, Nick listened for what Captain Mundy was going to say. They'd reached a point where they were going to have to try some other way of opening the negotiations with Dotson up there. It was like with the sharpshooting teams around this building: they had enough firepower to blast half a regiment into Christendom, but if Dotson wouldn't show himself, they couldn't hit him. In the case of the negotiating team they had had a formidable assembly of psychiatrists, psychologists, experienced police negotiators and the top decision-making brass of the department, with a calculated scenario of argument and persuasion and strategy all worked out and ready to go, but if Dotson didn't pick up a telephone they were all of them deaf and dumb.

Mundy knew that Valenti was waiting for some kind of new approach to this thing, but he didn't have any. As he prowled up and down the confining hallway of the fifty-first floor, looking upwards all the time and seeing only the ceiling, he felt that Dotson and his hostage were a thousand miles away. It was a gap they'd have to close, if they wanted to get that woman out of there still alive and with her sanity intact, if it wasn't already too late.

"I want to *see* that guy," he said again. "We have to know he's there, and real, and approachable. So we're getting out of here."

As the first light of the new day began flowing across Long Island and into the narrow chasms of the city's streets, the negotiating team settled into its new quarters on the roof of the building opposite Park Tower—now known officially as the command building—six hundred and seventy feet above the garbage trucks and yellow cabs and police vehicles moving sluggishly past the barricades and through the intersection of Fifth Avenue and Fifty-seventh Street. The complement was the same: Captain Mundy, commanding the overall field; Detective Lieutenant Nick Valenti as primary negotiator; Al Groot as secondary negotiator; Tony Rimkus as the reserve; two members of the Emergency Services Division armed with deer rifles; two FBI sharpshooters with their Remingtons; and now an additional two detectives to act as physical liaison and messengers. In this building, at least, they had access to

the elevators: a middle-aged patrolman had been rushed to
the intensive-care unit of the Medical Arts Hospital with a
heart attack after climbing the steps to the fifty-first floor
at Park Tower in a hurry; he was still in critical condition.

Mundy felt better up here. Across the street and on
almost the same level he could see the twelve tinted windows of the Park Tower penthouse, the four on the left
uncurtained but with the interior obscure because there
were no lights burning. From his knowledge of the floor
plans the city engineer had obtained for him, he knew he
was now overlooking the enormous living room of the
penthouse, the music room, the library, a study and a
bedroom, each with windows on the east side and facing
the command building. The living room occupied the southeast corner of Park Tower, and these were the windows
that had no drapes or blinds across them; but as the pale
sun rose from behind him, all Mundy could see was the
reflection of the command-building rooftop, where he was
standing now.

He'd ordered seven telephone lines to be brought up
here, three of them connected to the penthouse in the
building opposite and the other four linking the hostage
team with the chief of detectives' office at One Police
Plaza, the Emergency Services central command post outside the entrance to Park Tower, and the New York Telephone exchange through two outside lines. If Dotson ever
made a call, they'd receive it here, and immediately.

"We weren't raising him," Mundy had reported an
hour ago to Chief of Detectives Daniel Warner. "I don't
think he could hear the speaker we'd put up there. Now
we're in the open on this rooftop we stand a chance of
actually seeing the man if he moves close to a window,
and even a chance of picking him off with a rifle if that's
what you finally decide; we can also use the bullhorn up
here, with the certainty of penetrating the east window

glass with enough volume to carry the message. We can also hope to see if the hostage is still alive, if she goes close to a window, and that's going to make the biggest difference to the team here: they've been trying to make contact for more than seven hours now and it's been like talking to a wall; if we can only just catch a glimpse of Dotson or the woman at a window we'll know we're not wasting our time.''

The chief had thought about this. ''Are you in full view of the other building, that's to say the penthouse?''

''No, sir. We're behind the natural cover up here: the elevator heads and the water tanks and the parapet. We—''

''How high's the parapet?''

''A couple of feet.''

''Perfect,'' the chief said.

''Sure thing, sir.'' Warner was thinking of cover for the snipers.

''Keep me in touch, Mundy.''

Soon after eight-thirty a report came through that Eugene C. St. Clair and his wife had landed at Kennedy in a private charter plane and were now on their way to police headquarters, where Chief Warner would brief them on events.

''The big question,'' the secondary negotiator, Al Groot, told the men around him, ''is how much?''

''It's going to be more than sixty-four thousand dollars.''

''Christ,'' one of the FBI men said, prone behind the parapet with his rifle alongside, ''just what does it feel like to have to put a price on your daughter's life?''

''They're a close family,'' Al Groot said. ''A man like him, he can go to fifty million, a hundred million, who knows what he can go to?''

Squatting low with his back to the water tower, Nick Valenti moved his field glasses across and across the row of tinted windows two hundred feet away, his eyes aching

71

for a glimpse of movement behind the glass, just a glimpse, that was all, so they could know there was life there.

"I don't think it matters how much he can pay," he said in a low voice. "I wish to God I could think it's going to be as simple as that."

7

HE WOKE WHILE IT WAS still dark, and watched the new day begin, the light creeping and touching on surfaces and angles and curves so slowly that he could play puzzle games, seeing an object and at first not knowing what it was in the first faint light, making three guesses, always three, like it was always three wishes in the fairy stories, and trying to beat the light to it, trying to guess what the object was before the light showed it up for him.

There were roses everywhere, and he watched them, in a way, blooming as the light grew stronger. He'd chosen this room after asking her which one she wanted to sleep in; she'd said she didn't mind. This one was like a garden, or a bower, with huge pink roses on the wallpaper, climbing through white trelliswork, even hanging overhead on the ceiling. The twin beds were bamboo and wicker, with rough white coverlets and a single enormous rose over the pillow.

He felt eased by all this; it reminded him of days in the country in New England, and lying in meadows with the sun in his eyes and birds calling, and a stream. Nothing bad could ever happen in a place like this.

It's almost square, with an angle, but a kind of curving angle, with the light making a faint line along the top bit, where the curve . . . *it's a bowl with something inside it* . . . no, that can't be it. There's a dark line, coming from one side, like a rope, or—*it's a telephone!* Right, it's the phone in here, the bedroom phone.

But it's not working.

He'd stopped all that business.

Coming down . . . he was coming down. It had taken quite a time for him to get back to—to where he was now. Where was he now? It didn't matter.

The light crept from the windows, flowing along things and making them float; they broke away from all the dark confusion and slowly, or sometimes suddenly, became what they were. That was what he was doing too. Coming back to where he was now.

In the night he'd woken up and remembered their faces and almost cried out. The men down there, the one with the peaked cap and the one with the badge sewn on his sleeve and the gun in its polished brown holster, their faces and their hands raised against him and their mouths saying he must go away, *and then the rage and the gun and the banging and the horrible idea that something was happening and that it was taking him back to where he must never—*

As long as you're okay, Joe.

I'm okay. Sure I'm okay.

He'd better get up because there was that fantastic new building to do on Fifth Avenue, and he was going to show Sam how the mullion guides— But that was crazy. That was yesterday. That was another world.

The light grew stronger, and now his head moved to the left and quietly he sat up, making himself comfortable with his bare arm hooked over the bamboo frame of the bed behind the pillows, where he could feel a sharp part of the bamboo sticking into his skin, though he didn't mind, or move his arm, because he was watching the miracle happening as the light went on flowing and touching and washing the shadows away, the miracle, the revelation, while his heart began thudding and he held his breath and waited and waited until suddenly . . .

There she was.

Sleeping.

He held himself perfectly still and let the feeling go through him like it had before, when he'd seen her for the first time, like his chest was filling with perfume, with the scent of roses, while the light flowed softly across the rough white coverlet and touched the dark wing of her hair that lay curled against it, and then the smooth curves and shadows of her face, her mouth tender, like a child's mouth at rest with no words ready, no kisses, her eyes closed, keeping the dreams hidden under the smoky shadows of their lashes while the light went on flowing, bringing the new day down from the sky and spreading it across the city and the windows and the room here and the miracle, the revelation, the face of Tina St. Clair.

I love you, he said, but not aloud, just in his mind, *I love you,* his mind pulling petals off the big pink roses and letting them fall across her a word at a time, *I love you.*

And then as the light grew brighter he saw that she wasn't asleep, but watching him.

"I don't believe it," she said.

"Don't believe it?"

"I don't believe any of this."

"How many eggs? Two?"

"God, I don't know," she said with almost a laugh, "I don't even remember what they taste like."

He cracked two eggs and dropped them into the pan, looking like any other man, somebody's young husband, dressed in one of Tom Lindquist's blue golf shirts—"D'you think he'd mind?" Joe had asked her earlier, "I put my things in the washer, so is that okay? I thought this was *your* place, I didn't know you were just staying here." Now he said as he dropped four slices of bread into the toaster: "Why don't you believe any of this?" He watched her intently, wanting to know.

"I can't explain." It would be like trying to explain sight to a blind man, though much more dangerous.

"You must," he said. The eggs sizzled, and he shook the pan.

Her hands tightened on the edge of the breakfast counter. She was leaning back against it, in one of the defensive attitudes she'd unconsciously adopted since he'd come here last night; perhaps her body knew, with its infinitely sensitive understanding of survival, that from here she could propel herself forward to spring against him, pushing hard with her hands and with her fingers clawing for his eyes, or to spring away if he came for her first.

"I expect I believe it really," she said. It was like talking to children: you had to talk down, avoiding long words and so on, but you also had to remember they were extremely bright, and were listening with a merciless attention. With this man she was already learning to avoid words that might offend him because he didn't understand them, like *normalcy*, and *reasonable*; because he wasn't normal, and couldn't reason. To anyone else she could have said well, I mean you're a total stranger and you probably killed two men last night and now the place is surrounded with police cars and I'm frightened to death, yet here you are frying eggs and making toast as if nothing had happened—don't you see it isn't normal?

Lying awake most of the night, she'd come to believe that they both had to protect him from finding out that he wasn't normal. Maybe he knew, somewhere at the back of his mind where it was too dark to see clearly, that he had done terrible things, and might do more terrible things; but he was turning his back on it all and looking the other way; and what she had to help him to do was never to turn around, because that would take away the last of his control.

Her life depended on the idea that it was perfectly normal for him to be here in the kitchen cooking breakfast.

"Sure you believe it," he said, with the sharpness gone from his voice. "I'm real, aren't I?"

"Oh yes, Joe, you're real."

And life was going on, whereas last night she'd thought it was going to be over. He hadn't even raped her, and that was unbelievable too. Maybe he was gay, though he didn't look it; he had the gentleness of the true male in his attitude toward her, a deference to her uniqueness as a woman that no woman ever failed to recognize. Or maybe she was just imagining it, feeling grateful for not having been raped. Early this morning when they'd put out the lights in the living room she'd gone quickly to the nearest guest suite where her things were and swallowed a pill, and had oiled herself in the bathroom, knowing she'd be absolutely dry if he forced himself on her. At first light, when she'd lain watching him through her almost closed lids, she'd felt almost ashamed for misjudging him.

But the police cars.

Oh yes, the police cars. This was Joe Dotson, cooking the breakfast and not touching her, looking at her with gentleness in his eyes; but the other Joe Dotson was here too, listening with a child's merciless attention to every word she said. One must be careful in speaking to Joe Dotson. Last night they'd said no, you can't see her, and they were dead.

"Over easy, or how?"

"What?"

"How d'you like—?"

"Oh, yes, just as they come."

The coffee was percolating and she went over to it, finding cups and things they'd need from the cabinets,

never quite turning her back to him, which was another
defensive attitude she'd adopted. She didn't think he'd
attack her when her back was turned; it was just the way
he'd looked at her last night when she was watching his
reflection in the window: his smile had gone, and he was
thinking, and she hadn't known what.

"Do you take cream, Joe?"

"Lots."

She opened the fridge. It was standing against the back
door now; at some time in the night he'd come in here and
moved it, even though it was enormous and must weigh a
ton. There were only two doors to this place, for security
reasons; the residents used the front door and the staff used
the back. He had probably explored, while she was sleeping,
and found no other exits. He hadn't bothered to explain
this morning that blocking the back door too would "stop
them getting in here," as he'd done when he'd moved the
huge box ottoman. She knew why he'd blocked the doors.

It was strange not to hear a telephone ringing. He'd
thought it was fun at first, going from room to room and
looking at the phones as they rang and rang like that; then
he'd gotten bored with it, and pulled all the jacks out,
putting only one of them back so she could call her
parents, then pulling it out again.

They'd already left Dorado Beach, because of "some
trouble with their daughter," as the desk clerk had said,
not knowing who was calling. It had been the most desolate moment of the whole night, because she'd been expecting to hear Daddy-O's strong and reassuring voice on the
line: it would have made her whole again and able to cope
with anything. But it must mean they'd flown to New
York; the police had gotten in touch with them; they could
even be here now, and not far away. Daddy-O could do
anything, move mountains, anything.

"You're okay, Joe," she said, putting the things on the table.

"What was that?"

She looked up. "I said you're okay."

He was watching her in perfect stillness, as if his breath were held. "You mean you like me some?"

"Of course."

Suddenly he was standing close to her, in that startling way he had of moving with a cat's quickness; his head was down and his eyes were squeezed shut and he was shaking all over and saying, "But I did things—"

She waited for him to go on, not knowing if it would be dangerous or if he needed to do it: to turn around and look behind him. But he just went on standing there shaking, his eyes clenched shut and his hands hanging by his sides, until for the first time she touched him, holding his arms and saying: "The thing is, Joe, not to do anything again."

"Oh, three or four years. Maybe four years." He spread butter on his toast.

"What made you take a job like that?"

"It was a job, I guess. You know, I'd been looking for a time, and—it was a job."

"You're obviously not afraid of heights."

"Heights?" He considered this, his knife poised over his plate, looking down and away like he sometimes did; and she knew she'd touched on something. "I guess not. I never thought about it."

She poured more coffee for him. "Do you always work alone?"

"Not always. There's a guy called Sam. And there were other guys. They don't last too long at that game, you know? There's a lot of stress. There was one guy who—" He looked up at her again with that sudden openness in his

79

face that she found attractive, or perhaps just reassuring. "Do you really want to talk about this?"

"Of course I do. I've never met a—I mean a man who spends his life scaling castles."

"Castles?" He didn't seem to get any connection. "There was this guy, and he looked okay, you know, absolutely okay, and we took him up some real high ones, thirty floors, forty floors, the GM and Citicorp and places like that, and then one day he was on his own up there, and when it was time for him to check in at the office, he didn't show up. So they sent me along there to see what was wrong, and when I got there I saw him way up there near the top of the building, clinging on—onto the—you know, the—" He tailed off, looking down at the table for a minute. "I don't think I want to tell you about him." Then he looked up again, and just sat perfectly still with his eyes on hers, and she made herself not look away, even though these changes of mood unsettled her so much; and in a moment he said, "It's not easy for me to talk to you, Tina, because you have the most beautiful face I have ever seen in my whole life, and I'm sitting here with you in this room, and we're alone, and you don't mind if I look at you like this, though I know it could be embarrassing, but I want to try and tell you how it—I mean it's more than just looks, you know? Looking at your face is like being bathed in light, colored light, and it kind of passes into me, and goes right through me till I'm, you know, vibrating with it. Do you have any idea what I'm trying to say?"

"Of course," she said gently, "and it sounds very nice." She watched his eyes, waiting for any change in them; she was learning to do that: to watch for his slightest reaction to the things she said; in this way she could learn the language he needed to hear, and avoid the dangerous sounds and tones that might trigger off an explosion in him.

"Do you know," he asked her, moving his chair back and watching her with his head on one side, "that I love you?"

But of course he did. That was what he'd come here for: to be with her for the rest of his life. But perhaps it wasn't the same; love was so many things. What he felt for her was some kind of adolescent idolatry, and she must find out how to handle it, to use it for her own survival.

"I think I know," she said, "yes."

He bowed his head slightly, as if receiving grace. "And you like me, a little. You said so." He couldn't wait, even for a second—"Didn't you?"

"Yes," she said quickly, "yes I did."

He left his chair and moved around the carved redwood table to stand behind her; she tried to get up before he reached her, but he always moved so deceptively fast and now she was trapped, and could only sit there waiting. His hands moved and cupped her face as he bent to kiss her hair.

"Then no one is ever going to take you away from me," he said. "No one, ever."

—— 8 ——

"THEN WE GET LOST AGAIN."

"Have you tried Interpol?"

"We're trying them right now." Lieutenant O'Rourke peeled some of the leaf from his cheroot and dropped it into the piston-top ashtray and fed "Dotsen" into the computer on the grounds that a lucky shot could sometimes beat six hours of intensive investigation, which was the period of time he'd been here at his desk in the Identification Section at One Police Plaza after Mundy had got him out of bed at one o'clock this morning. "I'm beginning to think he's either changed his name or he went overseas at some time." He ran his fingers through his stiff black hair and struck another match and got the end of the stub glowing again and squinted through the smoke at the stack of files on his desk. "Or he could've changed his identity altogether."

Detective Spiro sat on the edge of the upright chair and watched him, in the same way that one might sit watching a hen on the nest. He was Captain Mundy's personal runner and he'd been told to sit in with O'Rourke however long it took to get the eggs. He hoped it wouldn't be too long; the smoke coming out of these cheroots was making him sick to his stomach.

Drunk-driving charge, the computer screen was reading out, *Hackensack, N.J., May 12, 1982. Conviction. Fine. License endorsed.*

The lieutenant crossed "Dotsen" off the list and fed in "Dolson."

"Spiro, you'd better go get yourself a cup of coffee."

"He told me to sit here till you got something, Lieutenant."

"Then don't breathe on me. You're making the air fresh."

Dolson had fenced stuff from robberies for two or three years in Queens and gone down for ten. O'Rourke penciled him out, picking up the phone as it rang.

"It's Joseph Paul Dotson, Lieutenant; it's on his work ident. papers. Okay?"

"The hell it's okay," he said and hung up, pulling a new cheroot out of its ripped cellophane pack and getting a match as Spiro moved his chair back and tightened his nostrils. "I'm going to try this Dozoretz guy, the window cleaner from Albany. It has to be a complete change of name or identity, or he went overseas. Go and tell Mundy."

"He said to sit, Lieutenant."

"Look, I can't concentrate with you perched on my shoulder like Long John Silver's parrot, so why don't you just get your ass out of here and batter the door of the girls' rest room down or ski on the stairs while I go into Zen with this thing."

"Is that an order, Lieutenant?"

"Better yet, it's a command."

He waited till Spiro had gone and then fed "Dozoretz" into the computer again and put the printout through the copier and sent five copies off, one of them to Mundy in the field and one to Interpol by telex. But even with Dozoretz there were two gaps, in 1967 and 1980, though there was one instance of a passport renewal in January 1970.

This was a few minutes past eight o'clock. At 9:13 one of the field men came in with a photograph in a dented silver frame and gave it to O'Rourke and he compared it with the mug shot in the yellow sheet file on Joseph Dozoretz and dropped his cheroot stub into the ashtray and kicked his chair back and got to the door in three strides and bawled out— "Spiro, where the fuck are you?"

"Oh my God," Mundy said.

On the roof of the command building the air was less cold as the sun cleared the city's profile to the east, and Nick Valenti had pulled his gloves off and was lifting the bullhorn again.

"Valenti!" called the captain, and beckoned him over to the water tower. "He changed his identity." While Valenti read the identity file, Mundy picked up the direct-line phone to the chief of detectives and started talking, sharing the file with the hostage negotiator. "Okay, sir, his name was Joseph Dozoretz originally, and in 1966 he was called as a witness in the death of one Mary Deborah Innes in Chicago, Illinois. For a time he was under suspicion of having caused her death: the woman fell from a balcony into the street after what the subject called a 'fit of depression.' No charge was made. In 1969—I'm giving you the salient points in this report, sir, but I can fill in the—"

"Go on as you are."

"Yes, sir. In 1969 he was convicted of first-degree murder in Trenton, New Jersey, when the victim, one of his work-mates, was seen in a café with Dozoretz's wife. He then skipped bail while appealing the verdict, and somehow managed to get to Europe—"

"Skipped bail on a *murder* verdict," came the chief's voice on the line, with a lot of anger in it. "By Holy God, I'd like to hang that judge, Mundy! Go on, dammit."

"Sir. The last file in Criminal Records has it that he was sent to King's County Hospital for medical tests and found mentally incompetent to stand trial on a charge of murdering a young woman named Sandy Baker, who fell to her death from a tower at an amusement park. Three witnesses said the accused was seen struggling with her before she fell. He was judged unable to understand the nature of the charges against him, or to assist in his own defense. He was sent to Mattewan State Hospital for the Criminally Insane and spent three years there before he escaped in a delivery van." Valenti held the report sheet still as the light wind ruffled the papers. "Nothing's been heard of him since that time: 1980."

There was a brief silence on the line. "So what are you going on?"

"They got the photograph from Robert Nicholas Dozoretz, a meat inspector in Manhattan, the father of Joseph Dozoretz. He hasn't seen his son for some years, but he had the photo among some stuff in an attic. I haven't seen it, sir, but O'Rourke in Identity says there's no question it's the same man as in the yellow-file mug shot—and there's no information about an identical twin or even a brother."

"What else?"

"The fingerprints on the dead security guard's gun holster and on the elevator call button at Park Tower match exactly with the prints in the Dozoretz file."

There was another silence. "He changed his name after his escape from Mattewan?"

"Everything points to that, sir, yes."

"All right, I want the file and the report in my office. Tell O'Rourke. And I have two other things to say. If these goddamned tenderfoot judges go on letting violent criminals loose on the streets, I think the New York Police Department might just as well retire. The second thing, Mundy, is that if that's the man who's up there at the top of that building, you'd better get him out before he does anything we're all going to regret. That's Tina St. Clair in there with him. It shouldn't matter, but it does."

Mundy let a brief silence of his own go by. "Yes, sir. And I have a daughter that age."

"I take your point, Mundy, but the difference is not humanistic, it's political. We're mounting this operation under the biggest public and media spotlight since the Reagan shooting, and the credibility of the police department is going to depend on whether we can get that girl out of there alive."

Less than an hour after Lieutenant O'Rourke had hit on the Dotson/Dozoretz connection, Mayor Abraham Levin called Police Commissioner Dakers and his top aides to a press conference at One Police Plaza. Before the press were invited into the main conference room, the mayor and the commissioner met with Eugene and Elizabeth St. Clair. The corporate banker had slept in his clothes on the plane in from Puerto Rico and his eyes were bloodshot, but his presence dominated the room. Beside him, his pretty wife was overshadowed, though Mayor Levin gave her marks for sheer style: she had actually managed to smile at them when she'd come into the room, and she was sitting with her small pale hands folded calmly together as she listened to the discussion and occasionally put in a word, her voice perfectly under control.

St. Clair swung his head alternately to look at the mayor and the commissioner, ignoring the five aides. When it became clear to him which of the two principals had the better ability to help him, he would be looking solely at one man.

"How much is he demanding?"

"We haven't yet made contact with him," Commissioner Dakers said, "since the outset. As soon as we can, we'll be asking his terms." Short, well-tailored and sunk into the kind of brooding calm his aides knew to be the eye of the storm, he returned the banker's glittering ocher gaze for a moment and then chose to look out of the window. He knew all the questions this man was going to ask him, and all the statements he was going to make. Dakers couldn't recall how many kidnap situations he'd had to deal with since he'd put on a badge, and he didn't want to. By their nature they were always the most harrowing, difficult and dangerous incidents the police ever handled. There was usually a life at stake; there was usually substantial money involved; and there was anguish of an order sometimes deeper than grief. After three weeks of silence, a mother had said of her missing son, "I'd almost rather he was found dead, than this. Then at least I'd know."

All Dakers wanted to do was end this interview, tell the press he was doing everything possible, and get over to the Park Tower stakeout and scare the hide off everyone there, from Mundy to the boys in the street. There wasn't anything they weren't doing that they could be doing, he knew that; all he could do himself was to step up their adrenaline production to keep them on their toes. The problem at the moment, Mundy had advised, was that nobody thought the hostage was still alive. They felt they were just beating the air.

St. Clair asked briefly: "What has to be done?"

"Just that, sir. We have to make contact. After that, there'll be—" he skidded past saying "much more chance" for the mother's sake, and finished "—much less of a problem."

"You've considered using the air conditioning?"

One of the questions Dakers knew he would ask. He was going to ask every single question that trained and experienced policemen had asked themselves, and already answered. "Nitrous oxide can be very toxic," he told St.

Clair. "We could evacuate the rest of the building and
feed the stuff through the air conditioning, but we'd be
unable to control the volume in terms of the gas/air ratio
inside the actual apartment. And people metabolize dif-
ferently: we could feed in enough to intoxicate your
daughter, perhaps fatally, and leave Dotson still walking
around."

He considered whether to pass St. Clair along to an aide
or give him a brief summary right now. He chose the
summary. The anguish in this room was tangible in the
nerves, and he had an urge to deal with it himself. "Mr.
St. Clair, we're doing everything possible. We considered
an anesthetic gas through the air conditioning; we've thought
of sending men in through the trapdoors and elevator
housings in the roof; we're aware that we can shut off the
heat, light, water, electricity and the telephones at a minute's
notice if we want to, if it would give us the slightest
advantage over Dotson. We could use ultra-sensitive microphones on the roof or in the apartment below; but I'm not
ordering any of my officers that close to a potential
explosion, not yet. We have upwards of one hundred and
fifty police officers of all ranks surrounding the building
and engaged in the task of resolving this situation safely;
in addition we have medical and fire teams immediately at
hand, with psychologists, psychiatrists, priests and our top
negotiating team standing by to apply their skills and
experience the minute they're given the chance." He turned
to the window again, preferring the view of Brooklyn
Bridge to the pain in this man's eyes. But he couldn't win:
the comfort he wanted to give could only be in terms of
the massive power of his police force, which was powerless at the present time to save one life. "That chance will
come the minute Dotson decides to pick up a phone."

Eugene St. Clair had the underlying message, but he

didn't turn away. It was his habit to stand with his feet evenly balanced and his head slightly lowered when there was something he had to face down.

"You are certain he took explosives up there with him?"

"Yes. We got a reaction from a sniffer dog. We also found sticks of dynamite in his rented apartment when we searched it. It seems he lives with the stuff."

St. Clair's wife spoke, slowly and with grace in her every intonation, as if wanting to spare these officers any suggestion of criticism. "You say you are trying to contact this man, Commissioner. How are you doing that?"

He turned to her at once. "With bullhorns, ma'am. Loudspeakers. There are four of them, across the street from each side of the building." He shrugged. "It sounds primitive. It is."

She unfolded her pale hands and folded them again. "But you have signs up somewhere, where he can—"

"Yes, we do. Whichever window he looks out of, he'll see a sign with the message on it. But I regard that as not much more than a backup device. He doesn't have to look out of any windows, but unless he's right in the center of the building, we believe he can hear the bullhorns."

"What is the message, on the sign? You said—"

"We're telling him we have some very important information for him, ma'am, that he ought not to miss." He turned to St. Clair. "That's on the assumption that you'd want to offer a ransom. You could help us there, with a specific figure to give him."

Watching him, Mayor Levin saw a flicker of surprise on the banker's face.

"Whatever he asks," St. Clair said. It sounded a simple enough answer, but Abe Levin knew that it wasn't, if Dakers wanted a specific figure. Eugene C. St. Clair had last month donated the round sum of fifty million dollars to the new state university for the endowment of scholarships and chairs. How much, then, would he give for his daughter's life?

"We need," the commissioner said carefully, "a specific sum in mind. When Dotson makes contact, he may have a sum in his own mind. If not, we'd like to suggest an offer. In hostage and kidnap situations we have to be very definite in everything we say; we have to establish trust, to give both parties solid ground to work on."

This is ridiculous, Mayor Levin thought. St. Clair could offer that freak enough to buy the Park Tower building, yet it seemed beyond him to think of an actual sum.

"I will give him whatever he wants," the banker said again. "Of course it would take many months to transfer any amount of property. It would require attorneys, accountants—" He waved a square thick-veined hand— the hand, Dakers thought, that had waved away the most monumental opposition at heated board meetings, the hand that was powerless now, unless that hostage-taker chose to pick up a phone. But Dakers saw the answer.

"We need to give him a sum he can understand. I doubt he's able to understand much more than a million dollars."

Surprise came again on the banker's face. "Is that—?" But he didn't finish, and the word *all* hung in the silence until he spoke again. "A million. Very well. But if he demands more than that—"

"Of course," the commissioner said quickly. "Now we have something to work on." He tried and failed to get any optimism into his tone. In the detailed record of Joseph Dozoretz there were two instances of attempted suicide, one immediately following the death of Sandy Baker in New Jersey. From the minute-by-minute reports reaching his office from Park Tower he knew that no one had seen either Dotson or his hostage at the windows since observation had commenced.

Hearing the flatness of the commissioner's tone, Eugene St. Clair remained facing him, his feet apart and his head slightly lowered. The time had come for him to take this matter further than these people could, by putting aside his pride and letting them know to what lengths he was prepared to go in order to protect his child. He must go like a merchant into the marketplace, and there bargain, if he could.

"If there is anything that could be done if certain funds were provided, Commissioner Dakers, I would expect you to inform me."

Dakers at once thought of the desperate need for renovations and additions to the Motor Transport Division's ten service and repair shops throughout the city, then realized he was on the wrong track: St. Clair must mean something more immediate.

"A police officer," the banker said, "is not expected to risk his life if he can avoid it. I realize that he does in fact risk his life in the normal course of duty; that is unavoidable. If one of your officers felt prepared to go into the apartment under arms and conclude the affair by force, I would be glad to know his name, and to consult with him in private." One man, he thought: perhaps that was all they needed; one young patrolman with enough courage, with enough sense of the heroic; perhaps his hesitation could be overcome with a fair offer of what to him would be riches. "If such an officer desired substantial life insurance, so that in the event of misfortune he would know his family would be left with generous resources, it could be arranged immediately."

Abraham Levin moved away from the windows, not so much to dissociate himself from the conversation as to give it some thought. They had to forget that anyone going into that apartment could blow it into the street, or that

Dotson could cut the girl's throat the moment a cop broke the door down; they had to accommodate the idea into their overall thinking that if there were *any* way of bringing Tina St. Clair out alive—any way that would for some reason require substantial funds—they must consider it. There were more people to profit from a safe conclusion to this incident than the St. Clairs: the mayor himself, the police commissioner, the chief of detectives, Captain Mundy, and in general the whole of the New York Police Department, and at a time when the new investigations into corruption were casting a shadow across every cop in the city, the good and the bad.

"It won't work," he heard Dakers saying bluntly. "The place is believed to be booby-trapped, and it's likely that if anyone tried to go in there he'd place your daughter's life in immediate hazard."

Watching him, St. Clair realized the commissioner was a practical man in a practical job, more of a tactician than a strategist like Abe Levin. Dakers could see only the terrain in front of him.

"I understand that," he told the commissioner, "yes. But if there are any possibilities of going in that you might not have considered so far, for reasons of inadequate funds or facilities, we might consider them now. It's clearly a case calling for extreme measures, even bizarre invention. An appeal is sometimes made to convicts, for instance, serving time in prison, to volunteer for an unusual enterprise; in this case, the additional incentive of great financial reward might help our cause."

Nobody in the room missed the message in the last two words; he didn't expect them to. There wasn't one of them who wouldn't dig into his own pocket, if a kitty were passed around, on the understanding that his contribution would help pay for a successful outcome to the problem.

They were all of them, in this room, involved in running a city that managed to survive its reputation by its own obstinate strength, and in a matter of hours New York would again make world headlines as a place where no one was safe, or emerge as a city where even a corrupt police force could prove itself still the finest. The fact that he could dig deeper into his own pocket was to their advantage. He could perhaps buy them what they all wanted: his daughter's life.

It had begun plaguing him, of late: the ability to buy whatever he wanted. At first, when he was young, he'd found it heady, and then later, valuable, and later still, convenient; now he carried it like a birthmark. People expected to be humiliated by his power over them; they did nothing for him except for money; more than half his mail, one of his secretaries had told him, consisted of appeals to his charity. But today he was ready to give everything he possessed.

Tina would hate that. *Daddy*, she'd once asked him, a straw hat swinging in her child's hand, *have we always got to be so rich?* "Daddy-O" had come later, when she was old enough to look on him as a friend, to understand he couldn't help being so rich, that it was simply his legacy. She'd learned to love him despite what he was. But today she'd hate what he was doing now.

"We'll bear in mind what you're saying," Commissioner Dakers told him. "Right now I'd just like to make it clear that there are plenty of my officers who'd be willing to go in there and risk their lives if they thought they could save your daughter."

"I'm certain of that, Commissioner. It's simply that there are sometimes circumstances where . . . extraordinary means can prove effective. I'll rely on you to tell me the instant you make contact with this man Dotson. I shall want him to know that I'm anxious to change places with my daughter as the hostage as soon as possible. He and I can then work out whatever deal he decides on.''

"You're willing to go in there yourself?"

"As soon as possible. It's the only solution, and if you'll order signs displayed to that effect, and put the same message over on the bullhorns, we can hope to finish with this whole thing in a matter of hours.''

9

THE BIG LALIQUE VASE HIT the mirrors and shattered them, and she saw his face become a dozen faces, bits of faces with the sharp bright fragments cutting them into weird surrealist patterns as he stared at her with his many eyes, shocked into stillness with his hands spread out to protect himself.

Then she fainted, or came close to it: images became jumbled and distorted until she was looking at a thousand eyes and a thousand hands growing bigger and bigger, staring right into her face, reaching out for her, while the voice rose and fell, beginning from a long way off and then loudening, booming at her—*Why did you do that? Why did you do that?*

To kill you, she heard her own answer in her mind, *to kill you,* while she tried to get up from the floor and saw flecks of blood coming from her hands and the glitter of glass splinters across the gray pile of the carpet, *to kill you,* she went on telling him, but silently in her mind, because she was only coming out of a faint: she still had enough grasp of things to know she daren't say it aloud.

"Why did you do that?" he asked her again, and he was really close now, pulling at her shoulders with some of his thousand hands as she felt herself dipping again into unconsciousness, but only for a moment because it was dangerous, and she felt glass in her fingers and realized she was trying to cut into him with it, pushing it like a knife. *"Don't do that!"* his voice came again, whispering and screaming and dying away. *"What are you trying to do?"* But he wasn't pulling at her anymore, just staring at her and waiting; and then his face became clear and his voice more normal. "Don't do anything like that, Tina, you'll only hurt yourself, don't you know that?"

"Oh God," she said, and managed to sit up, her mind working fast and on several levels. "What happened? What happened, Joe?" On several levels: she still felt weird and not really conscious, but she was thinking consciously all right and even with cunning—this man could kill her for attacking him like that unless she made out it was some kind of mental aberration; and on another level she was aware of this, of how cunning she was being despite the waves of being and not-being that came and went like clouds through her head, "Joe, what did I do?"

"Jesus," he said almost quietly, and the whole scene suddenly locked into reality for her like a split image coming together, and she was sitting up, with Joe crouching on the floor and staring at her. "Jesus, you threw a vase at me, Tina, that's what you did." And she felt bright, very bright, seeing something quite clear in his eyes: that he was wavering between rage and reason. Her memory was back in place now, and she knew exactly what had happened, what she'd done. But he mustn't know that.

"I threw a what?"

"A vase. At me."

"Oh, God. I'm sorry, Joe. I can't think what made me do that. It's the strain of being—you know, I mean not quite understanding you yet, the way you say you love me, when—" She gave a shudder, her whole body shaking suddenly, and felt immediately better, like coming out of a fever. "I'm sorry, Joe, please forgive me—I didn't mean to do a thing like that."

Apologize. Cringe. Survive.

"I didn't know you were so strong," he said, wariness in his voice. "That's a heavy vase."

"I didn't really throw it at you, Joe. I just threw it. Can you understand that? Like people finally have to scream?" He was helping her up, and she thought that was incredible. If that vase had hit the back of his head he'd be dead by now, or lying on the floor while she stepped over him and went along to the kitchen and got a broom and levered the fridge out of the way and walked out of the door and into the elevator—but he was simply and courteously helping her up, and that was incredible. Didn't he know he'd almost lost her? Or did he think she wouldn't have walked out? *What did psychopaths think?*

"I guess I'll have to tie you up," Joe said, still shaken but prepared to laugh it off, to work it into his bizarre sense of humor and make a joke of it.

"I'll be good," she said, "in future. That was just— let's call it a tantrum. God, I could use a cigarette. Will you find me one?" She couldn't look into his eyes because he'd see the fear in her own, because of what he'd said about tying her up. The idea was associated with narrow cells and leg irons and a tin cup and no lavatory: she found her imagination took off with a terrible ease, since this thing had started. Worse than that: if he tied her up she couldn't throw anything again or use a knife or do whatever she'd finally have to do. "There are some over there."

It was a mess, over there: the gold-tinted mirrors paneled one entire wall of the living room, and although only four of them had been smashed the glass was all over the place and the Lalique vase had ricocheted across the shelf and smashed into the telephone, sending it down. There was no sound coming from it because Joe had pulled all the jacks out last night.

There'd been of course a perfectly good reason for throwing that vase. *No one is ever going to take you away from me*, he'd told her this morning. *No one, ever*. So she'd had to start doing something. The police out there obviously couldn't do anything, except hang out signs on the buildings opposite and expect Joe to react. It wasn't very complimentary: here she was trapped with a dangerous lunatic and all they could do was hang out signs. Couldn't they send helicopters in and make an armed assault through the skylight or something?

The gold box had a dent in it. Joe was holding it out to her with the lid raised. A dent like that one, in the back of his skull, would have . . . "Thanks." She took a cigarette and he lit it for her, watching her with an expression she hadn't seen before and couldn't fathom; was he admiring the way she'd suddenly decided to hit back, or was he considering carefully in that strange sick mind of his whether he should tie her to the big brass bed in the rose room and go in at regular intervals to feed her? "Don't you smoke, Joe?"

"I quit." His smile was so horribly attractive, horrible because inappropriate.

"These are awful. Egyptian. Can we go out and get some Bensons or something, later?" Reality was slipping out of focus again. He'd been going to put some Grieg on the record player for her, then she'd seen her chance and thrown the vase and hoped it would kill him, and now he was politely lighting her cigarette, all in the space of ten minutes. Perhaps she'd just go quietly mad as time went on, so that when he finished her off she'd hardly feel a thing.

He didn't answer that; she hadn't expected him to. Now and then she tested him out with a stray idea, and when it was the wrong one—like going out for some cigarettes—he just ignored it.

"What the hell are they doing now?" he asked suddenly. He was looking toward the windows. He never went close to them, even though they all had the thin glass-fiber curtains drawn across. He never let her go close either. When she turned to look, she saw some men hanging another canvas sign along the opposite building, pulling the old one up to the roof. She and Joe had to wait till all the folds were out and the ropes drawn taut before they could read this one properly:

WE OFFER $1 MILLION FOR TINA'S RELEASE

She could hardly believe it. It didn't seem to have anything to do with the fact that she was standing here smoking a cigarette with Joe, getting over their little tiff. It looked monstrous, like a cheap commercial. She was up for sale.

This was Daddy-O. He was back in town, and doing the only thing he could think of doing.

"Will you just *look* at that!" she heard Joe saying.

Don't just buy me, Daddy-O.

But what else could he do? It might even work. But if it did, what would she feel like afterward? Tabloid: *St. Clair Bids a Million Cash for Tina*. Question Time in the rumpus rooms all over the country, the young eyes troubled: Dad, what would have happened to her if he didn't have a million dollars? If a man took me, would you have all that much to get me back?

The pale October sun came sifting through the glass fibers, lighting the silence. There was no sound anywhere, and when it came it was the slightest creak of a tendon in Joe's leg as he moved suddenly toward the telephone on the floor. "A million dollars," he said disbelievingly. "Jesus." Through the smoke from her cigarette she watched him as he put the phone back on its base and found the end of the cord among all the broken glass and pushed the jack into the outlet and lifted the phone and began dialing.

At 10:45 A.M. the alert call went through the entire radio network from the three command posts to the street and sniper stations and One Police Plaza. The hostage-taker had made contact.

Dotson's voice was heard over a dozen telephone amplifiers and the ensuing conversation was monitored and recorded on tape. At police headquarters Commissioner Dakers swung around to look at the radio, and on the thirteenth floor the chief of detectives spilled some coffee in the saucer as the call came through. Everyone knew which telephone had begun ringing: it was the open-priority line from Park Tower.

For the first time since the chief hostage negotiator for the New York Police Department had been rushed to the scene ten hours ago, he picked up the phone by his side and spoke into it.

"Hi. This is Nick Valenti. Is that you, Joe?"

For the past thirty minutes Nick had been crouched against the base of the water tower, going over in his mind the score of different scenarios that had been worked out to cover a score of different contingencies; now he moved, standing up so that Dotson could see him if he was looking this way. As he waited to hear Dotson's voice, he tried to believe what was happening at last. They now knew Dotson was alive; there hadn't been a murder/suicide enacted during the night. And this call had come only minutes after they'd hung out the new message. Dotson was interested. . . .

Not far from Nick, Eugene and Elizabeth St. Clair heard the voice of the man who held their daughter's life in his hands.

"Yes, this is Joe. Who's Nick Valenti?"

Another phone had begun ringing, distracting Nick; then

someone answered it and he could concentrate again. He had already approached the first hurdle, and it consisted of one word. He didn't want to say it. He wanted Dotson to say it. There was the risk that in the next few seconds Dotson would slam the phone down, because of that one word.

"I'm doing the negotiating," Nick said. "Did you see the sign we hung out for you?"

There was a pause, then: "Are you the police?"

That was the word, and Nick took a quick breath and said:

"Yes. We're looking after things this end, Joe, because we're the right people to do it; we have the authority to do just anything you want, or get it done. Make sense?"

Rule 1: Don't say the word *police*, because it can scare the man off, or anger him. Let him say it first: he usually does. Rule 2: If he says it, tell him the truth and immediately go on from there, don't leave it at simply *yes*. Take his mind off it and keep him going; at all costs keep him on the line; it's usually a lifeline.

"A million dollars," the voice of the hostage-taker came over the amplifiers. "That's a lot of money."

"You better believe it, Joe."

Very quietly Captain Mundy moved across to where Eugene St. Clair and his wife were standing against one of the elevator housings. "I'd say we have him. He's interested. And we can rely on the negotiator to steer this through: he's the best we have—the best anywhere in the world."

Elizabeth felt tears coming and turned away. Eugene went on staring across at the row of windows lit by the morning sun. He'd not expected it to come this fast. Miracles, someone had once said in a war, take a little longer.

Nick Valenti approached another hurdle. Dotson was

still alive. That didn't mean the hostage was still alive. "Hey," he asked cheerfully, "how's Tina?"

In the streets, where the police and media crews and an estimated five hundred bystanders were now gathered, a silence drew down; on the rooftops of the four buildings adjacent to Park Tower, where police and FBI sharpshooters lay prone behind the parapets or crouched in the shelter of towers and elevator hatches, men lowered their rifles an inch as the silence went on.

Dotson's voice matched Valenti's in tone as it came over the amplifiers. "She's fine."

Reporters were breaking for the cordoned exits from the Park Tower area, racing for the half dozen telephones they'd already staked out. Others held back, not certain there was a story yet: a headline wasn't a story. But the headline was going out within minutes over the international wire services: "TINA ALIVE."

Nick Valenti's voice came over the amplifiers. "She's fine? That's great. Can we see her, Joe?"

There was a pause again. The police knew that even if he'd killed the hostage during the night or this morning, he might easily say she was fine. He'd be likely to work for the million dollars first, and demand a plane. He wouldn't get it, but he'd try.

There was still no answer on the line from Dotson, but the snipers, whose orders were never for an instant to take their eyes off the row of blue-tinted windows, were the first to see the curtains being drawn back from the third window from the southeast corner of the building, and a woman's figure appear there. Police with field glasses narrowed their eyes, watching intently; but at this distance any kind of manequin or dummy would never fool anyone.

Elizabeth St. Clair was openly weeping now, and Eugene went over to her and embraced her. Nick Valenti found himself nursing a strange feeling of letdown. For the last ten hours he'd been rehearsing and preparing for a long, exhausting struggle with the mind of that psychopath over there, pulling the lifeline inch by inch until Tina was safe. Now it was almost over, within minutes of starting out. But it didn't bother him; he'd experienced this feeling before, when a hostage situation suddenly finished and they all went home. He watched the girl in the window as she went on waving; then she half-turned her head, and moved away.

On the rooftops every sharpshooter lifted his rifle at once. The orders were precise: if they saw Dotson at a window they were to prepare to fire, but wait for the signal. Only four of them—the world-class marksman of the FBI's special assault force and three ranking police officers with international awards—were to fire at their own discretion and without waiting for the signal, and then only if they could see Dotson clearly and could see also that the hostage was clear of their line of fire; she would need to be visible, and not standing behind him, where she could be hit by a bullet passing through his body.

The window was blank now. The observers had seen that Dotson had ordered her away: there'd been that quick half-turn of her head as he'd spoken to her. Now the filmy curtains were drawing across the glass as she pulled on the cords: Dotson was still deeper inside the room, and his voice came on the line while the curtains were still moving.

"How does she look?"

"Fine, Joe. Just like you said. We know we can trust you now." Nick had begun relaxing his muscles over the last few minutes as the high tension went out of him. They'd cleared the first two hurdles and were beginning to establish the one primordial condition of all hostage negotiating: trust. "And you can trust me, Joe. I want you to know that."

"Well sure. Why shouldn't I?"

Nick jumped in quickly before the question could linger in Dotson's mind. "No reason, Joe. No reason at all. We want to cooperate with you, just like you're cooperating with us." The change was subtle: from "me" to "us," letting Dotson know that not only could he trust this one guy called Nick, but the whole of the police department. It was going smoothly now, and Nick breathed deeper, more slowly. "And we're glad you're interested in our message," he said. "We can do business now."

"A million dollars," the amplified voice came over the line. "That's—gee, I mean how would you move that amount of cash?"

"It's already set up, Joe. Several banks have cooperated, and the cash is in a security van right down there in the street on Fifth Avenue, waiting for you. We thought maybe you'd agree to the deal. After all, who wouldn't?"

They'd discussed this point for an hour together: Chief Warner, Mundy, and Nick. Mundy had been for hanging things out and tempting Dotson by saying, sure, they'd get the cash along here but it'd take a little time; meanwhile, they'd like Dotson to bring Tina into the hallway of the apartment, where she could call to them through the elevator shaft to say she was all right. Nick had finally said: "The cash is what we're trading. He has to believe in it. And we have to get it there, in the street. He's liable to ask us to open up the van and have a bystander or two look inside and then come on the line to him, saying it's real, a huge stack of C-notes." Nick had felt strongly about this, and held out. Mundy was his superior, but Nick was the negotiator, the key man in this whole operation. "We have to zap him with the idea of all that physical loot. We're not just playing games."

"Down there in the street?" Dotson's voice came. "You didn't waste any time, Nick."

Another success: the hostage-taker had called the negotiator by his name. "We're not here to waste anyone's time, Joe. Listen, we've all been hanging around here for Tina since midnight last night, you know that? We all want to go home now, like you do. We have the cash waiting for you. We have a plane readied too. Okay?"

"A plane?"

"To take you wherever you want to go. You won't want to hang around New York. What we're going to do is see you and Tina onto the plane, with your solemn promise to release her as soon as you land, wherever it is, so she can take the same plane home. You keep the million dollars. That's a fair deal, Joe."

He waited. They would have to get Dotson somewhere between Park Tower and the airport, or even at the airport itself. The FBI would never let a hostage-taker board a plane in the continental United States: in the event of a struggle on the flight deck it could come down anywhere, on houses or a city street. They weren't going to send Dotson anywhere; they just had to get him out of that building with Tina, where they could see him. Again, Mundy hadn't understood the situation. "We should talk him out of there, without this charade of hauling a million dollars through the streets. It's not necessary." Nick had needed patience. Mundy was here to supervise this whole operation, to keep order in the streets, contain the scene in safety, deploy the assault teams to new positions if necessary, maintain communications with One Police Plaza—he was here to do *everything*. Except negotiate. "Sir," Nick had told him, "to talk down a hostage-taker you have to have something to trade. There has to be something he wants, that you can maybe give him in return for the hostage. But all he wants right now is Tina St. Clair. And he's got her. So we've nothing to trade—except cash."

Dotson's voice came on the line again. "A plane. Where would we fly?"

"We'd suggest anywhere outside this country, Joe. Then you'll be safe. You won't ever be hassled. With that kind of money, I'd pick Acapulco or somewhere. Swaying palms, silver beaches—you know something? You've got it made."

A short distance from where he stood, Elizabeth St. Clair asked Captain Mundy: "But what if he doesn't let her come back?"

"He's not going anywhere, ma'am, and neither is she. Don't worry, leave it to us. Would you like some coffee or anything?" They'd brought a whole canteen up here to the roof, in case of a long negotiation.

"No, thank you." The tears had left smudges on her face, but her smile was less strained now.

"Acapulco," Dotson's voice came, "that sounds a nice place, yes. I've heard a lot about it. In Mexico, right?"

"Right." Nick waited.

In the street below, where the TV cameras were zooming from close-ups of the crowd to the row of windows at the top of the Park Tower building, reporters were reaching their editors and the wire services almost simultaneously with material, using their two-way radios to repeat the conversation coming out of the telephone amplifiers while their colleagues were standing in the pay-phone booths relaying the copy coming from their radios.

The major wire services were receiving much the same copy but with an additional emphasis on the work of the New York Police Department. *Associated Press* put it: *The relaxed tone of the negotiations confirms the established capability of the New York City police to bring down the tensions and the temperature of a situation that for the past ten hours has threatened to end in stark tragedy.* From *United Press International* the angle was only slightly different: *This is a good time to remember that it was the New York Police Department that initiated the low-profile, low-key negotiating procedure that has to date saved many lives. But it must be pointed out that this is no longer a hostage situation but a kidnapping, which is now reaching a successful conclusion by the payment of ransom. This is not to say that the police are not doing an extremely competent job in defusing a potentially disastrous situation.*

The moment the mention of Acapulco was heard over the telephone amplifiers and relayed to the media, editors and agents in their Manhattan offices instructed journalists and representatives to board a plane immediately for the Mexican resort and stand by to meet Dotson and Tina St. Clair when they landed there; offers for the exclusive story in magazine, serial and book form were reported to be in the region of seven figures. Even those editors who realized that the FBI was unlikely to allow Dotson inside an airplane still hoped that by some unusual dispensation he might arrive at Acapulco. The same arrangements were being made in other major cities of the United States and in London, Paris, Rome, Berlin and Tokyo.

Meanwhile in the tiny area that was the focus of world-wide media attention the voice of Joseph Dotson was heard again over the amplifiers. "How would we get to the airport?"

"Under police protection," Nick told him, keeping to the dialogue they'd worked over for hours. "There'll be no problem, Joe. We're in your hands, and we recognize that. This is your party."

There was another of Dotson's now familiar pauses, and Nick Valenti waited again, no longer troubled; he knew that Joe took a little time to think things through before he committed himself to speech, and that was okay, that was absolutely fine; it kept the exchange low-key and unhurried.

"My party," he heard Joe say in a moment, his tone light and amused. "That's nice. I like that. I like parties."

"Sure. And you're calling the shots. The only thing

is—and this is just helpful advice, Joe—the sooner we get this thing over, the better it's going to be for you and everyone else. So just say the word and we'll meet you and Tina down in the entrance lobby. Okay?''

"Down in the lobby?''

"That's right. We have a limo for you, and it's pointed at the airport.''

The time the pause was a little longer. "I see. Okay, but listen, I was just interested in how you'd planned things out, that's all. I don't need a million dollars. I have Tina, and we're not going anyplace.''

The amplifiers clicked as the line went dead.

— 10 —

HE WAS FLOATING.

She watched him, for the first time dispassionately, as if he were just a man she knew slightly, not a man who was her slave-master. She watched him floating.

Muted daylight was coming from above, through a false ceiling. Tom Lindquist had told her how it worked: the architect had installed a series of mirrors lined up at angles with a checkerboard of skylights in the roof; in this way it had been possible to make an artificial sky above the swimming pool, a sky which could be darkened at the height of summer—in the unlikely event that anyone would be here in New York in the height of summer—and brightened in the winter when the sun was low; there was also a system of slats and alternating lamps that could make it seem that the puffs of white cumulus cloud were moving across the sky.

Joe was floating exactly in the center of the pool, which was Grecian and symmetrical; he was floating on his back with his arms out sideways and his feet together, like a fallen Christ, his eyes closed and his face in peace. In the last few minutes she had been measuring possibilities in her mind: the distance from here to the kitchen door and the time it would take her to run there and get a broom and lever the refrigerator away, and the time it would take for him to swim to the poolside and climb out and catch up

with her. There was an imponderable factor: the time lapse
before he opened his eyes and realized she had gone. It
was, she was quite aware, an academic exercise. He knew
the measurement of possibilities himself, in any situation,
and that she couldn't escape. His eyes at this moment were
probably not quite closed; he could be watching her from
the slits between his lids, as she'd watched him at dawn
this morning. Before she'd thrown the glass vase there
might have been a chance. Not now.

Except perhaps tonight, while he was sleeping.

The water lapped at his body, which was surprisingly
tan. He was wearing one of Tom's French bikinis, the
choice of which had also surprised her until she went
through the classic equation: some fags wore small turquoise bikinis but all men who wore small turquoise bikinis weren't fags. The measurement of possibilities over,
she could now watch Joe as if they were strangers at—oh,
God—Acapulco, just staying at the same hotel. Would it
be amusing to spend the evening with this tan compact-
limbed Adonis in the azure pool, or the night?

She must be losing her mind, to think this way. Or
perhaps she realized it was too late now for escape. The
only hope had gone: he'd refused a million dollars, and
would therefore refuse a hundred million, or a thousand
million. She was priceless.

Daddy-O, you couldn't buy me after all. I feel good
about that, but I'd never be able to explain it to you: it
sounds like a suicide talking. But it's happened at last, and
my childhood dream has come true: we're not so rich
anymore; there's something you can't buy. But I never
thought it would be me.

"C'mon on in, Sandy."

He rolled suddenly upright, his face toward her, smiling.

"What?" Her whole body shook to a spasm. She'd
learned over the hours of this day that while her mind went

careering around looking for escape and inventing hair-raising scenarios like concealing a razor blade and waiting until he made love to her, an infinitely more subtle intelligence was at work at the cell level in her body, scanning and computing stimuli so sensitive that she didn't consciously receive them; and her body knew that it was going to die.

"I said c'mon in." His quiet voice stirred echoes among the marble columns and the arches at the end of the terrace.

"You—" And she stopped right there. *You called me Sandy. Why?*

He might not like to be asked. It was a strange thing to have done, to call her by a different name. He was a strange man, and would become most dangerous when she brought attention to his strangeness, which he was trying all the time to forget. She was beginning to know him.

The water broke as she slid into it and swam towards him, while he gently dog-paddled, waiting, his smile more gentle than she had ever seen on a man's face. It was as if his heart were coming out to meet her, floating on the water for her to hold.

Drown it. Quick.

"You look—" she said, and stopped again. She did this quite often, being often uncertain whether it were wise to say what she was about to; it had become a habit now, and a useful one: it drew his thoughts from him, and they were almost always different from what she believed. In this way too she could know him.

"In love," he said.

He took her hands and they floated together, dancing. "I had a thought," she told him surprising herself.

"For me?" His smile was quiet sunlight on his face.

"Yes. I imagined your heart was floating on the water, for me to hold." *And I thought, also, of drowning it.*

"And now you're holding it." His voice was hushed, as if they were speaking in a cathedral. "I can feel it in your hands."

Crush it.

"Don't bruise it, Tina."

Shock buffeted her. *He couldn't know. Yes, he knew.* He was catching vibrations with the infinitely subtle intelligence at work in his own body. And that was infinitely dangerous.

"Where shall we dine tonight?" he asked her.

"What did you say?"

Her surprise pleased him. "In the gold room, or the drawing room, or the small and more intimate dining room through the archway where . . ." But that was all she heard, because she was having to pull her mind back from the impossible dream of a table for two at Sardi's or the Four Seasons, with the nightmare over and a different man escorting her.

"I don't mind," she whispered, "I don't mind."

When she opened her eyes he was gazing at her thoughtfully, lifting a hand to her face. "Where did you get those scars?"

"A car crash." She hadn't put on any makeup this morning; she'd thought it wise to look as unattractive as she could.

There was pain in his eyes, and his wet hand cupped her face as he kissed her lips with a tenderness that was like a blessing. *I've locked the door to the stairs and I've stacked forty pounds of explosive against it, and if you or anyone else tries breaking it open then you'll blow the top floor of this building right across Central Park.* His kisses touched her softly, meeting her mouth and parting and meeting again as the water lapped against their bodies, and when she let her eyes close again she could see only the face with the smile on it, and not the face that had watched her reflection in the window last night, perhaps considering murder.

"I love you, Tina."

Then leave me alive. But it was only a small voice now in her mind, a small red flag waving a long way off as he turned in the water and took her hand and led her to the lapis-lazuli steps that came down from the terrace between the two bronze dolphins.

She stood under the canopy of the changing rooms, drying herself and letting him draw the halter strings of her swimsuit down across her shoulders, not helping him and not hindering, feeling his arousal as he stood against her and kissed her throat and her breasts; and when she was naked she thought: so here we are again with the answer to everything, just as Mother Nature bids us—when in doubt, copulate. They'd done it, she'd read, in the packed cattle trucks on their way to the camps in Germany and Poland; they'd done it in the thick of every war, their bodies leaping half with passion and half to the shuddering of the bombs. But she wasn't ready to do it now, with a man who had killed two other males of his species and was ready to kill more if they tried to take away his seized privilege to couple with her.

The thing was, could she stop him? If *they* hadn't, could she?

She was lying on the damp towel now with her eyes open to watch him, admiring his body even as she resented the sovereign right of his sheer masculine strength. This was what he had come here for, what he had killed for and what he was prepared to die for. So how in God's name could she stop him?

"I love you," he said again.

What exactly did that mean? Anything? If it really meant anything, there was hope. There was a hope of stopping him doing this, if there were any control left in him; and later, of stopping him doing other things, like, for instance, killing her.

Put it to the test. This question was going to be important. Vital. Life-and-death.

"Joe. What if I said that I don't want to? Not yet?"

He lay against her, his tongue coming away from her nipple and his face resting as if he were now asleep, his ear cold from the water and his breath stirring on her skin, his hand cupping her face as it had done before in the pool, when there had been such tenderness in his eyes that she'd been defenseless, the same tenderness that she could feel in his hand now as the silence drew out. Was this his answer? So it was perfectly okay, then, was it—she just had to say no, and he'd leave her alone, right? Wrong. He was a fully aroused male, hard against her, and any doctor would tell you that after tumescence there has to be detumescence, and not with a dying fall. If she kept on saying no, he'd have to rape her, that was all.

Behind them she could hear the quiet sucking of the water at the pool outlets, and the lapping of small waves along the steps; there was no sound from anywhere else; the pool was in the center of the apartment, itself soundproofed from the rooms and passages surrounding it. When she began screaming, while he raped her, clawing at her and drawing blood and ripping into her in a frenzy of rage at her denial of him, no one would hear, no one who cared.

"Then we won't," he said.

—— 11 ——

"AND THE OBSESSION?" CAPTAIN MUNDY asked.

"Is classical." Dr. Weinberg started walking around again, picking his way with short steps among the telephone cables and camp stools and cartons of cigarettes. Mundy stayed by his side, wanting to know it all.

Below the main elevator housing Nick Valenti stared at the rising moon with his back to the others. He didn't know it all, but he knew enough to understand the negotiations were over now, and had been over since Dotson had hung up on them almost twelve hours ago and they'd hauled in the banner about the million dollars and St. Clair had taken his weeping wife down the emergency stairs. The banner about how St. Clair was ready to take the place of his daughter was still up there. Big deal. Dotson wanted the girl, not her old man.

"What does 'classical' mean?" he heard Mundy demanding, his voice impatient.

"It's an established syndrome," the psychiatrist told him placatingly. He stopped walking around, out of consideration for the others. Eugene St. Clair was up here again on the command-building rooftop; here also were Commissioner Dakers, two of his aides, the police psychologist and the two backup negotiators. Some distance from the group lay the FBI and police gun teams, their Ithaca rifles resting across the parapet and their night glasses raised to watch the row of windows opposite.

"We're talking here of the 'love-object choice,' " Dr. Weinberg went on. "There are many reasons why we make the choice that we do—the romantic choice or the sexual choice. The most common reason is identification with a parent: a woman with her father, a man with his mother. We must also bear in mind the psychodynamics of vision. Visual stimuli are vastly more important to a man than to a woman— hence the plethora of advertisements displaying pretty girls; but of course we are talking here of even deeper urges and associations and desires: from the information we have about Joseph Dotson we can be certain of one thing. When he saw Tina St. Clair at the window up there, he saw the unattainable."

Dr. Saul Weinberg thought back to the day when he'd gone into the small green-painted room at King's County Hospital and seen Joseph Dotson for the first time: a young attractive-looking man who seemed to understand only the logic and the reasonableness of the appalling things he had done. It had needed barely a few hours to be quite certain that he wasn't fit to plead. It was only this afternoon that Weinberg had learned from the lieutenant in the Identification Section at police headquarters that something had happened to this young man that was of itself able to explain his behavior.

"He is what we might loosely refer to as a borderline personality," he went on, looking up at the faces around him in the moonlight. "He is not manic-depressive, but he has a very distinct mnemonic prima, akin in many respects to psychosis schizophrenia. There are feelings of depersonalization; these people become strangers to themselves— or more accurately—*strange* to themselves. There is usually a degree of paranoia present in the general syndrome; borderline personalities tend to be gregarious, but their relationships are shallow; they have many 'friends' but leave no impression on them. The salient feature, of course, in the case of Dotson is that he was just nine years old when his mother fell from that balcony.''

Among the group who listened to him was Lieutenant O'Rourke of the Identification Section, who had spent most of the day interviewing Robert Dozoretz, Joe's father, at his home in Jackson Heights. "It was an accident,'' he'd told O'Rourke, "a pure accident. The balcony gave way. It broke.''

O'Rourke had persisted in coming back to the incident, asking for more details, working around it until Dozoretz had managed to find the yellowed news clippings in a box in the attic, where the family album had been. "Look,'' he said in a tone of wearied finality, '' 'BALCONY COLLAPSES: WOMAN FATALLY INJURED BY FALL.' I don't like talking about this, you know? It was twenty-five years ago, a quarter of a century, but I loved my wife. She was my first wife, and she was beautiful. I still don't like talking about that day. It was ten years before I married again. Ten years.'' He dropped the clipping back into the box, as if into a grave. "And I know what you're thinking, but the boy was inside the house at that time. I heard the wood-work breaking. I saw my wife go down. I saw the boy run out to see what had happened. Then he began screaming. He screamed for two hours, until a doctor sedated him. He would have gone on screaming all night. I knew him. He was my own boy. I knew what he suffered, what we both suffered. But he . . . was young. It's hard for the young, when a thing like that happens.''

O'Rourke had left him, to go down to City Hall and check the records of the case. It had been an old house, and Dozoretz had done it up, or most of it. The balcony had adjoined a room they never used, and in his testimony Dozoretz had said he had warned his wife and son never to

go into that room until he'd had time to fix the balcony.
Why had his wife stepped onto a balcony she knew was
dilapidated and unsafe? There were other balconies below,
where they used to sit sometimes; they were perfectly safe.
Before she had died at the hospital in Jackson Heights, his
wife had been able to tell them that she had heard the
sound of an accident in the street, and a child crying out.
She was on the third floor and without thinking ran through
the unused room and onto the balcony, fearing it was Joe,
her son. But Joe had been in his room at the other side of
the house with a playmate, a neighbor's boy. He hadn't
cried out. But he'd heard the balcony breaking, and his
mother's screams.

"In my opinion it began then," Dr. Weinberg told his
listeners, his short figure turning in the moonlight to address each of them. "And if we look even cursorily at the
pattern of subsequent events in Joseph Dotson's life we
can see the cause and effect at work. This man lost his
mother, traumatically. He has been searching for her ever
since, in other women. We have seen the remarkable
likeness in the photographs of the other women who met
with a similar fate in falling from a height. We have seen
the remarkable likeness of his dead mother to Tina St.
Clair, and I believe the conclusions are inarguable."

Nobody spoke immediately. When Captain Mundy broke
the silence it was with a question most of them had in their
minds. "Dotson professes to love the girl up there, and
you say obsessively. Won't that stop him killing her?"

"Some of you may remember what John Hinckley Jr.
wrote to Evan Thomas, *Time*'s Washington correspondent
at the time of the attempt on President Reagan's life.
Hinckley said that the most important thing in his life was
Jodie Foster's love and admiration, and that if he couldn't
have them, neither could anyone else. He said that his
devotion for Jodie became an obsession—an erotomanic

obsession, according to some. He wrote her hundreds of poems and letters, expressing his profound love. But he ended by saying that the ultimate expression of his love would be to take her away from the world permanently. No, Captain Mundy, Joseph Dotson's obsessive love will not necessarily stop his killing her. We are talking here of the classic murder-suicide syndrome. There is a final point. I believe that Dotson's psychosis was brought on by the tragic death of his mother, which he almost witnessed—and certainly he saw her body lying there below the balcony—and which deprived him of her. She became unattainable to him, leading him to search for her in other women who resembled her." He turned suddenly to look across the street at the row of darkened windows. "I would propose that few women are more unattainable to a hardworking window cleaner than the most glamorous heiress in all New York City. Now that he has, in his way, attained her, he won't readily let her go."

Nick Valenti sat huddled against the elevator housing, a plaid rug around him and a half-empty cup of coffee by his side. Mundy wasn't liking this very much. He was a man of action, the kind who went at a situation with a battering ram if he could get one. But you couldn't batter down the walls of psychotic obsession in a man's mind. The strain was beginning to show up in some of them by now, especially in Mundy, deprived of action. "I think it was a mistake to make all that play with putting real money into a van and telling Dotson it was there. It was too pat. He suspected something. And now we've lost him."

He'd made that little speech to Commissioner Dakers, in front of Nick and several other people. Okay. Maybe he was right. Maybe they should have taken more time, teasing Dotson into taking the money and running. Or maybe Mundy was wrong. At this stage it was anybody's guess. Dotson was unpredictable, and they hadn't had a chance to learn much about him. But Nick had learned something about Captain Mundy. He was a shit.

It was Mundy who'd "forgotten" to tell him that Karen had called again. She'd called twice so far, the first time when they'd just opened what they thought were negotiations with Joe Dotson. Maybe Mundy had really forgotten. Once negotiations have started, Jesus Christ can call up and you have to put him on hold. But Mundy was still a shit, and it would be well to remember it, when this whole operation got into the really critical stages and you needed to know who your friends were.

The second time Karen had called, he'd just had to tell her he couldn't make it.

"But you promised."

"I promised. And I have to break my promise, and I have to break it to you. That makes me feel like hell, but it doesn't change anything. You know what we've got going on here. There's a human life at stake; there always is, in this job."

In a moment she'd just said: "I'm scared, that's all."

"It's only for a final checkup, sweetheart, and then they'll start inducing labor. That's what Doc Marcellino told me. Isn't that what he told you?"

"Well, sure. But he mentioned the possibility of complications."

"He told me that, too. But I asked him if I should go along there, and he just said it was up to me. He said there wasn't anything I could do there."

"Except be with me for a while, Nick."

She said it naturally; she wasn't needling him, or trying to make him feel guilty—at least, not much—or trying to wheedle him off the job. And that made it difficult. She was such a fantastic girl. But she was scared. And it broke his heart.

"Karen, this thing shouldn't take too long now. There

has to be a breakthrough pretty soon, and when it comes, I have to be here. He's gotten used to my voice now and he's starting to trust me, and that's important. It could save her life.''

She'd just said yes, she understood. He'd told her again he'd be along at the clinic the moment he could get away; then she'd hung up, just saying good-bye. The word was still echoing in his mind as he listened to the psychiatrist and Mundy talking, with Mundy's voice rising sometimes in impatience, and Weinberg's bringing him down again. They were talking about the Acapulco charade, and Nick went over it all again in his mind, but couldn't reach any new conclusion: it pointed up an important aspect of Joe Dotson's character, though. The guy was a clown. He liked jokes.

Two relief sharpshooters came out of the stairhead, bringing their own guns; they crossed the roof with the typical crouching lope that training had turned into habit.

''Seen any pigeons?''

The two men going off duty got to their feet, stretching.

''If I saw so much as a goddamn pigeon over there, I'd blow its beak plumb through its asshole.''

Mundy had ordered regular duty hours first thing this morning, but now he was changing guns at one-hour intervals. You get a man too bored and he'll start wanting to shoot at any damned thing, his fatigue presenting false targets. The same feeling had started coming into Nick, hours ago; he'd gone over the techniques he wanted to use with Joe Dotson so often that he'd begun thinking they weren't going to work. But they'd have to work. The reason why he was indispensable to himself right now was that he couldn't leave here whatever happened. So far, he'd failed in the negotiations, and if they had Al Groot or Tony Rimkus take over, they might succeed. His reputation couldn't stand that. Nor could his pride. And the first thing he'd learned in negotiating was that you can't be honest with that guy out there on the other side if you can't be honest with yourself.

Soon after ten-thirty Captain Mundy was called down to the street command post and Nick got up and did a dozen knee-bends and went over to the group around Dr. Weinberg.

"But if you want a considered opinion," he was telling the commissioner, "I would say that rape and torture are very unlikely, very unlikely indeed." His sharp features now angled toward Eugene St. Clair. "This man appears to be a total romanticist, a perfectionist. To him, as a boy of nine, his mother was perfect, as most mothers are to boys that age. She was his ideal, just as your daughter has now become his ideal. I doubt if he thinks of her sexually, even though she happens to be an exceedingly attractive young woman; the much more important thing to him is that she resembles his dead mother. The danger," he said with considerate reluctance, "is that Tina will inevitably show imperfections as time goes on: she'll say things and do things that he can't approve of, and once he begins to lose his romantic obsession with her, he's liable to swing right across in the opposite direction. I believe that is what might have occurred with the other two women, Mary Innes and Sandy Baker: they became imperfect—as they were bound to—and he rejected them."

"What about Bobbie?" Nick asked.

"From the reports I've been given, she simply left him. Possibly in time."

O'Rourke had dug up two more items early this evening, one of them hopeful, one disquieting. "There's a girl named Bobbie Gifford," he'd told Nick over the phone. "She was living with Dotson for six or seven months, here in New York. From people who saw them together I'm getting the impression he was crazy about her, lots of kissing at the corner café and the bowling alley and the drive-in, and for most of the time she seemed crazy about him, even though there was a big age gap: she's only eighteen and looks even younger, built like a doll. She—"

"Can you get a photograph?"

"Huh? We're trying."

"Any facial description?"

"The words I'm getting are like pretty, precocious, a real little homecoming queen—some say she's dark, others say she's kind of brunette, you know how people can't even describe their own mother when—"

"I'm thinking about Joe Dotson's mother," Nick said.

"You're what?"

"Okay, the shrink's telling us that it's Joe's dead mother he's got up there. She looked like Tina."

"Jesus, you know I really think some of those shrinks need cleaning out. And if Bobbie Gifford looks anything like Tina, people would have said so. I mean they'd've said she looks like something right out of this world and into the next."

"Is she still in New York?"

"Nobody knows. We've got an all-points tracer on her. Missing Persons is checking institutions, hospitals, morgues, the whole bit. But they can't put flyers out because she's not officially missing. Nobody's reported her as such. Her mother hasn't seen her since she joined up with Dotson. No father or close relatives in the city. McNeil's pushing us hard, through the top brass."

"McNeil?" He was the police psychologist.

"He's working on the idea that when this kid left Dotson three months back, it broke him up. If we can find her, and get her to tell him she's ready to come back to him, he might release Tina."

"That'd be nice," Nick said. His business as a negotiator was trading, and this was a trade that could really work. There wasn't even any risk attached: if this kid

Bobbie agreed to meet Joe Dotson, even if only for a minute or two, she'd be under strong covert surveillance and protection.

The second item O'Rourke had dug up was causing tremors throughout the whole network. "A couple of newspapers came up with a point nobody else noticed at the time of Sandy Baker's death fall," he told Nick. "I read the clippings. Both she and the other girl, Mary Innes, died at full moon."

"How's that again?"

"They died on a night when the moon was full. Dotson was in the tabloids as the 'full-moon killer.' "

Soon after getting off the phone with O'Rourke, Nick had asked Dr. Weinberg about that. "What we read in the tabloids," he'd said after reflection, "doesn't often relate very closely to reality, but if we assume it was a fact that those young women died—"

"We've checked the records, Doc."

"Very well. It might be significant. The borderline personality isn't specifically conditioned by the lunar cycle, as far as anyone has discovered; but any kind of stress, any kind of mental abnormality can be aggravated by the moon's gravitational influence. And if *both* those women died at such a time, it might not be just coincidence."

Captain Mundy had called it bullshit, though not to the psychiatrist's face. "The moon won't be full until the night after tomorrow, and by that time we'll have got that freak out of there even if we have to drag him out at gunpoint."

Earlier in the day, an hour-long conference had been held by Police Commissioner Dakers; those present had been his aides, Chief of Detectives Dan Warner, Captain Mundy and the Hostage Negotiating Team led by Lieutenant Nick Valenti. Eugene St. Clair and his wife had urgently requested to make an appeal to Joe Dotson on television, and after a formal agreement the arrangements were made. The message on the banners was brief: "WATCH NEWS CHANNELS AT 11:00." It was deliberately enigmatic, since Nick Valenti had argued convincingly that any elaboration would decrease Dotson's interest; the idea was to intrigue him with a mystery he could solve only by switching on a TV set at the stated time. The banker had been warned that since these arrangements had been made at his own request, he must also bear the responsibility for any harmful consequences. This he had agreed to. The special news flash was scheduled to go out from the three major and two local networks, following a fifteen-second introductory announcement to alert their viewers.

At 11:00 P.M. Eugene St. Clair entered the Park Tower lobby under the close protection of police officers, and at the scene of the double killing of the doorman and security guard just twenty-four hours earlier, went in front of the cameras to make an appeal to Joseph Dotson to spare the life of his only child, Tina.

12

"Bijan," JOE SAID, AND SPRAYED some onto his sleeve, like it was a testing sample in a store. "Fantastic!" He could see her in the mirror through the open doorway, the mirror in the corridor. She was smiling. *"Kouros."* He splashed this one on to the back of his hand, making the hairs go dark. "By Yves Saint Laurent." He waved his hand around, sniffing the air. "You like that?" He saw her nodding in the mirror, nodding and smiling. It had been a terrific evening. Dinner and everything. Not terrific. Very . . . elegant. And romantic. "Terrific" and "great" and words like that meant nothing; you could apply them to any damned thing. Elegant and romantic, right. *"Givenchy Gentleman!"* It was another spray, and he was about to spray it around the bathroom like it was for killing flies when he thought, no, that'd be cheap too. He sprayed it on his other sleeve. "Mary?" He put the bottle of perfume back onto the shelf against the leather padding. Everything was leather in here—a man's bathroom, sure, leather and gold, smooth gold, not like in the huge living room. She hadn't answered him and he glanced up at her face in the mirror. She wasn't smiling anymore. She looked more like Tina now. "Tina? How much did this place cost?"

After a while she said, "I've no idea."

"Okay, I mean approximately. I mean you know about how much things cost, right? Your old—your father's a banker." He remembered that. She was Tina St. Clair with the rich father. But she wasn't answering his—

"I'd say about twenty million."

Joe laughed. "I don't mean the building. Just the apartment." He went out to the corridor and saw her living and breathing, not in the mirror anymore. "Or d'you mean the apartment cost that?"

"Yes, as a rough figure. I really don't—"

"As a rough *figure*?" He laughed an awful lot now, hearing the sound of it go shouting along the corridor. "Jesus Christ, twenty *million*?" Then he stopped laughing suddenly and looked away from her. She didn't think it was funny. It wasn't elegant to laugh at a thing like that.

"Joe, can we look at the news?"

"News?"

"It's almost eleven. Remember?"

He couldn't answer because she looked so incredibly beautiful standing there with the rose-colored lamp on the wall bringing a flush to her skin, and the archway behind her making a frame for her head. She'd put on a filmy white dress for their dinner party, with a gold belt. Did rich people always use a lot of gold? It'd figure, and besides, it looked very nice.

"Eleven?" He didn't like knowing the time, the hours or the days. Time had stopped now. "Oh, sure. You want to? You mean look at the news?" Those screwballs had put new banners out across the street, about watching the news at eleven. He wasn't interested, but if she wanted to see it, then okay. She could have anything at all.

"Is Mary a friend of yours?" she asked him as they went into the library. It was the first room they came to with a TV in it. Most rooms—*Mary?*—most rooms had a TV, all over the whole apartment. "I don't have a friend, no," he said, "called that. Don't sit over there. Sit right here with me." She shouldn't talk about dead people.

127

He'd been on a real high all evening, way up there after their dinner with oysters and quiche and wine and with the roses on the table and her looking the way she did, the way that sent him curving through rainbows and back, not believing he was so close to her—

"Joe?"

—and not believing she was going to be close to him forever *but not if she talked about dead people*, bringing him down from the high, all the way down, like diving, like falling.

"On?" he said. "Switch it on? You mean?"

"I'll do it." Her voice was quite faint, like she was outside the room. He didn't feel very good. Not sick or anything, just not quite focused.

"Okay," he said and watched the screen. A news flash, the woman was saying, and then they cut and there was a man looking at them, a man wearing a topcoat and looking solemn. Then the feeling went and he was back to where it all was, with Tina's hand feeling for his. They sat holding hands like that, like they would forever.

"She is all we have, Mr. Dotson. We have no other children. We love her deeply, just as you do, and we know you'll take great care of her." He spoke with his head down a bit and his eyes up, like he wanted to say other things but had decided not to. "But we'd like to see her for a while, and talk to her, because she's back from overseas and there are so many things she'll be wanting to tell us. We—"

"Hey! Is he your dad?"

"Yes," she said with her voice very low and vibrating. She turned her wet face to look at him. "I'd like you to meet him, Joe."

"Why are you crying?" He touched the tears, smoothing them on her cheeks. He didn't like her being hurt. He didn't like anyone hurting her. He would kill them.

"I miss him," she said. "Do you understand that? Did you ever miss your father?"

He looked away, back at the screen.

"Of course," the banker was saying, "we would want to meet you too, Joe. We'd all have an hour or two together, you and Tina and ourselves. We would appreciate it deeply, Joe, if you'd talk to us on the telephone, and tell us when we can see our daughter. Would you let her talk to us, on the phone? That would be generous of you. In the meantime, my wife, Elizabeth, and I know that we can rely on your natural human decency not to harm our child in any way, but to show her, and all of us, how much you really love her."

He saw the man lift his head a little in the moment after he stopped speaking, with his glittering dark eyes looking straight out from the screen at the man he was talking to. As the image faded Joe took three strides to the TV set and pulled it off the ebony cabinet and swung it across the room and saw it crash into the lower shelves of calf-bound books and crush them, spreading them against the wall with their leaves bursting open like white flesh laid raw from the leathery skin.

"What the hell are you talking about?" The period brass telephone was in his hand before he knew what he was going to do. *"Why do you keep saying you don't want me to harm her, for Christ's sake?"* The sweat poured from him, running into his eyes, while his breath shook loose in his body like a gale had come up and was blasting through him, carrying away hair and blood and bones. "Listen to me—"

"We're listening, Joe."

"Who the hell—?"

"This is Nick. You remember me."

Nick? The guy who'd said all that crap about Acapulco. "You listen to me, Nick. You people can stop giving me all this shit about hurting Tina. You know who's hurting her right now? Her own father! She's sitting here crying her heart out because of what he said, you know that?'' Not sitting here, no, but standing up now, standing against the wall where the archway led into the next room, watching him with her head back to touch the wall and her green eyes looking at him at an angle like she was half turned away and ready to run, the mess, maybe, he'd made a mess with that fucking TV set, it had brought down a whole slew of books and smashed away the shelving and left splinters and chips of lacquer all over the carpet, okay, it was a big set, a twenty-five-inch, and weighed a ton, it was bound to make a mess—*why couldn't people seem to understand anything*, if you start throwing something that heavy around you're going to make a fucking mess, right?

''She misses her dad,'' the voice came over the phone, ''that's why she's crying, Joe.''

''Will you just shut your goddamned mouth?''

It was such a beautiful evening with the wine and the roses and then she had to talk about dead people and the man had to come on the screen and make her cry and now this jerk was trying to feed him a lot of guff about why she was crying, and now he'd smashed the TV and scared her and she was staring at him like he was—like he was— crazy or—

White light burst and showered him with ice and left him shaking with his teeth clenched trying to keep everything still, the phone slippery in his fingers and the sharp smell of acids churning in his body that always happened when people made him remember things he needed to forget, *so long as you're okay, Joe,* sure I'm okay, you just have to leave me alone, I just need to come down slowly, it's happened before, slowly, come down on my own, *so long as you're okay, Joe,* sure I'm okay, just leave me alone—

"It's good to hear your voice again, Joe, and I'm really glad you accepted our invitation to look at the news. It's made everyone a lot happier, even Tina, who's only crying because she hasn't seen her folks for a while now. We—"

"I want you people to leave us alone. Are you listening to me? I want—"

"I'm listening, Joe—"

"I want you to get the hell out, you understand me? I don't want to see any more stuff written across the buildings for me to read, okay, and I want you to take all those fucking police cars away and get those people off the top of the buildings and all those people out of the streets down there, because you know something, if any harm comes to Tina it's going to be your fault, are you listening to me, it's going to be your own goddamned fault."

Her green eyes were very big, watching him like soft lights from the shadow of the archway; he could see the white folds of her dress moving to the movement of her breasts as she breathed deeply, like she'd been running, or was going to run, she mustn't do that, there was nowhere she could run to, she was his forever, and they should know that by now.

"All I'm asking you, Joe, is to keep the line open, so I can talk to you and get to understand your feelings, which are very important to me . . ."

The phone down, the slippery phone down.

". . . and to all of us. We want to do everything we can to help, Joe, but we can't do that if . . ."

The phone down in the brass hooks of the base.

". . . you don't keep the line open. . . ."

The phone down.

Alone.

*   *   *

He stood watching the moon.

It was lopsided, hanging over the buildings with some of its edge missing, as if in rising it had caught on their dark peaks and had some of its roundness torn away.

"There's something wrong with me," he said.

From beside him she put her arm around and held him. "Is there?"

The moon went up so fast; he could see the gap widening between the bottom rim and the buildings. Everything was turning, the earth, the moon, the stars, his round brain in his round head, with some of it torn away, some of it missing.

"It's a bad time for me." He spoke very softly, not wanting to disturb anything within himself: he had to tiptoe across volcanoes down there. But he felt perfectly clear about everything, as it sometimes happened, like he was standing in some other place and seeing himself, and knowing himself, from a distance, and understanding it all. These were good times, because of being able to know what he was, so clearly; but they were also bad times, because of what he knew.

"These are bad times for you?" she asked him.

He even knew about other people, at these times. "You can ask me about it," he told her. "You don't have to be scared."

"You mean"—her hand strengthened against him as if she could trust him now—"it's a bad time when there's a moon?"

He breathed in her scent. It wasn't Givenchy or Yves Saint Laurent or anything; it was Tina St. Clair, with her tawny skin and her smoky hair and her long lithe body with its curves and hollows and its slow hidden fires, *let me show you,* where nobody else had ever understood.

"Yes. When there's a moon. There's something wrong with me. You must know that."

After a while she said very quietly, "The best thing is to keep in touch with Nick, on the phone. Ask him to work everything out."

He could hear the hope in her voice, as clearly as if it were his own voice, his own hope. He felt very close to her.

"They can't do anything," he said.

"If you'd let them, I think they could."

"No. It's the bad time, you see. There's me, and there's this—there's some other—"

The word went falling into the shadows, echoing . . . *other* . . . the one who made him do things he didn't want to do, but had to do, because of the . . . *other* . . .

"I can help you," she said, the hope still there in her voice, like a bird trying to fly.

"No one can help me." He'd like people to help him, but the *other* didn't let them.

Standing in the quiet room with the woman he loved more than life itself, he felt a desolation so deep and so cold that it was like being up there on the moon, alone. "But everything will work out," he said, "when we leave here."

He felt a tremor in her hand.

"We're going to leave here?"

In her voice he heard the bird trying to fly again; but it felt itself trapped.

"Yes. Just the two of us."

"When?"

"Soon." The light of the murderous moon washed over him, and he closed his eyes in despair. "And no one will ever know where we've gone."

— 13 —

THE MATCH FLARED AGAINST NICK Valenti's face, then smoke drifted past the moonlit brickwork of the elevator housing as he drew on the cigarette. Five ripped packs of Winstons had gone into the garbage bin by the stairhead since eight o'clock this morning and the smoke had gone into his lungs. Two whole percolators of coffee had gone into his nerves, while Joseph Paul Dotson and Tina Diane St. Clair had moved through his head in a shadow play he couldn't stop watching, in case he missed something: a thought from nowhere, a theory, an idea, something, anything he might be able to work on, and end the waiting.

"There's snow, upstate," a voice touched the edge of his attention.

"Any other good news?"

Two men were moving, two snipers changing shifts, the man coming on duty wearing black woolen gloves with the fingers cut off. The seven other people up here were all wearing their uniform greatcoats; the sky was brilliant with stars, even with the moon's ashen light pervading the night and casting sharp-cut shadows of building on building on building across the city's heights. But even with the wave of cold coming in from the northlands, the current reports estimated the crowd down there in the streets at several hundred strong, at almost midnight. What were they doing there? Hoping for? Throughout today the police switchboards had been handling fifty calls an hour from all over the country from people wanting to get into the act—psychology juniors, evangelists, cabdrivers, most of them asking to be patched in on the telephone with Joe Dotson so they could persuade him to see reason.

That would be nice, Nick thought as he dragged smoke in, that would really be nice, to persuade Joe to see reason. There was just one little snag. He wouldn't recognize it.

They'd called the penthouse the moment Joe had hung up on them an hour and a half ago, but there'd been only a couple of rings before he pulled out the jack. There were no rules anymore. Dotson didn't want anything, so they'd got nothing to trade. Commissioner Dakers had been up here again, brief with his questions but wanting long answers.

"What *exactly* is the holdup, Valenti?"

"There's nothing he wants."

"That doesn't tell me a great deal." He was well wrapped up in his expensive black overcoat and black calf gloves, the moonlight whitening his thick head of hair and his bright stare as he listened with the attentiveness of calm desperation. O'Rourke, closer than Nick to the administrative brass, had said the commissioner was going to get bounced right out of office if Tina died.

"Okay, sir. We started out with what we thought was a hostage situation. A hostage-taker always makes demands: his freedom, the release of a political prisoner, the custody of his child, whatever. Or he's calling attention to something he thinks is unjust: he's been thrown out of his apartment or fired from his job or his wife's left him. There's always something he wants, and there's always, therefore, something we can give him, if we decide to. Dotson wants Tina St. Clair, and he's got her, so we've nothing to trade."

The heavy-shouldered man in the dark coat stood silhouetted against the spill of light from Fifth Avenue's glimmering ravine, a monument to impotence, the commander of thirty thousand armed men held in check by the invincible adversary, a mentally disturbed window cleaner.

"Then it's a kidnap situation?" he asked the lieutenant.

"No, sir." Nick moved to stand closer to him and lowered his voice. Some of the people here on the rooftop were rooting for Captain Mundy, who was waiting for the order he felt sure he'd finally get: to send in the assault teams and bring out Tina St. Clair before Dotson knew what was happening. But they couldn't hope to do that. "Dotson may be crazy," the police psychologist had said, "but he's not stupid." He'd know what was happening, all right, if the assault teams went in. "We tried to sell him the idea of a kidnap situation," Nick went on, "but he wouldn't buy it. We had a million dollars to trade, and it was too much."

The bright stare dwelt on him as Dakers turned his head. "You think we should have started with less? A more credible sum?"

"No, sir. The man wants nothing he doesn't already have. So anything we can offer him is too much." From the distance along Fifth Avenue came the sound of tires shrilling and then the crunch of metal on metal, and someone in the night patrol below the building here must have heard it and hit the dispatchers at the precinct with his radio: in less than ten seconds a siren started up near the intersection of Fifth and Forty-sixth and lights began flashing on a south-bound prowler. You get instant assistance in this fair city, for we are the Finest. Just take care who washes your windows. "If we could call him up and talk to him, we'd have a chance. We can't. If he'd jack in just one of those phones and leave it off the hook by accident, we could bug the system and hear what he's saying to her, and what she's saying to him. But then we couldn't call him. Captain Mundy's decided that in another hour he's going to bring some pressure on, to make Dotson call us up.''

''What kind of pressure?''

''Cut off the lights over there, or the water. Cut off the heat.''

''D'you agree with that?''

More sirens sounded from the distance, and an ambulance horn. Someone for Bellevue. ''I don't see any point in getting the guy mad at us. Were you listening to his last call, sir?''

''Yes.''

''Then you know the mood he's in. If we cut off the facilities across there he'll call us up, sure, but only to tell us to switch them on again, or else. We only have one thing to work with, and I'd like to hang on to it.''

''One thing?''

''Time.''

''Lieutenant, I want you to be more informative. I want more than one-word answers.''

''Yes, sir.'' Dakers had come up here to listen, but Nick wasn't ready to talk. The police department had been donated the use of empty office space two floors below the roof of the building and a furniture store had grabbed itself some publicity by sending in beds and chairs and tables; Nick and some of the Emergency Services squad had been snatching a half-hour's sleep down there when they could, but he wasn't refreshed; he was feeling more than just fatigue: in a protracted hostage negotiation the worst enemy was frustration, the gradual loss of confidence in yourself and the gradual realization that you were going to fail, and the knowledge that your failure was going to be marked, for someone, by a cross. But he needed to help the commissioner, who was here to cooperate: he'd asked him if he agreed with Mundy's decision to cut off the facilities over there; the commissioner wasn't listening only to the captain; he'd listen hardest to the man who could offer the best chance. "Time is the one thing we've got on our side," Nick told him. "If Dotson had gone in there to rape and kill in some kind of psychotic rage he'd have got it over with by now. If he'd wanted some kind of attention he'd have told us, and we could have lowered a camera from the roof over there and put him on TV and screened him worldwide in exchange for the hostage—"

"Or put a shot through him at the window?"

"If that had been the decision, sure, but my sole function is to save life—even his—by talking. When I have to stop talking, that's when the shooting starts. But he doesn't want attention: he's asked us to leave him alone. So there's no rush on. Nobody has to panic or run out of patience and send the troops in and risk hitting that explosive. There's no reason, right now, why we shouldn't go on waiting. I'm just as frustrated as everyone else, but sir, when you let frustration get on top of you, you're going to fail. If we owe Tina St. Clair anything, it's patience. And if we just hold on, there's going to be something that guy over there discovers he wants, after all; then he'll tell us; and we can go to work and trade."

Dakers got out his cigarette case and flipped it open and found it empty and snapped it shut and accepted one of Nick's filter-tips and lit up. "What can he possibly discover he wants? You say he already has it."

"I don't know, sir. He's a psychotic; he may find he wants something that anyone normal wouldn't think about. He may suddenly want out—that's happened plenty of times. We're building up a lot of pressure on him just by being here, and that's draining his psychic energy and working on his emotions. He could finally just want someone to talk to—someone with authority, like the police, his doctor, a priest, someone who can handle this whole thing he's gotten into. That's happened before, too. It could happen right now.''

He wanted badly to sell Dakers the idea of patience. Dotson had called up twice and each time Nick had failed to keep the line open, and if it happened again, Mundy could get what he wanted: an order to go in there despite the risks. Because they were running a risk already, and suddenly Dakers was talking about that.

''It's not the only thing that could happen right now, Valenti. That screwball could kill Tina anytime at all, at any next minute while we're all hanging around doing nothing. That's Mundy's point: waiting could kill her, too.''

Soon after midnight Nick took a call from the maternity clinic where they'd taken Karen, and after a few seconds she came on the line herself, though he hardly recognized her voice.

''I'm scared, Nick.''

The Dotson-Tina thing got blown clean out of his mind. ''You don't have to be scared, sweetheart. I was talking to Doc Marcellino earlier tonight; he says everything's in good shape.''

''I'm still scared.'' Her voice crept out of the phone in a whisper, and he knew he'd have to get right over there, and knew that he wouldn't.

''Your mom's there, isn't she?''

''Yes, but—''

''There isn't anything I can do that she can't, sweetheart. And you know how much we trust the doc. He's the best in the business, and he's going to be the godfather, remember?''

''He says that to everyone. How long will you be there, Nick?''

"It can be over anytime at all. Just as soon——"

"They might have to operate. It might have to be a cesarean, and that's why I'm so——"

"They'll let me know, sweetheart. I'm right here on the end of the phone and they know that, and if there's any question of operating I'll be over there right away——Code Four."

And he would do that, if it was going to be a cesarean. But once he left here he wouldn't be able to come back. Mundy would trade on his absence; with the chief negotiator off the scene he wouldn't leave it to the backups: he'd hustle the top brass into launching an assault on the penthouse over there and for the first time the Hostage Negotiating Team would mark up a failure. And just incidentally, Tina could get killed.

"It's just if anything happens," he heard the soft scared voice in his ear again, "it'd mean I never had another chance to see you, Nick." Then she began crying, and he sat listening in silence, wanting to hold her and kiss her better and soothe her to sleep, till the idea of letting Mundy go in and blow that bastard's head off grew very attractive.

"You'll be seeing me the minute this thing's over, sweetheart," he said at last, but she didn't answer, just went on crying; and suddenly there was another voice on the line——her mom's.

"Are you there, Nick?"

"Yes," he said.

"She needs to see you."

"I know. But——"

"Listen, Nick. I think you're okay, you know that. So don't get me wrong, because I'm going to hang up the minute I've said this. You'll have to decide what you want to be for the next couple of hours, a cop or a husband."

*   *   *

Sitting with his back to the elevator head, the plaid rug wound around him and his legs stretched out among the mess of phone cables and camp stools and coffee cups and cigarette butts, Nick Valenti dozed, his head nodding and jerking up again, nodding again. He could go below and curl up on a bed down there, jacking the hotline into the wall so he'd be right on the spot if Joe Dotson called; but they were all watching him now, waiting for him to show any sign of giving up. Mundy, with his plans ready to send in the assault teams the instant the word came through; Al Groot, the secondary negotiator, waiting to take over at a second's notice and snatch the credit if Tina survived; Tony Rimkus, the backup negotiator, hot on Groot's heels; and somewhere across the city, Maria, a good woman, a good mother, proud of him up to now but just as scared as her daughter that something might go wrong—*which it could*. And that fucking basket case over there screwing the daylights out of the city's sweetheart, St. Tina, while she lay underneath him wondering how much longer she had to live.

Mundy, Groot, Rimkus, Maria, *Karen* . . . His head dropped again and the lights of the city swung up and scattered against the sky and then swung down again as he opened his eyes for as long as he could till his head went down again. . . . Mundy, Groot, Rimkus . . .

"Nick?"

"Huh?" He sat up with a jerk and got Al Groot's face into focus.

"Lindquist is on his way. Be here in maybe an hour."

"Where was he, all this time?"

"Hong Kong."

Nick lurched to his feet and took the mug of hot chocolate Al had brought him. Al was okay, a good negotiator and a good guy all round; he wasn't looking to snatch any credit from anyone, and if he came in for any, he would have earned it. Those had been half-dozing thoughts, brought on by stress.

"Thanks." Nick took a sip at the hot chocolate and burned his lips. "Let's hope Lindquist can tell us something." Thomas Lindquist was the owner of the penthouse, and maybe he could give them some information about the layout that didn't show in the city engineer's plans: were there any rooms or closets with outside or two-way locks, where Tina could entice Dotson and lock him in? Were there any hiding places she could use where he could never find her? They were hungry for the smallest clue to anything that could give them leverage to work with.

"Whatever he tells us," Al said, "couldn't ever match up to what we told him." The poor s.o.b. had been halfway around the world when the NYPD had traced him and called him up to tell him his apartment was full of dynamite and surrounded by police and the FBI.

"Have they found Bobbie Gifford yet?" Nick asked him.

"Nope. They're still trying, though."

"Where's Mundy?" he asked Al.

"Putting the gun teams through their drill. That guy's raring to go."

"Maybe it's going to be the only way."

"Bullshit. All Mundy's working on is a picture of him on the front page tomorrow with Tina drowning him in tears of gratitude. Thing is, he's more liable to blow the top of that building all over us." He crouched beside Nick, watching the windows across the street, the moonlight turning his red hair to copper and sparking on the rim of his watch. "We're here to talk to Dotson. That's the only way."

Nick wished he had Al's confidence, his faith in the orderliness of human nature. Al had seen half a dozen negotiations since he'd joined the team but they hadn't been complicated; three of them he'd handled himself, but they'd been domestic cases like the black kid on the bridge all those years ago; and none of them had involved a psychotic. Al's short experience had taught him that you could talk *anybody* down, anybody at all, given enough time and enough patience. Maybe he was right.

"Karen just called," Nick told him, before he knew he was going to.

"She okay?"

"She's at the clinic now. Some kind of complications, though the doc says he was ready for them; she's small."

"Sure. Gee"—Al was watching him in the moonlight—"you want to go over there?"

"Yes."

After a slight pause Al said: "Okay."

"But I'm not going. Not yet."

"Okay," Al said again. "If you want me to take over, you just have to say. The thing—I mean sure, I'm ready when you are, Nick."

Nick drained his cup of chocolate and put it down among the cigarette butts. "The thing—?" he asked in a moment.

"Thing is, if you left here, and he called us—you know?"

"Yes. I know." Al hadn't had a lot of experience in the field but he knew the psychology, and he'd learned from cases written up in the training manuals; and two of the major failures in negotiating had been caused by switching members of the team at a crucial point: just when the hostage-taker had seemed ready to give up, he'd been thrown by hearing a different voice on the telephone—the voice of someone he didn't know. In each case the aspect of trust had been negated; the hostage-taker had got scared and suspicious and had taken a life just to prove he was still in charge. "If he called us," Nick said quietly, "and I wasn't here, you'd do a good job."

"That isn't what we're talking about, Nick."

"Okay." But he'd wanted him to know he was ready to trust him to take over. "What we're really talking about is whether a cop should marry."

Al was quiet for a while, then asked him: "Is Maria with her?"

"Yes."

"I guess she's the most important person for Karen to have around. And there's nothing you can do anyway, is there? It's in the doc's hands, right? And he really loves that girl—who doesn't?"

There was a silence again; then Nick said: "I don't, if I don't go over there and see her."

"Jesus, it's not as simple as that, Nick. Where are those fucking cigarettes?" He scratched around in the faint light, and a match flared. "Pregnant women get scared as hell, and this is Karen's first time."

"Sure." Karen, scared as hell, with her small white face— It didn't bear thinking about. It was tough even for Al; the two families were close to each other: when cops were partners, their families became partners. But Al had a different worry: that Nick might hand Tina St. Clair's life over to him and he might lose it. "It's her first time," Nick said, "and I'm not there. Of course"—and he realized he was deliberately needling Al, because Al wasn't giving him the answers he wanted—"it's partly a crapshoot."

"For Christ's sake, we all know that." Al was filling the air with smoke now, dragging the tobacco out of the paper.

"I mean," Nick told him in a tone of feigned detachment, "there's no question I could get permission to go over to

144

the clinic, and while I was over there, everything would be perfectly okay, so long as Dotson didn't call. Right?"

"I wish to Christ—"

"On the other hand, if I was over there and he called, that would be it. I'd leave the team. I'd have to. It's a crapshoot, Al. And I'm going to play."

He got to his feet, and Al stood up with him. "Shit," he said, "do you mean that?"

"Yes." Karen, scared, with her small hand clenched on the bedsheet, missing his. No way. "I want you to take over, just till I'm back."

Al dropped his cigarette and ground it out with his shoe. "Okay."

Then one of the phones began ringing, the one standing with the flashlight shining on it so Nick could get to it fast. He picked it up and spoke. "Hello?"

The caller's voice came over the amplifiers, but it wasn't Joe Dotson's. It was Tina St. Clair's.

14

THE MOONLIGHT CAME THROUGH THE two narrow windows, bright enough to pick out the lettering on the Roman plaque over the shower doors, burning on the gold faucets and the gold box of tissues and the lever on the toilet head. She hadn't put the lights on, in case he woke and began looking for her. She had locked the door.

It hadn't been done without thinking. Last night he'd slept deeply for a time while she'd lain awake, too frightened to sleep herself, so frightened that she'd said his name, hoping to wake him so that she could talk to him and hear the sound of another human voice, even his. Tonight, ten minutes ago, she'd called to him again, saying his name twice, the second time louder. It hadn't woken him, so she had slipped out of her own bed and gone through the dressing room and into the carpeted passage, passing the first bathroom and going to the next, to this one. She would say, if he ever asked, that it was because if she'd used the first bathroom the noise of the flush might have awakened him. She would say a lot of things, make a lot of excuses, if he ever asked her; but if he heard she was on the phone there'd be nothing she could say, and no excuse.

He was so strong. He'd lifted the TV set, that time, and simply *thrown* it across the library. It had been heavier than she was. She weighed a hundred and twenty-five, despite her height, and she had small bones. It would be like a maddened child smashing a doll.

She had seen a long jeweled paper knife on one of the desks in the library, and there were bread knives and butcher knives in the kitchen that she could have fetched and brought in here; but that would have meant blood, and hers, not his; even if she could bring herself to attack him with a knife she wouldn't have the strength of total commitment to drive it into his body fast enough to take him by surprise; he would have time to turn it against her, with a strength she didn't possess. If this weren't so, and if she weren't perfectly sure she was right, she needn't have come in here at all; she'd passed his bed, stopping for a moment to think it through: if she were standing there with a long sharp butcher knife in her hand, looking down at him, his throat bared, his mind drugged by sleep, she would have the necessary time: but the strength? Not muscular strength, but the strength of *will*. No.

It had been this way throughout history; it wasn't so much the greater physical strength of the male that had given him domination; it was the woman's reluctance to hurt, to kill. Otherwise men by the million would have died in their sleep: there were as many ways of killing a man as killing a cat.

So if he woke now, and missed her, and began hunting for her and found her here, there was nothing she could do against him; there was no chance of her hearing his bare feet on the carpeting outside the bathroom before he heard her voice on the phone, through the door. If he came here, she wouldn't be able to put the phone down and flush the toilet and make her natural excuses. He would know.

For a while she waited, listening for him, still safe on this side of the decision, watching the moonlit shape of the hinged onyx shell that housed the telephone; then she took a breath and raised the fluted lid of the shell and picked up the phone, the nerves rushing cold along her spine.

"This is Tina St. Clair."

As the soft voice was heard over the amplifiers at the two street command posts a shock wave of sound rose from the hundreds of people still keeping vigil at the cordons: the expression of mingled surprise, relief and awe.

It was also the trigger for police action on a wide scale in response to plans already made for this contingency, and the two-way radios and closed-circuit telephones came alive.

"Kill the amplifiers."

"Hit the press with a blackout: no questions answered."

"Lieutenant McNeil to command post, please."

"Is Doc Schultz patched in?"

"Yes, sir."

"Is Dr. Weinberg at his home right now?"

"Yes, sir."

"Wake him up and patch him in."

"Will do."

"Where's Lieutenant O'Rourke?"

"He's at Park Tower lobby."

"I want him at Command. And keep control of those crowds down there."

There were things that were going to be said to Tina St. Clair that had to be private; there were things she'd say to the police that could wreck any chance of success if the press overheard and a leak was sprung and the TV newscasters aired it and Joe Dotson saw it on the screen.

"Who's there at headquarters?"

"I'm here," a voice answered, unmistakably the police commissioner's. The mood tautened another degree at the street and mobile command posts, in the entrance lobby of Park Tower and at the two posts high in the opposite building, one on the fiftieth floor and one on the roof.

Most of the radio and telephone calls had hit the networks simultaneously as orders and information were passed; only those officers directly involved with the penthouse were listening to the voices coming over the hotline.

"Hello, Tina. This is Nick Valenti, police."

He left it right there. There was no talking-down to be done with Tina on the line; they wanted every single bit of information she could give them before she had to hang up or Dotson unjacked the phone; and they wanted Tina to have all the information she needed from their side.

Her voice came in almost a whisper. "This is as loud as I can talk. Can you hear me?"

"Yes we can."

Across the roof from where Nick was standing with the phone in his hand, the snipers were at the sights with the long barrels of their Ithacas swinging to aim along the row of windows opposite. "When something happens," the Emergency Services chief had briefed them when the roof posts had been set up, "you train your sights along those windows and prepare to fire on orders. When *anything* new happens we could shift into an entirely different phase and maybe have Dotson alone at a window, if only for a few seconds. In those few seconds we might have a chance at dropping him."

"I'm in one of the bathrooms," the soft voice came. "Joe is asleep, but he might wake and miss me."

The men listening were aware of the electricity in their nerves as they realized what was happening. Tina had not only managed to get to a phone but she was alert to the necessity of a rapid and economical interchange. Already she was giving them information she knew they needed, without waiting for questions.

"I'm in good shape. He hasn't been violent, not to me. But he says he won't let anyone take me away from him, ever." There was a pause, and they could hear her quick nervous breathing. "He says we're leaving here together, where no one can find us. I think—I think he means he's going to kill me and then himself." Another pause came, and they waited, sickened.

On the command-building roof a radio came to life and Detective Spiro hit the knurled knob and turned the volume down.

"Dr. Weinberg is patched in, sir."

"Very good," Mundy's voice came over the network.

Nick Valenti decided to give Tina another five seconds; then he'd speak; she might be needing the moral support of his voice. But she came on again.

"He says there's—there's something wrong with him. But he says nobody can help him. I told him you could help him, but he said this is a bad time for him because of the moon. There's some other—I don't know quite what he meant— some other pressure on him, or—"

"Some other personality?" It was Saul Weinberg's voice.

"He didn't use that word, no."

In the swing-tilt radio chair inside the enormous mobile HQ van standing outside the Park Tower entrance, Captain Mundy waited impatiently. If the psychiatrist was going to hold the air discussing clinical mishmash he was going to cut in very fast; they needed to know a lot of practical things from Tina while they had the chance: and it could be the chance of a lifetime.

A voice sounded from the radio console in front of him.

"Lieutenant McNeil has arrived at the command post."

"Very good."

The psychiatrist's voice came again. "But he mentioned the moon, specifically?"

"Yes."

"Has he mentioned taking his own life?"

"Not in so many words. He just implied it."

"Tina, this is Police Captain Mundy. Does he have a gun?"

"I haven't seen one."

"Have you been outside in the lobby on that floor?"

"No. He's blocked both entrances with heavy furniture. He—"

"What material?" He was thinking of bullet penetration. "Is it wooden furniture or—"

"Front door, a hardwood chest and a ceramic vase, a big one. Kitchen door, a refrigerator."

A voice came again from the console. "Dr. Schultz is patched in, sir."

"Very good" He turned away from the speaker and said into the phone: "When he came into the apartment, did you see anything through the open doorway, in the lobby? Any kind of bag, bundle, or a box—"

"No. But I saw the elevator doors were open."

"Wide open?"

"No. A few inches."

"Was he carrying anything when he came in?"

There was a pause again, and the silence drew out, except for the fluttering of her breath close to the mouthpiece. On the rooftop Nick began sweating; the silence seemed to spread from the phone in his hand to the other rooftops and right across the sleeping city.

"I—I thought I heard him." This time they could barely catch the whisper; then she was saying softly, "I don't want to die . . . I don't want to die . . ."

"You won't have to," Nick cut in at once. "We're right on top of the situation, Tina, and there are police officers as close to you as the stairs just outside the lobby of your apartment. We simply have to be patient, and so do you."

Two floors below the rooftop where Nick was speaking to Tina St. Clair, her father stood facing Lieutenant McNeil, the police-department psychologist attached to the Hostage Negotiating Team. Elizabeth St. Clair was still asleep in one of the offices where beds had been brought in for anyone who could snatch an hour's respite; but Eugene had caught the sound of his daughter's voice a few moments ago, before the amplifiers had been shut down on Captain Mundy's orders.

"I must speak to her," Eugene told the lieutenant. "Surely you can understand that."

McNeil studied the drawn, sleepless face of the banker, the hotline phone in his hand. "Yes, sir, I understand how you feel. But there's a risk we don't want to take." He was holding the phone to his ear, blocking the mouthpiece with his free hand, half his mind waiting for what Tina would say next.

"What risk?" Eugene asked him impatiently.

"I realize the sound of your voice might give her comfort and hope, but she's critically emotional right now and it might send her clean over the top and provoke some kind of a showdown with Dotson—and his own emotional state could trigger a manic explosion. We can't—"

Tina's voice came again.

"I'm okay again now. I thought I could hear him coming, and—got scared. He hasn't hurt me yet, but I have the definite feeling he'd do something violent if I provoked him. It's like being close to a bomb."

Lieutenant McNeil kept the phone close against his ear, to save St. Clair's pain; if he could hear what his daughter was saying now it could turn his mind.

Eugene watched the thin studious face of the lieutenant, wondering how good he was, how talented; he didn't have a high rank, but then he looked young and could have left a successful private practice to join the department. "I can't believe," he told McNeil, "that a few words of comfort would entail any risk. My own emotions are totally under control, and my daughter is highly intelligent."

McNeil heard another voice on the line now, and recognized the bright, articulated tones of the private M.D. who'd been the chief medical consultant to the police department for the past three years.

"Tina, this is Dr. Harry Schultz. You say you're in a bathroom: can you reach the medicine cabinet from where you are?"

"Yes."

"Please open it and tell me what's there."

"I'd have to put the lights on."

"Would that worry you?"

In a moment she said: "I guess not. But I'll want to switch them off again as soon as I can."

"Whenever you want."

"Okay."

On the rooftop two floors above where Eugene and the lieutenant stood facing each other, four rifle barrels swung across the parapet to sight on the narrow oblong of light that began glowing on the face of the building opposite. To those listening on the hotline, the impression of vague distance between them and Tina St. Clair closed in a flash to something measurable; her voice on the telephone could have been coming from a thousand miles away, but that one small light going on over there brought her suddenly close, and suddenly real again.

Nick Valenti blocked the mouthpiece of his phone and called across to the gun team. "Take it easy, you guys. That's not Dotson, it's Tina."

The four barrels moved again, and a man called back: "She still okay?"

"Doing fine."

Two floors below, Lieutenant McNeil watched the strained

and red-rimmed eyes of Eugene St. Clair, trying to judge how far gone he was after twenty-four hours of not knowing whether his only child was going to live or die. McNeil didn't have to bring St. Clair or his wife into his considerations: his total concern was Tina; but he knew how the man in front of him was feeling.

"Your emotions are under control right now, Mr. St. Clair," he said evenly, "but once you started talking to her, that could change. I've seen it happen."

The banker's gray head went down a little, and the strength went out of his shoulders. McNeil had seen the force go out of this man in the last few hours; he hadn't eaten and he hadn't slept; on top of his own fears for Tina he'd had the anguish of seeing his wife heartsick, and the burden of trying to give her comfort. Like the rest of them, St. Clair didn't have anything to do. Given the chance, he would fight for his child, die for her, kill for her, and find a strength that could match even a madman's; but a standoff situation where life was at stake called for courage of a different kind: this man had been required only to wait, and go on waiting, while the telephones and two-way radios came to life and fell silent again, while men moved around him with their faces set and their eyes avoiding each other's, some of them offering him a cup of coffee, telling him everything was going to be okay, they'd handled dozens of situations like this one before and they knew what they were doing. But they were doing nothing, and they couldn't hide it from him.

"Then let me listen to what she's saying," he told the lieutenant. "At least let me hear her voice."

McNeil considered the idea. Every aspect of this standoff was sensitive; every minute of time passing, every word that was said, every new phase in the confrontation was critical; it was in the very nature of the standoff situation; nerves were strained, emotions were hot, and a life could be lost to a wrong word or a wrong assumption. The inevitable onset of fatigue, boredom, lassitude, could be dangerous; most dangerous of all was the sudden mood of "the hell with it—we've got to do *something*, and I don't care what it is." If he made any concession to the man in front of him it would have to be calculated, weighed and assessed.

"If you listened to her, Mr. St. Clair, you'd be tempted to talk to her, even if only a word or two."

"Yes, I would be tempted."

"But you think you could resist?"

"Yes. I would resist. And successfully." He said it with deliberation; if he let himself show a trace of emotion to this cold-eyed policeman, there'd be no chance.

"Can you give me your word on that?"

"Yes. I give you my word."

Lieutenant McNeil spent a last few seconds on it, and didn't try kidding himself along. He felt confident that a man of St. Clair's caliber could keep control of himself, and particularly if his personal word had been given. It wouldn't, then, bring any harm to the girl over there with her life in the balance: she wouldn't know her father was listening. But what it would do to the man himself was unpredictable; it might reassure him to hear she was still able to work things out for herself and use her wits to survive, but if she said anything again like *I don't want to die*, it could send this man into a crisis. But again, there was no point telling him that. More than anything else in this world he wanted to hear his child's voice, and he wouldn't care what it did to him. It wasn't much to ask, and as McNeil looked into the haunted face of his fellow human being, he felt he couldn't withhold it.

"Bob," he told one of the plainclothes detectives at the makeshift communications table, "jack on that spare phone on the hotline circuit and give it to Mr. St. Clair."

Unblocking the mouthpiece, he raised the phone to his ear again, and listened to Tina's low voice.

"There's a box of Triaminic, and a bottle of Nyquil."

Sixteen blocks away to the northeast on Park Avenue and Seventieth Street, Dr. Harry Schultz was sitting up in bed with the phone in his hand, nodding to his wife as she gestured the familiar question: Would he like some Ovaltine? Since he'd become consultant to the NYPD on twenty-four-hour call three years ago their consumption of Ovaltine and milk had gone up enough to make it a tax-deductible expense.

"Okay, Tina. Go on." The first two drugs she'd read out were for coughs and colds. What they needed was a really powerful sedative, which Lindquist probably didn't have.

"There's Contac," he heard on the line, "and Neo . . . Neosynephrine. And Mylicon-8."

"Keep going," he said, "till I ask a question." They might not have long on the line, and he admired the reticence the top brass were showing by not cutting in; they realized the question of drugs could be important, even vital. He went on listening, getting a fairly accurate picture of Thomas Lindquist's routine health problems. Mylicon-8 was for gas, and so were Mylanta and Camalox, which were the next couple of labels she was reading out. Merthiolate, Lanacane, Mycitracin . . . Sal Hepatica, Excedrin, Desenex, Mitrolan . . . This was a pretty typical list for a wealthy New Yorker who lived too well and traveled too often and breathed too much of the air and took too many sauna baths: he was prone to colds, sinus irritation, acid stomach, athlete's foot, dry skin and constipation—so far.

"Nervine, Somnicaps—"

"Hold it," Schultz told her. "What strength is the Nervine? It'll tell you in milligrams."

"Twenty-five milligrams."

"How many in the bottle?"

"Fifty capsules."

"How full is the bottle?"

"Wait. About half full."

"Okay, go on." Twenty-five capsules of 25-mg pyrilamine maleate wouldn't knock Dotson out with any certainty, even if he didn't notice the bitterness. Somnicaps wouldn't be any more useful—they were both nonprescription. He didn't stop her again till she got to Pentobarbital Sodium. That might— Jesus, no, not a barbituric for a man with Dotson's mental history: it could blow him into a manic state.

"You don't need to read anything with the word 'barbiturate' in it," he said. It might save a few seconds.

"Okay."

He waited, but she didn't go on. He could hear Katie stirring the Ovaltine into the hot milk in the little kitchenette they'd installed on this floor; he could hear the tires of a car squealing faintly on the corner three stories below; he couldn't hear anything else.

On the roof of the command building, Nick Valenti's fingers began gripping the phone progressively harder as he too waited. Two floors below the roof, Eugene St. Clair turned his head slowly to look across at the police psychologist, but McNeil was watching the narrow oblong of light glowing on the face of the building opposite. Everyone was waiting, at the street and mobile command posts, on the rooftops where the snipers lay prone at the parapets, at One Police Plaza, where Commissioner Dakers was perched on the edge of the bed in the small night room next to his office, a cigarette growing short between his stained fingers.

The window high in the Park Tower building was still lit, but that didn't necessarily mean Tina was still there in the bathroom. The distance was drawing out again as the silence on the telephone lengthened, and the waiting police crews were made to realize again how fragile the lifeline was; the voice on the telephone had stopped; the light over there could go dark at any second; and they could lose everything.

It was Nick who spoke first, very quietly.

"Tina?"

Silence.

"Tina, are you there?"

They waited.

"Yes. I—" But many of them missed the next few words as they drew in a breath and let it out again. "I have to listen for him. If he finds me in here at the phone, he'll—he might—"

"Okay," Nick said reassuringly, "we understand." He fumbled for a cigarette and put the wrong end in his mouth and lit the filter tip and said, *"Shit,"* forgetting to cover the phone.

"There's some Navane," Dr. Schultz heard her voice again, and cut in at once.

"What strength and contents?"

There was a pause. "Five milligrams, fifty capsules. The bottle's almost full."

Schultz sat up straighter in bed. He hadn't met Thomas Lindquist but he was said to be a busy and enterprising figure in the art world, combing the world's museums and antique markets for private collectors at home. Navane, a thioxanthine derivative, was chiefly effective in cases of psychotic disorders, which didn't fit the personality pattern of a busy and successful connoisseur, unless he was one of those men who weren't happy even when they'd notched up their first fifty million dollars. But there were doctors around who'd prescribe the major tranquilizers for overactive teenagers, depressed housewives and hard-driving executives: there was more drug abuse in doctors' prescriptions than in their patients' medicine chests. But that was incidental: could Tina slip that guy over there a gross overdose? Depending on his metabolic function, a dozen of those capsules could take him through anything from CNS depression to coma. But the taste . . . She'd have to open the capsules and give him the powder in honey, and even then he wouldn't miss it.

"Okay, Tina," he said, "please go on." He could come back to the Navane idea later, while she was talking with the police.

The only other drug of interest was Artane, a synthetic antispasmodic—Parkinsonism in some form?—but its effect on Joseph Dotson's specific organism was almost unpredictable; it could weaken the muscle tissue enough to leave him physically vulnerable, giving Tina a chance of overpowering him; but there'd be the same problem in administration as with the Navane: he'd taste the bitterness, however she tried to mask it.

"Okay," he told her. "I might get back to you, if I can; in the meantime, you mentioned Valium. You could use that if you wanted, for yourself—"

"Not unless you really have to," Captain Mundy's voice came on the line. "We'd like you to stay as alert as you can." Those goddamn medics couldn't ever think beyond drugs. "Doc, are you through with the medicine cabinet?"

"Is that it, Tina?" Schultz asked her.

"Yes."

"Then I'm through. But Captain Mundy, give me another chance on the line when I've done some thinking."

"Will do."

Tina came in again. "I'm switching the lights off now."

"Okay."

On the fiftieth floor of the command building, Eugene

St. Clair saw the window across the street go dark. Standing with the telephone in his hand, so close aurally to Tina that sometimes he could hear her nervous breathing, he couldn't understand how he could have given his word to Lieutenant McNeil that he wouldn't speak on the phone; nor could he understand why he was not now cutting in and saying her name, just her name . . . *Tina* . . . the name for all the things she was and had been to him and to Elizabeth for twenty-nine years, the enchanting child swinging her big straw hat; the blossoming teenager suddenly galvanized with ambitions and dreams, troubled by mysteries she was too young before to recognize; the slender, leggy debutante with her mother's beauty and reticent charm; and now Tina . . . the name for a light going out.

Across the room from him he saw the police lieutenant watching him, his thin face expressionless, a reflection of the streetlights turning his glasses to a mask, but his head moving slightly from side to side . . . *Don't. You gave me your word. Keep it.*

Very well. His word had bought this chance of hearing his child's voice; that was the deal. Very well. But later, if anything happened to her, *if she died,* he would go through the rest of his life, through the darkened summers and the haunted nights, knowing he could have said her name, and told her he was there, close to her, giving her comfort in the last hours of her life. Very well. That too was in the deal.

15

THERE WAS THE SCREAM AND then doors were slamming and Dad was running down the stairs and shouting *Oh God no, no, oh my God no, don't let anything*—and someone else screaming from down there and Billy looking at him in the room with the sun coming in it, his small pointed face going slowly white, *Billy, what happened, Billy, what are they*—then the room on the other side of the house with the door wide open, *the room they mustn't go in,* with the balcony all broken away and the bits of wood sticking out from the wall with white splinters at the ends, *Joe, it was your mom, it must have been your*—

No! No! It mustn't be my—all the way down the stairs with not enough breath to go fast enough, hands flying out and hitting the wall and the smell of onions because Mom was cooking a—*Mom! Mom! Mommeeee*—down and down with a hot wet salty face and no more breath and the horrible black dreadfulness of *knowing, knowing*—

Joe, it was your—

No, no, no, it mustn't—through the front door and Dad there bending down by—bending down over—*Oh my God, Oh sacred Jesus—Joe, keep away, boy, keep away—someone keep him away!* Like she was dancing but flat on the ground, on the gray flinty paving stones with her arms and legs out and the lucky charm on the gold necklace lying in a twisted curve and a pearl button pulled off and winking in the sun and the blood coming out of the side of her head and creeping in a moving kind of blot across the gray stone, meeting and touching the lucky charm and melting over it, and her eyes looking at him but not looking at him like she didn't know he was there, and Dad talking to people with a noise like when a dog whimpers— *Billy, take him away, take him to your place, Billy! And get a priest here, somebody—get Father Laughlin!*

Joe!

Running into the wall—

Joe! Catch him, some—

It's all right, boy, you—

Running into the wall, into the window with the glass flying up bright—

For God's sake stop him—Joe, it's—

Running running running into things with the sky spinning and the long hot howling in his throat and into the wall again, crash—then their arms, *Okay, I've got him, I've got him, it's all right, Joe, she had a—she just had a fall, she'll be all right when—*

Blood on his hands and glass and the shouting in his throat, not stopping, not stopping, then a woman with her arms around him and his face burrowing into her apron till he couldn't shout anymore, couldn't breathe, with only the hot salt waves pouring and pouring in the dark against her warm body while her arms held him and—

I'll look after you, my little Joey, I'll look after you.

Shaking, shaking all the time, the whole of him shaking like an engine, like the school-bus engine, with the hot salt soaking into the pillow and his mouth open in a shout but not shouting, just moaning, *oh my God, there's something—* and the moonlight in his eyes as he turned his head and shuddered with his whole body like a dog coming out of the water, *oh my God, I wish I didn't have to go on living,* the moonlight shining through the waves of tears and the taste of acid in his mouth, his breath still coming so fast that his throat was sore, *there's something wrong*, the bed drenched in his sweat as he lay there not knowing why it was, why he kept having these horrible nightmares after all this time, in Mattewan they'd shoved a needle in but he didn't want that again.

So long as you're okay, Joe.

Sure I'm—no. No.

There's something wrong with me.

"Have you thought of any way you could overpower him?"

Listening to Mundy, Nick was appalled, and waited to hear one of the brass cut in on that; but nobody did. That was appalling too. All Mundy could think of was force. That girl over there was shut in with a homicidal maniac and if she made any attempt at *overpowering* him—Jesus, what a word to use!—he'd just go for her.

"Yes," her voice came in a whisper. "I've thought of trying to do that."

"There are weapons there at your disposal," Mundy said carefully, "but you'd have to make sure you could knock him out the first time." There must be drawers full of kitchen knives, heavy ornaments, glass she could break and use: the guy wasn't wearing a suit of armor.

"I threw something at him. A vase." There was a sound low in her throat, almost laughter. "I missed."

"What was his reaction?" Dr. Weinberg cut in at once.

"He just said I shouldn't have done it."

"He didn't get mad at you?"

"No. He's very gentle with me."

"All the time?"

"Yes."

"What are your personal feelings towards Dotson at this time?"

On the roof of the command building, Nick Valenti grew suddenly impatient. Even someone as specialized as a psychiatrist should have heard about the Stockholm syndrome in hostage situations.

The soft voice came. "I'm terrified of him."

"And yet you tell me—"

"You're the psychiatrist?" she asked him.

"Yes."

"Then listen. Joe has been gentle with me because he loves me. But that doesn't mean I'm not terrified of him."

Weinberg noticed automatically that the soft voice on the line had not changed in tone, but in timbre: she was forcing herself to speak normally, but the fear had increased in her during the last few words she'd spoken.

He asked her evenly:

"And despite his apparent love for you, you believe he still means to kill you?"

There was the sound of her drawn breath and then she was whittling the next words out, her tone sharp with anger. "For God's sake, don't you realize he's mad? He's trapped me in here and barricaded the doors and put explosives in the lobby somewhere and told me he's not going to let anyone take me away from him—isn't that being mad? Mad enough to kill me? Can't you understand he scares the shit out of me?" Then she was sobbing, and they listened to it until she covered the mouthpiece and left them with dead silence, and when Lieutenant McNeil turned to ease his leg muscles he saw Eugene St. Clair hunched over the telephone with the tears glistening on his face.

In his office at One Police Plaza, Commissioner Dakers lit a fresh cigarette from the butt of the last. He was a public servant, the head of a thirty-thousand-strong force designed to keep peace and control crime in a city where there were six thousand people living in every square mile and dependent on him for their safety; he was also a man who would lose his job if he permitted this unique situation to end in murder under the glare of the international media spotlight; and now, for the first time, he was a man listening to a young woman crying with fear over a telephone, and he began to understand.

He'd have to send someone in there to get Dotson and wipe him out, and not just because otherwise he was going to lose his job.

From the huge headquarters van standing outside Park Tower on Fifth Avenue, Captain Mundy had much the same attitude of mind. These fucking negotiators and headshrinkers could keep on rapping till the full moon came up tomorrow night and Dotson made his kill: his third in the Park Tower building.

"Tina," he spoke into the hotline phone at the console, "can you hear me? This is Captain Mundy."

The silence went on for another five or six seconds, then her voice came shakily, "Yes. I can hear you."

"Do you think you could entice Dotson to show himself at a window?"

"I don't know. Why do you need to see him?"

Mundy said with care: "If you think he's liable to kill you, we've got to do everything we can to stop him. And we don't have too many options. It's you or him—try to look at it that way."

"You mean you'd shoot him?"

"We'd do what experience has taught us we have to do, and what the law allows us to do. You're not involved."

Crouched against the elevator head on the roof, Nick closed his eyes wearily. Mundy was out of his mind. He hadn't learned the simplest things about human nature, like that when a man's scared, he'll kill, while a woman just lives with it.

"I couldn't do it," they heard Tina saying. "I don't want him hurt."

Stockholm, Nick thought in resignation, Stockholm all the way. That too was a basic quirk of human nature that Mundy didn't understand: the gradual identification of a victim with his captor. A gunman in Stockholm had forced three women and a man into a bank vault and subjected them to extreme psychological brutality for almost a week, and when they were finally released, the four hostages pleaded with the police not to harm the gunman, and after he was convicted one of the women said she'd wait for his parole and marry him. They were expressing their everlasting gratitude to a man who had held their lives in his hands for six days and allowed them to live. And it happened, with variations, in almost every protracted hostage situation. It was happening now, and Mundy would have to realize that from here on out, the real threat to Tina St. Clair's life wasn't Dotson, but herself.

"If you don't want him hurt," Mundy's voice came on the line, "it puts a limit on what we can do for you."

"I know. But he has a life too."

Mundy took a second to think before he spoke again, in case the commissioner or Chief of Detectives Warner felt like cutting in here. Nobody did. "Tina, we decided to keep certain information from you, for your own peace of mind; but I think it's time you were told that Joseph Dotson was involved in the deaths of two women, was convicted of killing a man, and is now suspected of shooting to death the doorman and a security guard only twenty-four hours ago in the building where he now has you captive. This should influence your attitude and behavior toward him."

There was a brief silence, then she broke.

"Oh Jesus Christ . . ."

Mundy pressed on with his argument. "If Dotson leaves that building alive, he's extremely likely to spend the rest

166

of his life in an insane asylum. You're not protecting anyone with much of a future. If you—''

"God damn you"—her voice came low in her throat—''don't you know what you're asking me to do?''

"I'm asking you to save yourself, Tina—''

"You want me to set him up as a live target for you and then stand back and watch his face when the bullets start going into him, but damn you, I'm a woman, don't you understand what I'm saying? A woman can't do a thing like that!''

"Not even to save her own life?''

"I don't want to die. I want you to save me. But you've got to save both of us. *Both* of us.''

Her voice was breaking into sobs again and Nick Valenti cut in quietly on the line: "Tina, don't let him hear you.''

There was the sound of a deep shuddering breath, then she said in a whisper again: "No. He mustn't hear me.''

Mundy came in again. "Tina, we have the plans of the apartment here, but they don't tell us everything. There must be a lot of rooms you and Joe never go into. Which side of the building would they be?''

She took her time, maybe suspecting the question was something to do with setting up Joe as a target. "We keep mostly to this side. The east side.''

"Okay. On the west side there are three guest suites, a game room and a large bar. You never go into any of those rooms? Neither one of you?''

"We haven't so far.''

"Thank you. Dr. Schultz, did you want to talk to Miss St. Clair again?''

"No. We have to work something out first, if we can.''

"Okay. Does anyone—?''

"I have some questions,'' Nick Valenti's voice came.

"Go ahead."

Nick knew they had to work as fast as they could in case Dotson woke and missed her, but he tried to keep his voice relaxed and reassuring; that klutz Mundy had gotten her riled up, and he'd have to bring her down again if he could. "Tina, this is Nick Valenti, the hostage negotiator. Try and remember the sound of our different voices, so you can identify us right away, okay?" It was important for her to know that Joe had a friend out here, and who that friend was.

"You were the man talking to Joe earlier, about the ransom idea?"

"Yes. And I think your own idea is a better one. We have to save you both. But to do that, I need Joe's trust. He's got to trust me to the point where he believes everything I tell him—and just incidentally, everything I tell him will be the absolute truth. He's got to trust me to the point where he'll listen to me when I tell him the only way out of all this is for him to open that door and bring you out to us, your hand in his. Make sense?"

She let out a breath. "A lot more sense, yes."

In his smoke-filled night room at One Police Plaza, Commissioner Dakers listened to the quiet and persuasive voice of his chief hostage negotiator and switched his attitude again. Listening to Captain Mundy—who last year had gone alone into a Bronx warehouse and won a shoot-out with three drug smugglers before the backups arrived—he felt the only way to save Tina St. Clair was by using his assault teams and going into Park Tower and blowing Dotson off his feet, somehow getting around the explosives problem and the risk of Dotson's killing the girl before anyone could reach them. Listening now to Lieutenant Valenti, he was already beginning to feel the only way of saving her was by working on Dotson's crazy mind and talking him into some kind of temporary sanity. There'd come a time, Dakers knew only too well, when it would be for him to choose between the only two options they had: and that time couldn't now be more than hours away.

Waking again with the moonlight on his face, he lay watching the roses on the ceiling, the moonlight on his eyelids, the same soft, ashy and very special luminescence that had lit the night for him since he was very young and had asked where it came from, and refused to believe it was indirectly from the sun; the sun shone on the daytime and that was okay and made sense, but light that could shine in the dark had to be magical, and—later, when he could form such ideas—unearthly, an outpouring of the cosmic soul to illumine the minds of men.

But the moon was powerful, too. It could draw him upwards and fill him with the strength of a whirlwind so he could do anything he wanted, even things that people weren't meant to do. It made him like a god.

Watching the roses, he felt at peace; when he'd woken the last time it had been horrible and he'd been drenched in sweat because of the screaming and the— But that was over now; it didn't always happen; it only happened sometimes. He felt such peace now that he turned his head to smile at Tina in the other bed, or to watch her face if she was asleep; but she wasn't there, and the shock went through him as the world became suddenly different, and empty.

"Tina?"

She'd gone to the bathroom, that was all; but he couldn't just leave it at that. Inside the part of his mind where he knew unknowable things, like what time it was when he woke, and when someone a long way off was thinking about him, he sensed she'd been gone from her bed a long time, longer than just going to the bathroom would take. A chill crept on him, icy on his skin and lifting the hairs on his arms. She mustn't go away. He couldn't live without Tina.

He threw the bedclothes back and his shadow moved across the wall, cast by the bright moon.

"The kind of things I need to know," Nick said on the line, "are the things that turn him on. Is he a car buff? Sports nut? Which sport? What has he talked about most?"

"He hasn't talked much," she told him. "I've had to ask him questions. He doesn't like talking about his past. But he runs a Corvette, and he belongs to the club."

"The Corvette Club?"

"Yes."

"You know anything about his car? Color, year, that kind of thing?"

After a pause she said, "No. He just said things like, 'She really goes.' Nothing technical. He hasn't talked about sports."

"Friends? Vacations, favorite eating places, movies, books, clothes? Anything, Tina. Anything at all."

From her pauses he understood she was scared of concentrating on his questions, of losing her alertness to her environment. As he repeated the key material, Al Groot chalked it on the big blackboard propped against the elevator head and moved the electric lantern to shine on it. *Corvette. Corvette Club.*

"He's talked about Florida. About fishing there. And he likes Chinese food."

Nick kept having to prompt her. The guys he worked with? His boss: good guy or bad guy? Medical problems, allergies, drink, smoke, drugs? She didn't know the answer to quite a few of the questions, and Nick was getting a picture of a man who didn't want to talk about himself, didn't want to give anything away. He hadn't even talked about religion or politics.

"He's asked me everything about myself," Tina said wryly. "I'm the only thing that really turns him on—aren't I lucky?"

"Yes, actually you are. Let him go on loving you, Tina. Be impressed, and touched. Encourage him. You can work on his heart more easily than we can work on his mind—on his reason. Let him love you so much he'll finally do anything you say: then tell him you want out."

"Why? Have you given up?" Her tone had tightened.

"We haven't even started. We start when I can get him to talk to me. You can help there. Tell him he has a friend out here: the guy who was trying to sell him the Acapulco deal. You weren't on the line that time, right?"

"No."

"But you heard his side of that conversation?"

"Yes."

"Okay. He knows you heard enough about that deal to talk about it. You thought it must be a real nice guy on the phone that time, the guy he was calling Nick. You think he should call Nick and talk to him, get his point of view on things, you know what I'm saying?"

"I think so."

"I've handled a lot of people like him, Tina. They want friends. They're lonely. But they're scared to trust anybody, least of all a cop. But cops are humans like him; they want to help him, and talk to him, exchange ideas. The first thing I'm going to talk to him about is *my* Corvette; because anyone with the kind of car he loves has to be human, and a possible friend. And I won't let him down. You know something? A guy who held three nurses hostage for nineteen hours in a hospital dormitory two years ago—this was at Bellevue, right here in Manhattan—he got off on a plea of temporary insanity, which was the legal term for overwhelming stress reaction: his wife had died on the operating table and he was demanding to have

171

the surgeon brought to him. And you know what? That guy takes me and my wife out to a slap-up dinner once a month regular, hasn't missed. I'd managed to convince him the surgeon wasn't to blame, which was the truth. And this guy had found a friend. Me. I can be Joe's friend too. Listen, Tina, that apartment is surrounded by highly trained and resourceful police officers, with the highest possible brass in charge—the police commissioner's listening to us on this line right now. And we're going to stay here until we get you out, safe and sound. But the biggest possible break you can give us is by working on Joe yourself. The first time he calls me up again and lets me talk to him, you're going to be on your way out of there. Really.''

There was a short silence again, and when she spoke, Nick heard at once the new note of calm in her voice. "I imagine you know how much better you've made me feel, Nick.''

"That wasn't my intention, but that's great to hear. You just get Joe to talk to me and we'll start wrapping this whole thing up. I've done it before, Tina, dozens of times.''

"All right. I'll tell him I want to talk to my father, and if he lets me do that, I'll just tell him it's you on the line, and—''

The crash came first, like an explosion, and then the screaming and then Eugene St. Clair's voice on the line: *"Dotson, if you touch her I'll—Oh God, oh my God, oh my God . . .''*

16

THERE WAS THIS PLACE La Ronde on Myrtle Avenue, and she came here twice a week when she had to pay, and three or four times a week when she could get a boy to bring her, which hadn't happened since Tony Nicolosi had tried to grope her in his TransAm on the way home: it had turned her clean off boys for a whole week because it was the first time he'd brought her here and he supposed that gave him a free ticket to her pussy in return for the free ticket he'd given her for the disco, *no way*, it was for her to start the action and that wouldn't ever be the first time they met unless of course it was Robert Redford but even there, he was too old now and wore glasses; and now there was this mile-high skinny black leaning all over her at the bar wanting to talk while she drank the Coke he'd brought for her—

"What's your name, anyway?"

"Jim Clark," he said, "what's yours?"

"Ellen."

"Ellen who?"

"What is this—a pot bust?"

He threw his head back and laughed again, which made her giggle through her straw: he was one of those guys who when they laughed you had to laugh too. He was good-looking in a skinny way, but so tall, it was like talking to a tree.

173

"Ellen," he said, smiling down at her, "how did you get so small? Your mom leave you out in the rain?"

"Well Jesus," she said, "I'm *normal*, and nobody's ever going to mistake *me* for a piece of string." She was beginning to enjoy herself. With most guys it was just "Hi, dance?" or "Hi, Coke?" This was actually conversation, nothing intellectual, but shit, you didn't go to a disco to puke Proust all over the place. But she had a reservation. "How old are you, Jim?" He didn't look as old as Robert Redford and he didn't have a creased face but there was something about him that made her think he was at least twenty-five.

"Me? I'm pushing ninety. What you're really looking at," he said with the shine coming into his dark brown eyes again, "is ten years of liquid protein plus ten years of Vitamin B_{15} and ten years of Transcendental Meditation plus a gallon a week of fortified homogenized ginseng, which means next year I'm going to be eighty, see, I'm actually on my way down. And I can dance, too. You wanna dance?"

"Are you kidding? I barely come up to your crotch."

"Sounds real interesting." But the way he laughed it didn't sound dirty; he was just having fun. So they did some stomping around to the heavy steel and he was fantastic, like a long rubber band with no bones or joints, just waves of black body under the colored lights and that big white grin of his that went on and off while he watched her: and the way he *watched* her, hey man, like she was something right out of *New York, New York,* making her feel really appreciated, up your ass, Tony the Grope, this is what I mean by being social before the fact.

Except, sure, this guy's too old. Or too something. Too kind of confident. Too . . . not the kind of guy you normally find in a disco.

"What do you do for work, Jim?" She got a reefer and

lit up and took a drag and held it out to him in her cupped hand and he shook his head and said with a grin:

"No thanks, I'm on duty."

"Oh *shit*!" she said and threw the reefer onto the floor and rocked off the stool and stared at him. "Are you the fucking fuzz?"

"Now that's no way," he said, smiling, and held her arm as she swung around, swinging her back.

"Is this an arrest?"

"Hey listen, Ellen," he said, "you don't have anything to worry over, nothing at all." He was looking at her big round eyes in her small white face and knew he'd come close to blowing it, because of that fucking joint.

"You guys okay?" the barhop was asking them, because Jim still had his hand on her arm, but not too firmly, letting her feel she could free herself if she wanted to.

"You tell him," he said as nicely as he could to the girl, and Ellen went on staring at him and got the distinct impression she oughtn't to make anything of this, or it'd get everyone excited and they'd think it was a fucking pot bust. *Maybe it was*, but she didn't think so: he was in here on his own.

"Sure," she told the barhop. "We're okay." Then she got back on the stool and lowered her voice and stared right into Jim's face and said, "But you're going to tell me what the fuck is going on."

"First thing is," he said with his dark face serious, "I'm your friend. I'm wearing a badge—which I'm not going to show you because it'd upset people in here—and by virtue of that badge I can guarantee your absolute protection and your absolute immunity to any kind of harassment by anybody whatsoever. I mean, this is the whole of the goddamn Constitution, Ellen, rewritten especially for you."

"You're full of shit."

"Second thing is, the police commissioner of New York City would personally appreciate you giving him a few minutes of your time."

She went on staring at him. "Look, I told you I want to know what the fuck—"

"He needs your help, Bobbie. We all need your help." He waited till she got the message, and kept his hand on her arm, because for Christ's sake, something like a thousand man-hours must have gone into just locating this little chick and he couldn't have her fly away now. "I can take you to see the commissioner right away, or if you like I'll tell him he has to come here to see you. We don't mind which way it has to be. You're the queen."

"The commissioner would come *here* and talk to *me* . . . ?" She pulled her arm free and turned away. "I don't know what the fuck you're trying to—"

"Bobbie," he said, "if you want to walk away from me, I can't stop you. I don't have a thing on you, okay?"

"What about that—?"

"Oh come on," he said and pulled out a joint, "have one of mine." She looked at it like it was a snake. "I'm not here to play games, Bobbie. I'm here trying to save someone's life, and if you walk away, I could lose it."

She stood with the play of colored light swirling across her face, like a doll in a window, unable to move. "Look," she said, "I haven't seen that guy for three months. And I don't want to see him. I didn't have any part of what he did, or what he's doing right now. I took a new name because I didn't want him to find me again. He's crazy, you know that? He scared the shit out of me. And now he's up there with her, and I don't wanna know—you get what I'm saying! *I don't wanna know.*"

She was white and drained and shaking and Jim held her arms to steady her and the barhop came over, two hundred and fifty pounds and with a face like a barnacled rock, and said, "Okay, buster, you just let go of this—" and Jim showed his badge and said, "Don't give me no grief, man," while Bobbie Gifford went on trying to handle the most frightening thing that had ever happened to her in all of her eighteen years, with this guy talking about the commissioner of police coming *here* to talk to her and that crazy son of a bitch up there in that building with Tina St. Clair and oh Christ, she wanted out, she just couldn't handle this.

"Bobbie"—the tall skinny black was holding her gently against him now—"I know you don't want to help us because you're scared of Joe, but you won't be anywhere near him, and all we want to do is talk to you and see if you can help us save a life. That's all we're trying to—"

"She's just a shitty little rich kid." Her voice was muffled against his chest.

"Why, sure she is, but does that mean she has to die?"

"You think he's going to kill her?" She was looking up at him now with her frightened child's eyes.

"We think so. But if you'd help us—"

"He scares me, Jim. He *scares*—"

"You won't even see him. And we'll look after you. We—"

"You didn't really mean the commissioner would get in a car and come here, if I didn't want to go see him?"

"Cross my heart, Bobbie, I got his orders to say that. Like I told you, you've got the whole of the New York Police Department right in your hand."

She was looking toward the doors. "Fuck the New York Police Department, but I guess I better go."

Shortly after one-thirty A.M. Chief of Detectives Daniel Warner got out of his official car at the intersection of Fifth Avenue and Fifty-sixth Street and made his way through the police cordon and the group of journalists with two officers keeping him separated and escorting him to the big mobile HQ van standing outside the entrance to the Park Tower Building.

"Where's Mundy?"

"In the lobby command post, sir."

He ducked out of the van and took the steps to the marble-floored entrance lobby, pushing his way through a knot of police officers and finding Captain Mundy holed up in a corner near the elevators with Captain Art Steziak, chief of the Emergency Services Division in the field.

"All right," Warner said as he came up, "what's your plan?"

"The idea is to send one man in, sir," Mundy told him, "from Emergency Services."

"How?"

Chief of Detectives Warner was a short, sharp-faced Canadian-born immigrant with Mojave Indian blood and bright black eyes and an unholy detestation for bureaucratic bullshit, which had earned him the admiration of the entire department. He was the father of three brilliant children, one of them a girl not much younger than Tina St. Clair; but among the seventy or so policemen personally involved in the Park Tower standoff it wasn't necessary to have a daughter not much younger than Tina St. Clair to feel this new onset of feverish anger that had spread through every unit an hour ago, when her screams had shrilled through the telephone network and brought the sweat out on them. Not all of them had been listening in, but the news had spread that Dotson had attacked her at last and that nobody could now be certain that she was still alive.

When the line had gone dead, Mundy had slammed the phone back onto its cradle and said: "Okay, that's it.

We're going to get that girl out of there.'' Then he'd called Warner.

"The window cleaner's stage Dotson was using," he told the chief of detectives now, "is still at roof level on the west side of the building. We'd put one man onto the roof by helicopter, and he'd winch the stage down to a penthouse window and cut a hole big enough to let him through: they're made of one-eighth-inch-thick tempered glass, double-glazed and insulated. We've got a man up there in the command building working with a diamond cutter at one of the windows now, to find out how long it takes and how much noise it makes."

"We don't know if Dotson is armed."

"No, sir, but—"

"Has the guard's gun been found yet?"

"No. They're still—"

"If they haven't found it yet, they never will: he couldn't have thrown it far. Until that gun's been found, we have to assume Dotson took it up there with him." He noticed the weary-looking man with the big black mustache standing there in a crumpled raincoat. "Who's this?"

"Marvin Rico, sir—he runs the window-cleaning company where Dotson worked."

"Dan Warner," the chief said and shook hands, turning a reluctant pressed man into an eager friend. They'd need his help tonight. "How do you aim to protect the man you're planning to send in?" he asked Mundy, swinging his sharp head to look at him.

"He'd be wearing a flak vest, sir, and he'd be armed."

"Was this your idea, Mundy?"

"Yes, sir."

Dan Warner looked at Steziak, the chief of the Emergency Services unit. "Do you think he's crazy?"

"I think someone has to be crazy, sir, if we're going to

save that girl. I mean it's risky, yes. but then so are most of the jobs we do. If you authorize this, I want to go in there myself."

"Going to be a night for heroes," Warner grunted. "Once you're inside, what then?"

"It'd be a question of stalking, sir. Room to room."

Warner studied him with his bright black eyes. Art Steziak was a former marine with a reputation for being a goddamn nuisance to everyone around him until he had a job to do, then he became a goddamn marvel and brought instant and abundant honors on the Emergency Services Division for his dramatic deeds. He was a thin pale ferret of a man with colorless eyes and a laugh that scared the shit out of people, because the only time he laughed was in the thick of a crisis when other men were running for cover or frozen stiff with panic. It occurred to Chief Warner that if they could get this man into the apartment at the top of Park Tower, Dotson wouldn't have a chance.

"I can't authorize anything at this stage," he told Mundy. "Go on with your preparations and be ready to send Steziak in there at a moment's notice. But wait for my signal."

"I keep a gun there," Lindquist said.

"Locked up?"

"In a safe."

Lieutenant McNeil nodded, and used one of the phones again. "Can anyone find Captain Mundy?" He blocked the mouthpiece and looked again at the man in the camel-hair coat. "Both Mr. and Mrs. St. Clair are here, in one of the spare rooms. I expect you know them."

"What? Yes." Lindquist was still trying to get a grasp of all this. Poor old George dead, and the security guard too, the whole place surrounded by police, and Tina up there with a bloody maniac, dear God in heaven. "I'm not thinking straight yet," he told McNeil. "Jet lag."

The police psychologist didn't agree. Lindquist had gotten right to the point the moment he was told the situation: he'd seen the need for a gun. But certainly he was still in shock, his eyes darting along the line of windows opposite, his ruff of pale hair sticking up around his head, his sensitive face vulnerable, as if he were expecting even worse news at any time.

"Sir?" a voice came on the phone. "Captain Mundy's in the lobby with Chief Warner."

"Tell them we have Mr. Lindquist up here at Command." He cradled the phone. "Would you like some coffee, sir?"

"What?" Lindquist jerked his worried eyes away from the building opposite. "Yes. Lots. Please." He saw Eugene St. Clair coming along the corridor, walking like an automaton, his pace fast enough to keep him from falling over. "My God," Lindquist said, "when did you last get any sleep?"

"Oh hello, Tom. Sleep? I don't remember." His red-rimmed eyes looked out from a gray face. "When did you arrive?"

"Ten minutes ago."

"How was Hong Kong?"

"What? Very noisy. She'll be all right—police everywhere, they know what they're doing."

For the young lieutenant's sake Eugene said: "Oh yes, I have every faith." He'd been in to see Elizabeth three times during the past few hours to comfort her; then, when Tina had screamed on the telephone, he'd gone to Elizabeth to hold her in his arms for his own comfort, saying nothing of what had happened but praying silently that their daughter was still alive and breathing, that there was a world that still had Tina in it.

When Mundy and his chief reached the fiftieth floor they took the visitor straight into the conference room on the west side of the building, which overlooked Park Tower: when this floor had been taken over by the police department there'd been no hesitation as to which offices they'd use: they had to keep those windows at the top of Park Tower in sight; however irrational the idea, they felt that once they turned their back on it, Dotson would do something dangerous.

"This is Captain Mundy. You know Mr. St. Clair? I'm Dan Warner, chief of detectives, in charge of the operation. Let's get some more coffee on the boil," he told one of the men.

They sat down where they could, on trestles and boxes left in here by the decorators when the fiftieth floor had been offered to the department.

McNeil said straightaway: "Mr. Lindquist says he keeps a gun in his apartment."

The chief's sharp head swung up. "What model?"

"It's a Browning nine-millimeter Renaissance."

"Pretty."

"And effective," Lindquist said. "My bodyguard put me through a training course."

"Where is it, Mr. Lindquist?"

"In a wall safe."

"You keep it cleaned?"

"It was cleaned after I'd use it for training, and it hasn't been used since." He sounded as if he resented the idea of his having a dirty gun, or a dirty anything.

"Thirteen shots?"

"Correct."

"Is it loaded now?"

"It has ten bullets in the chamber. My bodyguard advised me that the spring would lose tension with—"

"Yes. Good." Warner sipped some coffee, working things out. This man kept the gun as a toy; nobody who expected to use it for his own protection ever kept a gun in a safe; and Lindquist kept it loaded because he had a sense of drama: there was no point keeping a loaded gun where you couldn't get at it in a hurry. "What sort of lock do you have on the safe?"

"A combination."

"You know the combination from memory?"

"Of course." He disliked the man's tone; it was as if they'd just arrested him for keeping a gun without a license.

"Is the safe concealed?"

"Yes."

"Where?"

"Before I give you any further information, I'd be interested in hearing your plans," he said pointedly.

Dan Warner flicked him a glance. "Mr. Lindquist, there hasn't been time to tell you how very grateful we are that you came here as fast as you could. It might well be that Tina St. Clair's life depends on this gun of yours, and therefore on your readiness to help. We all deeply appreciate it." He put out his hand. He needed friends tonight, from wherever he could find them.

"I'm still in shock," Lindquist apologized.

"But of course you are." Warner swung his head to look at Eugene St. Clair, his heart going out to him as he saw the pain in the man. "Mr. St. Clair, has your daughter ever used a firearm, to your knowledge?"

"I can't say. She may have, in the Arctic: she went on an expedition."

"They'd have taken rifles."

"Probably."

"It was a tough experience for her, that trip?"

"They were stranded at one time, and had to be flown out."

"She doesn't sound as if it'd worry her, to face a man down with a gun."

"She's quite resourceful." He waved a proffered cup of coffee away: he didn't need it. He wouldn't sleep again until Tina was safe.

"Now, sir," the chief of detectives said more slowly, "if she was able to get hold of Mr. Lindquist's gun, and control Dotson with it until we broke in, there'd be a risk attached. He's unbalanced. It's unlikely she'd miss the target if he went for her: it's an automatic with ten shots in the clip; but he just might think she was bluffing and go for her and get to her before she could stop him, even with a nine-millimeter."

"Or more likely, sir," McNeil put in quietly, "she wouldn't even fire at all."

"Because she's a woman."

"Because she's *this* woman."

Eugene was sitting upright on one of the decorators' crates, his hands folded on his lap, his red eyes narrowed against the glare of the fluorescent lighting. He was going to be asked to make a decision, or to help them make a decision, and it was already on his mind. How would Tina perform, in a shoot-out with a man who had no gun but had other deadly weapons: demoniacal strength, speed, and indifference to whether he lived or died?

"We are assuming," he said with the impression that he was lighting a long-burn fuse, "that Dotson would be unarmed. That he'd have no time to reach a gun himself."

"Yes." Chief Warner watched the man on the crate, noting how upright he sat, how steadily he spoke. "Tina has told us she hasn't seen anything of a gun in Dotson's possession."

"I believe this gentleman—" Eugene said, squinting up at the police psychologist.

"McNeil, sir."

"Thank you, yes. I believe Mr. McNeil might be right, when he says she might not shoot at all. She's an adventurous girl, and resourceful; but she has a gentle nature." His mouth took the shape of something like a smile. "She abhors violence."

"Chief?"

Warner's head swung to look at Captain Mundy. "Well?"

"The way I see it, should we deny her the *chance*? I mean she's drowning, and there's a life belt. Shouldn't we throw it?"

Silence came down in the cavernous room, and the men sat without moving, like sculptures that had been taken out of the crates to be arranged for an exhibition. The light tubes hummed, and a moth circled them, bumping at them again and again, dropping motes of gold from its wings. The telephone McNeil had brought in on its long extension cable was silent, as if it were disconnected.

"All right," Warner said at last. "We need to decide whether she should at least be *told* there's a gun at her disposal. We need to decide whether we should send a man in through a window to confront Dotson. Mr. St. Clair, it's for the police department to make decisions like this, and to act on them, entirely on its own initiative, without reference to you or to anyone else. That doesn't mean you won't be consulted, or that your considered opinion won't weigh with us in the final decision-making." For St. Clair's sake he didn't point out that one of their decisions could be academic: unless they were able to talk privately with Tina again, she'd never know the gun was there in the safe. "It looks like the waiting's over. We can't hope to negotiate if Dotson won't talk to us. So now we've got to push forward.'' To McNeil he said: "Get the commissioner on the line.''

As the lieutenant reached for the phone it began ringing, and the shock jolted their nerves. He picked it up, listened briefly and hung up. "They've located Bobbie Gifford. She's on her way here now.''

—— 17 ——

SHE WAS LOOKING AT SOMEONE she didn't recognize.

He stood in the open doorway, gigantic, his huge body filling it, his eyes appearing like holes in his skull revealing the white-hot fires of rage within; his teeth were bared and pointed, and she lifted a hand to her throat, thinking he would bite there first, and to kill.

The silence was appalling, as if she'd gone suddenly deaf and couldn't hear the roaring that was going on in him, the voiced rage. She could smell him; it was an animal smell, raw and of the wild. When the silence broke, it was to the sound of his breathing, low in his throat, reminding her instantly of the tiger's voice she'd heard one night in India, only a mile away across the dark plain, a sound that had chilled her blood.

A sliver of wood fell from the jamb of the door that the closed lock had smashed away when he'd hurled himself against it without warning, so that she'd thought the explosives had gone off and she was to be flung into the disintegrating night; the wood sliver fell with a fluttering motion like a tiny toy airplane. There was no more sound from the telephone; her hand must have dropped it back onto the cradle without conscious command: it had been her idea to do this if she heard him coming.

She'd been afraid Joe would come here and find her; but this wasn't Joe; it was a creature, an apparition; and then the thought came to her that she'd lost her mind at last and wasn't really seeing him, and the tears came pouring from her eyes without any warning, because nothing could help her now if she'd lost her reason.

There was the strong smell of carpeting and she realized vaguely that she must be lying on the floor: the refuge she'd known as a child, the place where you can't fall any farther, the kindly floor where everything comes to a stop until somebody finds you and picks you up; but that didn't work anymore; she was a grown-up now, and when he touched her she screamed again, remembering what he looked like, monstrous, a creature out of a nightmare.

"Tina . . ."

She didn't move; the shock of his touch had gone through her body like a stroke of lightning, leaving her weak; she lay there for minutes, maybe hours, she couldn't tell, while he kept saying her name, his voice coming from a long way off; for a while she thought it sounded like Joe's voice, because it was gentle.

"Tina . . ."

"Oh my God," another voice was saying, "I can't take it anymore." It sounded like her own voice but it had stopped now. His hand began stroking her bare shoulder; she was in her nightdress and lying on one side. This must be Joe, then, and not that ghastly creature who— But that had been Joe too, of course: she'd been out of her mind from the shock when he'd smashed the door down, and she'd seen him as a monster, towering with rage. He was bending over her now, with the moonlight silvering his skin; she remembered he slept naked, and must have come here straight from bed.

"Don't hurt me, Joe."

"Of course I won't. I love you."

"Oh Christ," she said weakly, and managed to sit up, leaning against the cold surface of the cabinets. "You've got a very odd way of showing it. Did you have to do that?''

"Do what?''

"Break the door down.''

"I thought you'd gone away. I thought I'd lost you.''

She saw into his mind for an instant and understood the infantile panic that must have been in him, demanding immediate relief; he would have smashed his way through a solid wall to find her, through the whole building, through the whole city.

"Couldn't you''—she began, but the idea was so absurdly formal that she felt laughter coming—"couldn't you have just knocked?''

"Just what?''

She was laughing almost helplessly now and he couldn't hear her properly. "Just what, Tina?'' He was joining her, not wanting to miss the joke, shaking her shoulder. "What did you—?''

"Just knocked, for God's sake, it's a bathroom, don't you—?'' But she couldn't finish; he was laughing with her now, putting his head down on her shoulder as they went through a whole paroxysm together, their tension breaking into hysteria as the tears rolled down her face and she wondered with half her mind whether this was the empty meaningless laughter of the mad. But it didn't matter; it felt good, and she sensed the hot blood moving through her body again after the chill of shock, and she gave herself to it, holding on to him and pressing her face against his and pulling him down across her at last with her hands running over his naked body.

"Joe,'' she said urgently, "I love you too, I love you . . .'' not because he was stiffened and ready against her but because they'd been laughing about something together, when minutes before she'd been quite certain he'd heard her talking on the phone and had stormed in here to kill her.

"Tina . . . what did you say?"

She felt his whole body go still, waiting. "I love you," she said, and he slumped against her, released, and suddenly she felt his tears on her face and realized with a shock that she'd never actually thought about him before, except as a crazy stranger who'd come here to rape and murder and blow the whole building down; now he was an ordinary man who could laugh and cry and make love, and it came as a revelation to her. He hadn't changed, but she had, and there'd be no going back. She would start learning to know Joe Dotson.

"I never thought I'd hear you say that, Tina."

She hooked her fingers into his hair and moved his head, finding his mouth and kissing him, reaching down for him and bringing him inside her, lying under his hard body and feeling its strength, moving with him and letting all thought dissolve away in the hot singing of the blood until they came, almost together, leaving her with only a distant awareness that as the seed of the man spurted inside her, the tears of the child were drying on her face.

"Look, do I get a backup or don't I?"

Jim Clark was heading north along the Brooklyn-Queens Expressway with his lights and siren going and most of the road to himself, but if a drunk or someone came out of nowhere and did any damage he'd need another car to get this little Kewpie doll to the command building where the commissioner said he'd be waiting.

"Gee," Bobbie said, "this is really okay, you know? I never did this before. Everyone pulling over, just for us!"

"Okay," Jim said into his mike, "I'm going left onto the Long Island and heading west. Can't anyone pick me up?" He glanced at the bunch of bobbing yellow curls in the passenger seat. "Everyone pulling over, sure, like I told you, you're the queen, but listen, take up the slack on that seat belt, will you?" A baby harness would've been a better fit on this little chick, she was almost a dwarf.

"Where's your partner?" She tugged at the belt and let the slack wind up. "Don't you always—?"

"I left him in the bar across the street from the disco, looking for you."

"You just *left* him there? I thought you guys were always as thick as faggots when you're on patrol."

"Now that ain't nice, coming from a queen. When he calls the station house they'll pick him up." He unclipped the mike again. "Okay, I'm going by Van Dam right now and heading for the Queensboro Bridge. If you can't— Okay, hold it, I have a backup now." He flashed his headlights and saw the cruiser ahead of him switch to codes and speed up to maintain the gap. "Two-oh-two, I have Bobbie Gifford on board here, did they fill you in?"

He got an affirmative and clipped the mike back, speeding up and pushing the other car harder. The instructions at the mass radio briefing had been very clear: "If you locate her, don't waste any time. Remember, time is critical."

"Are they going to give me something to eat? I'm starving."

Jim thought of the franks he'd parked in a paper bag under the seat, but it'd look kind of sleazy, raking them out for her to eat; people didn't understand that the inside of a busy cruiser tended to get like a garbage bin by the end of the tour. "What'll you have?" he asked her as they hit the long echoing perspective of the tunnel. "Pâté de foie gras or a little caviar with truffles? You name it, you got it. You're the queen."

"You know something, Jim? You're making me suspicious. I don't get treated like this for nothing."

"But sweetheart, this is the New York Police Department.

We always treat people this way." The cruiser ahead of him made a left onto Second Avenue and a right onto Fifty-seventh, and when Bobbie saw the crowds of people at the intersection of Fifth and Fifty-sixth she popped her eyes open wide and held on to the handgrip.

"Oh Christ, he's done it . . . ."

"Huh?"

"Pushed her through a window, look at those crowds!"

"They're just the remnant, baby. Come on, we move now."

People pressed forward as he made way for her, calling for help from the press-relations team guarding the entrance to the command building. Photojournalists began popping their flash equipment, surging forward against the ropes as the TV camera crews swung their floods and zoomed in on the tiny figure of the girl in the sequined dance dress, half-hidden by the police as she was escorted through a mass of people who'd ducked under the ropes and swarmed onto the steps from the sidewalk.

"Who is she?"

"We don't know."

"Is she a relative?"

"We'll be putting out a statement for you, but not till you get back behind the ropes, c'mon now, try and cooperate."

When she reached the fiftieth floor of the command building, Bobbie Gifford suddenly forgot all about how really okay it was to be whizzed into town in a cruiser to visit with the commissioner of police with a promise of pâté de foie gras and caviar on the side: as the door of the unfurnished office was closed by a uniformed cop who took up guard duty inside it, all she could see was a huddle of red-eyed men with set faces chain-smoking themselves to death under the glare of the fluorescent tubes, most of them in shirtsleeves and some with their shoes off. They sat on camp stools, benches and the floor. One of them spoke.

"Miss Gifford, we really appreciate your coming here to help us. We don't have any time to lose, so I'm going to ask you another big favor, to begin with. If we can get Joe Dotson on the telephone, will you talk to him?"

She stared at him. "Are you the commissioner?"

"Yes." He stood up and took one of her hands in both his own and kicked his camp stool at an angle. "Why don't you sit right here, and can I call you Bobbie?"

"Jesus, I guess—well, sure. Okay. I don't want to talk to him, no."

"You know what the situation is, Bobbie, at the top of Park Tower. That girl up there could get herself killed, any minute. You might be able to save her."

She stared around at their faces, sniffing at the smoke-saturated air, trying to get a fix on things; she felt like a small child among a bunch of wolves, all of whom said they were just Little Red Ridinghood's grandmother. They were the fucking fuzz.

"If you can't save her, I don't see how I can. I mean, we split, six months back. I walked out on him."

The man who said he was the commissioner nodded. "We think it unbalanced him. We think he'd pull out of this crisis if he thought you might go back to him. He—"

"Shit, if you think—"

"All we're asking you to do, Bobbie, is to promise him, on the phone, to go back to him. And make him believe you."

"Look, that guy scares the *hell* out of me. That's why—"

"You won't even see him. You're under our protection."

"Like *she's* under your protection?"

The man closed his eyes wearily, then opened them again, squinting at her through the cigarette smoke. "You won't have to leave this room, until you're taken home with a police escort. Dotson will be spending many years in prison, or in an asylum. You'll never see him around." He waited, watching her.

He reminded her of the way people waited in Atlantic City, when they'd laid their bet and the ball was in the wheel and they had to wait and do nothing, because there was nothing they could do to change anything now. It made her feel important again: shit, this was the commissioner, and he was having to wait for *her* to make up her mind!

"You know something, Commissioner? That guy scares me so much that if I heard his voice on the phone again, I'd just do it in my pants. That isn't a very nice way of— But I mean, you know? He really *scares* me."

One of the other men in here, the thin one in glasses, bent over the commissioner and murmured something. "This is Lieutenant McNeil," the commissioner said. "He'd like to talk to you."

"I don't care who does the—"

"If you don't want to help us," the thin man said nicely, "we'd quite understand. It's just that there's nobody else we can turn to. To be frank, I told the commissioner it'd take someone pretty—well, heroic—to do something like this. And let's face it, very few of us are a hero when it really comes to the crunch."

"Who said so?"

"I beg pardon?"

"You never met me before, so what makes you think you know what kind of person I am?" He was a typical slimy bastard; she'd listened to people like him at the courthouse after a pot bust. "Are you a lawyer?"

"No. I'm a police officer."

"So what's this shit about being a hero?"

"It isn't just the matter of talking to Dotson on the telephone," he said, worried now. "It's our duty to be absolutely honest with you. If you're instrumental in saving the life of Tina St. Clair, we can't shield you from the inevitable publicity; the press are going to eat you alive—you know, front-page photographs, exclusive interviews, TV appearances—and there's just nothing we can do to stop them. You have to know what to expect."

Before she had time to think about that, another man spoke.

"Bobbie, we have upwards of seventy police officers deployed in this area, hoping desperately to save Tina's life. They can't do anything. But you can."

The thin one spoke again. "Captain Mundy, I really don't think we should press the point. Tina St. Clair doesn't mean anything to Bobbie—how can she? She's never met her, and—"

"Will you for Christ's sake stop telling me what I am and what I am not?" The camp stool tipped over as she got to her feet and stared up at the lieutenant with fury stinging her eyes.

"I'm sorry," he said ruefully, and glanced at the cop by the door. "I want you to arrange a car for Bobbie, with a motorcycle escort to take her—"

"I'm not going anywhere." She was looking at the commissioner now. "Will you be listening in to the call?"

"Yes, Bobbie." He stubbed out another cigarette, looking too tired to care whether she stayed or quit. "We'd give you visual signals, when to say yes and no, things like that."

"But you can't call him. I saw it on TV all the time. He doesn't answer your calls."

"We'll let him know you're here. We'll put your name on the banners out there at the top of the building. Then hopefully he'll call us. Call you."

"Okay," she said. "Then let's go. I'll talk to him." She swung her head to look up at the thin guy, surprised to be seeing him through a blur of tears. "And don't think it's because of all that shit you were conning me into about the publicity, smart-ass. I just wanna know what it feels like to save someone's life."

"There are complications," Maria said, her voice dull.

"What are they?" Nick shifted his legs under the rug, watching the four prone men at the parapet, and beyond them the two lighted windows of the building across the street. They'd started glowing ten minutes ago and the word had flashed through the communications network: someone was still alive in there. According to the engineer's plan of the penthouse, they were the lights of one of the kitchens on the east side.

Maria's voice came again. "The doc told me what they were, but you know me, I can't remember anything technical." He saw her in his mind, Karen's mother, the mother of the girl he loved, the wife he loved, with her plump surprisable face and her hesitant eyes, always glancing away to look for the answers to questions she never really understood, closed now, maybe, to shut out the answer she didn't want to know: that he wasn't coming to the clinic, not yet, not till this was over.

"Is she asleep, Mom?" He'd never called her that until his own mother had died, five weeks after the wedding; and he only called Maria that when there was a closeness between them, when they were saying something really important to them both. He loved this large, permanently bewildered woman with her bountiful kitchen she used as a refuge from the greater complications of life, and her trace of a Neapolitan accent and her black gloves for church even in the wet heat of August; he loved her almost as much as Karen, her daughter with the pretty Scandinavian name and the cornflower-blue eyes (her dad came from Stockholm), because Maria was probably the kindest woman

Nick had ever met, and the most vulnerable, which was why he was bleeding unseen and scorching tears as he talked to her. She'd made her statement, earlier: "You'd better find out which you want to be, a cop or a husband." Now she was lost again, and vulnerable.

"Yes," she said. "She's under some kind of dope."

That let him off the hook a little. Karen wouldn't know it even if he went along there and held her hand on the bedclothes, so he didn't have to go. *But as she fell asleep, she remembered he hadn't come.* His heart came apart again, but that wasn't anything new; it'd been doing that for a long time now, ever since he'd married Karen and found he had to deny her things so often—not presents or anything money could buy, but things like a phone call when there wasn't time, a few minutes of his company when he couldn't be there, and reassurance when she was quietly desperate to know if he was okay and not suddenly shot to death by some poor demented son of a bitch he'd been facing hour after hour, trying to bring him down from a murderous high.

Nothing of this had come as a surprise to him; he'd married late, because he'd seen so many marriages go down the drain in the department; policemen were stressed citizens, like lawyers and doctors and dentists, and they spent their whole working life with other policemen and criminals, building up anger and frustration and sometimes taking it out on themselves, or their partners or their wives and kids; but when they put on the badge they were also expected to put on a pair of wings and rise above it all. "We're not pigs," he'd heard a narcotics detective say in court, "but we're not angels either. People expect too much."

Maria wouldn't understand things like that; all she understood right now was that her little girl was in the special ward of a maternity clinic, sick and endangered, while the

man who professed to love her wouldn't even come along
to hold her hand.

"Mom," Nick told her slowly, "there's something I'd
like you to think about. Karen has the best doctor around,
and she's in the best clinic. There'd be nothing I could do
if I went along there, except share the waiting with you—
which, believe me, I would like to do. But if I left here
now, I'd have to quit my job, and in this particular job
I've proved I'm the best there is. That's why I'm here
right now. So when Karen comes through this, as we
know she will, and we're all looking at our fantastic
baby—it's going to be my kid, too, Mom—I'm going to
think, this is terrific, and I'm the happiest guy in the
world, except that I lost my job. And what I want you to
understand is, it won't have been necessary. I'll have just
thrown it away."

There was a long silence, almost like she was deliberately giving him time to listen to the echoes of what he'd
just said, and hear now spurious it was, how cunning, how
like the wheedling bullshit he'd used for years now as a
professional con man as a means of saving lives; but she
wasn't doing that to him; she was just trying to think
things through.

"Why would you have to quit your job, Nick?"

"There happens to be so much publicity with this situation we've got now that the whole of the police department's
under a microscope; it just happened to come together that
way; and what we do now is going to make a really big
difference to the way people feel about us—about how
safe they are with us around. If I walked out on this thing,
it'd look like we'd failed, like we'd decided to give up.
And I couldn't go back, after that. I wouldn't want to. I'd
have to quit." He waited again, wondering how it was that
he'd so often talked strangers down and made them
understand—strangers with a gun on him or a knife at

someone's throat or a kid dangling over a bridge—and couldn't make this kindly, huge-hearted woman, who loved him, see what he was trying to say. "You have to know this, too, Mom. That guy up there is out of his mind; he's put dynamite against the only door we could go in by; he shot two men to death just to get in there; and he told Tina he won't ever let anyone take her away from him. So there isn't any way, any way in this world, we can go in there and confront him physically, without she dies. That's why I've got to stay here. It's the only chance for her, and I can't take it away."

He shifted his legs again, watching the two lit windows across the street, one of them with the thin silhouette of a rifle showing against it on the parapet here. A gust of wind blew across the rooftop, tugging at his hair and chilling his face; in the end window of the penthouse was the bone-white reflection of the moon.

"I'm thinking of you too, Nick," the slow and thoughtful voice came on the line. "It would be bad, sure, to have to quit your job, especially a job with so much responsibility. But if—if Karen died, and you weren't there . . . don't you understand?"

"You're such a fantastic cook!"

She poured some more coffee for him. "A retarded chimpanzee could do eggs and bacon."

"But I didn't know rich girls ever had to cook."

"Sometimes they make an attempt at knocking some of the retarded champanzees out of first place. It's quite a challenge, of course, for anyone as monumentally stupid as a rich girl."

"Gee, I didn't mean—"

"I know you didn't." She flashed him a smile and watched him react; her smile always seemed to do something to him. Or maybe for him. It was like giving someone a present when it wasn't Christmas.

So here we are eating our eggs and bacon, a long way yet to breakfast time—the clock on the wall says 2:17—and his seed's still in me and his tears have dried on my face and we're sharing the childlike excitement of having gotten ravenously hungry all of a sudden and having rushed in here to raid the fridge like a couple of kids at a secret feast while everyone else is asleep—which everyone else is, as a matter of fact, the entire city outside there, except for the police.

She'd have to call them somehow and tell them she was still okay, because that scream she'd let out when he'd busted the door down would have made them think she was dead by now. She didn't care so much about the police worrying; they were used to screams in the night and they probably couldn't have cared less, for all their big show of trying to do something for her. But she didn't want her parents to worry. Daddy-O would think— But suddenly she couldn't imagine what he'd think, or even see him in her mind. Everyone out there in the city was becoming unreal to her; people she loved were becoming just the names for the people she loved, as if she'd created them out of her imagination. And the frightening thing was, it wasn't frightening.

Isolation did things to you. It was part of the routine for breaking spies and people under interrogation: they'd isolate them until they lost their sense of identity.

"You want some more jam, Tina?"

"No. How about you?"

"Okay, I'll get it."

She didn't want any more jam but today she wanted to know what was actually going on, whether he meant to kill her or not. She would ask him. There'd have to be a breakthrough and she felt she was ready for it. And if he said yes, he did mean to kill her, at least the prisoner would have eaten a hearty breakfast.

Detachment like this was dangerous.

Everything was dangerous, but most dangerous of all was losing her mind, very gradually, step by step, until she came to believe the city was "out there" and no longer surrounding her, that Daddy-O was just a name for someone she'd created from her imagination, and that she didn't care any longer whether this young, charming and very gentle man was going to be the last person she would ever see in her life as he finally came to take it away from her.

"Joe."

"Yes?" He was spreading the jam on his rye toast.

"Are you still planning to kill me?"

The silence moved in and surrounded her, as if she had suddenly plunged into deep water where everything was soundless. It had been something like panic that had forced the question out of her, and she had enough reason left to realize it. She had to get out of danger—of the danger of not caring anymore whether she lived or died, simply because she knew she could do nothing about it.

The red jam dripped from his knife. There'd been a school play she remembered, about a murdered antique dealer; and the party shop had been clean out of vampire blood and time was so short that they'd had to use strawberry jam. Funny, the things you remembered.

"What a horrible thing to say." He was staring at her, appalled, his body crouched over the shock. But it was a breakthrough, just as she'd sensed there could be. His eyes hadn't dipped away as his mind dodged the question; they were still on her face, the eyes of a child whose deepest secret had been discovered: the nudie magazine under the mattress; the ten-dollar bill that Gran had missed from her purse. The kind of secret that was not only no longer sacrosanct but also undeniable.

"When?" she asked him.

He looked upwards, above her head, and she shivered as she realized that behind her and above her were the windows, and the moon.

"You mustn't think of it that way," he said slowly, looking down at her again. "It's not going to be like that."

With a strange urge to laugh, she asked him: "Then what is it going to be like?"

He went on staring at her, as if trying to figure out how it could be explained; and she noticed he was beginning to tremble.

"We're just going away together, that's all."

"Where, Joe?"

It was a time for truth. She was making progress at last, getting into his mind, now that he was no longer dodging the issue. But the trembling bothered her: his hand was still holding the knife, and its blade had started ringing against the porcelain plate. She hoped he wasn't going to lose control; this thing had to be planned, if it were going to happen at all; she didn't want to end up in a bloody mess all over the kitchen floor with undigested eggs and bacon in her stomach to be noted by the pathologist at the morgue. There'd have to be some degree of dignity.

"We're just going away," he said, his eyes staring at her face but seeing something else, in the place where he was now, in his thoughts.

"Well that's okay," she said. "We'll have a whole lot of fun. But you don't have to kill me first, Joe. Why don't you just marry me?"

His eyes focused suddenly as the words found a response in his mind. "What did you say?"

"We could get married. I'd like that. Wouldn't you?"

In a moment he said: "You love me. You told me."

"Yes." A time for truth, however crazy. But also for definitions. There was no such thing as love; it was a name for so many things: need, admiration, lust, compassion; or a mixture of all those things plus so many more; the label did a good job, though: it wasn't false. People killed for love, died for it, broke their hearts over it. What was the love she felt for this mad stranger? Mostly the growing compassion that had driven out the fear as she came to know that even in his rages he never hurt her; and sex, because he was a male of the species, and attractive, and potent; and something else, more complex, more important. "Yes," she said again, "I love you."

That brought him all the way back to her from the haunted wastelands of his lunacy; his eyes were tender again, and the trembling had stopped. It occurred to her that this power that she had over him might be enough to save her. *I love you, but I'm going to stop loving you unless you let me out of here.*

Too big a risk to take, yet. It would be the last throw, to say *I love you*, as the blade of the knife drove down, as the strong hands tightened on her throat, *I love you*, the knife veering to one side in the last instant, the hands loosening.

Something more complex, yes, this love of hers for him, more important than compassion and sex. *She was in thrall of him.* The trite phrase came into her mind: "You mean so much to me." But that could be it. Joe meant a lot of things to her, but chiefly things like danger, risk, the power of life over death. That was exciting; it had the excitement of the flame for the moth.

That was what those people were doing, down in the street. This was better than the ball game and the TV and any goddamned movie show in town. This was the most exciting thing of all: the closeness, the awareness, the recognition, the thralldom, of death.

"So why don't you marry me, Joe?"

But already, even as she said it, the idea had the sound of a cheap joke. He knew why she'd suggested it: to trick him into setting her free. He was planning a different kind of marriage for them, with the shadow of death for her bridal gown, white lilies for her corsage, and the sound of dark wings beating to bear them away.

Blood wedding.

"It's no good," he said. "We can't do that."

"Why not?"

"Because"—he looked lost for a moment—"there's something wrong with me."

"I know."

He looked almost eager now. "You know?"

Dear God, how difficult it is to stop the laughter coming, when you've nothing to lose. "Yes, Joe. You told me there's something wrong. And you're keeping me a prisoner here. That's wrong."

"I know," he said earnestly. "And I'm sorry. But everything's going to get straightened out, when we leave here. You'll see."

She sat feeling almost content. The relief of being able to talk about it—of hearing *him* talk about it, where before he'd always evaded it—had brought a strange kind of sanity. They were talking about death, okay, but now it was like having to face up to a diagnosis of incurable cancer; you finally had to get to grips with it, and recognize it, and therefore diminish its power over you, and thus defeat it.

"When we leave here," she repeated. "Okay, Joe. When will that be?"

He looked above her head again, and she noticed how quickly his eyes changed. She'd had a dog, three years ago when Michelle, her closest friend, had killed herself on the slopes at Aspen. The dog had been sitting on its haunches in front of her, hoping to go out for a walk, and she'd said to it: "Prince, Michelle's dead." And being stupid with grief she'd half-expected to see some kind of reaction in the dog's eyes; but of course he'd just wagged his tail because she was speaking to him. That brain of his, which could recognize words like "walks" and "supper" and "fetch," hadn't been conditioned to understand words like "Michelle" and "dead." He'd gone on watching her, mindlessly; and she now looked into the eyes of the attractive young man opposite her at the table and saw the same thing, and knew that she would never be able to make him understand that she didn't want to die.

"When the moon comes around again," he said.

"Tomorrow night?" But that wasn't quite accurate. "I mean, tonight?"

He looked down at her, and she shivered again because his eyes were so like the dog's had been.

"We don't have to worry about when we'll be going, Tina. Don't complicate things."

That terrible urge to laugh again. "All right. I was just interested, that's all." But perhaps he was right, in the light of the special wisdom of the mad; to die wasn't very complicated.

"Don't be scared," he said. A single drop of jam dripped from the blade of his knife, gleaming in the light as it touched the white porcelain of the plate and spread against it; she saw it on the periphery of her vision, just as she saw his strong hands lying loosely on the checkered cloth, and behind him the outline of the huge refrigerator that was blocking the door.

"I'm not scared," she said, for the sake of her pride; but she could smell death now in the very air; it would be easy to think it was simply the odor of her own fear rising from her skin, but it was more than that; it was coming out of the walls, clouding down from the ceiling, turning the air into the reeking fumes of a crematorium. She knew now that nothing had changed. When she had first seen him standing inside the doorway, the rain dripping from his hair, she had asked him why he'd come here, and he'd said: *To be with you. To be with you, for the rest of my life*. And nothing had changed: they'd eaten food together, swum in the pool, slept in the same room, made love, but it wasn't going to make any difference. He'd known that, but she hadn't been certain until now; and now she could smell the death that was going to come to this place, the death he'd brought in here from the rain; she sensed the warping of time, and heard their voices, the voices of the people outside there in the city as they broke in here at last . . . *Oh Jesus, they're both* . . . The muted voices of the future that wasn't for her . . . *Okay, get an ambulance to the door* . . . *Don't touch anything yet* . . .

Then the shock of it hit her stomach and she lurched away from the table with her chair crashing over as she ran for the door and along the passage with her hands out to keep her from hitting the wall, making the bathroom in time and heaving again and again into the john, bracing herself against the bowl and thinking *I hope he doesn't come and see me like this*, giving herself to the paroxysms and feeling the raw relief, as if by emptying her stomach she could empty her mind of the foulness that was in there, the knowledge, the recognition, the intimacy of her coming death.

They were sitting in the big gold salon, drinking brandy, which Joe had prescribed for her, distressed at what had happened.

"Was it something in the eggs? They didn't taste—"

"I shouldn't have eaten"—she smiled—"so soon after making love."

She'd seen her face in the mirror, deathly white and

pinched, as it must have looked when she was a child. She still wasn't very old. Those whom the gods love . . .

But the brandy felt good inside her. Maybe it'd be an idea to get absolutely smashed, so that she'd never know what happened.

No. That wasn't the way. She'd rather face it.

"Refill?"

"What? Yes. But not too much. I don't want to get smashed."

He was tilting the bottle carefully over the balloon glass when the voice came from outside, calling for Joe Dotson. A look of impatience crossed his face but he put the cognac down and went across to the windows with her. The amplified voice was reading the words they'd put on the banner against the building opposite, bright under the spotlights.

BOBBIE IS HERE   SHE WANTS TO TALK TO YOU

—— 18 ——

THE TELEPHONE WITH THE RED tape around the base began ringing at 2:34 A.M. and Nick Valenti reached out to grab it and stopped his hand in midair and looked across the room to where Bobbie Gifford was resting on the bunk, propped on two cushions. Fright came into her face and for a moment she did nothing, then as the phone went on ringing Nick gave her a quick grin and put his thumb up, and she relaxed a little and picked up the phone, holding it as if it were red hot.

Everyone else stopped pacing or sat up straight in his chair or came slowly away from the coffee machine and stood listening, watching the girl.

"Hello?"

It wasn't much more than a whisper, and Chief Warner compressed his lips. He and the commissioner had briefed Bobbie on every possible reaction Joe Dotson could give: if he were angry at her for walking out on him, she should be contrite, but not humble; if he seemed eager to see her again, she should be willing, but not without token reservations designed to make him all the more eager; if he threatened her with revenge for leaving him, she should seem worried about it, but try her hardest to soften him. But the one problem they couldn't overcome with any certainty was her fear of Dotson. "I'm going to tell you guys something," she'd said ten minutes ago. "If that phone rings and it's him, I'm liable to just hit the ceiling without even getting up.''

"Is that you, Bobbie?''

As had happened before when Dotson had called, the sound of his voice sent a tremor throughout the communications network, and the monitors down in the big mobile headquarters van turned down the amplifiers so that only those within a few yards of them could hear. Earlier tonight an order had gone out from Commissioner Dakers that every effort should be made to keep the general public ignorant of what was going on; the press would be given routine handouts but told nothing of any new development until its projected repercussions had been assessed. "This whole situation is now so hair-trigger,'' the media-relations officer had been told, "that even a minor occurrence, like a spontaneous reaction from the crowds in the street that Dotson might hear, could cause a disaster.'' As Lieutenant McNeil had put it in a private aside to Tom Lindquist, "We're less concerned now with that bundle of dynamite he says he's put inside the door; we're concerned something might touch off the nerve synapses inside his brain and send him into a killing phase.''

So already we know two things, Nick Valenti thought as he watched the pale-faced kid at the phone: Dotson himself is still alive, and he's still interested in Bobbie. For the first time since the Acapulco charade had failed, he felt a breath of hope come into him, as potent as sea air.

"Yeah,'' Bobbie said tightly, "it's me.''

Dan Warner quietly pulled up one of the chrome-and-vinyl office chairs and sat down on it the wrong way around, leaning his folded arms across its back and watching the girl, ready to guide her as Dotson's voice sounded over the room-model amplifier they'd set up in here.

"Are you okay, Bobbie?''

She felt less scared now, because Joe didn't sound at all

mad at her; he was talking quite soft, and she remembered him as he'd always been with her: he'd never talked loud, and he'd always been gentle, except that time . . .

"I'm fine, Joe," she said.

But she felt awkward, because she and Joe had been living together and everything, and this was suddenly a kind of private conversation again, and there were all these guys in here listening in like it was a radio program.

"Are you really?" Joe asked her. He sounded pleased about her being fine. He was the same old Joe; he used to call her up every day, after they'd first met, to ask her how she was, and he'd just gone on talking and talking in that soft voice of his and she hadn't wanted to do anything else but go on listening and listening. But he couldn't be the same old Joe really, because they said he'd shot those poor guys to death in the lobby over there. Jesus Christ, she'd done the right thing to quit on him, especially after that time when he— "Gee," he was saying now, "I never thought you'd want to call me, Bobbie. I never hoped for that."

"I didn't call you," she said, kind of making a joke to stop the queasiness in her stomach, "it was you that called me."

"At your gracious invitation," he said, and she thought *Wow*, there he goes again with his fancy talk. He'd told her his secret once, how he'd seen an ad in *Reader's Digest* for a book on everyday etiquette, and sent for it, and mugged up a new thing to say every night when he went to bed—"Instead of my prayers," he'd joked, because he wasn't religious.

Sitting a little way behind Chief Warner, Eugene St. Clair watched the scared-looking young woman with his brilliant black eyes unblinking as he tried to project a thought into her mind: *Ask him if Tina is all right.*

"You still got your book on you-know-what?"

"My book on—?" Then he gave a soft laugh. "Oh, *that* book. No, I guess I used up all the things to say on you, Bobbie. Remember how you used to call me Prince Charming?"

"Sure, I remember." She felt the urge to ask him if Tina was okay, but Nike Valenti, the cop who did negotiating, had warned her about that. "Don't mention Tina, or anything to do with what's happening over there, unless he starts talking about it first." But it'd be nice to hear him say, oh, she's fine. That's what they'd brought her here for, to help save Tina.

One of the other phones began ringing and Captain Mundy picked it up at once.

"This is Siegel, FBI, on the roof."

"Yes?"

"I can see Dotson."

Mundy bent low over the phone, blocking his free ear to shut out Bobbie's voice across the room. "How clear?"

"Not dead clear. That Captain Mundy?"

"Right. Clear enough to kill?" His pulse had started throbbing at the side of his neck and he was holding his breath. This whole thing could be over in a couple of seconds now, if . . . Jesus Christ, he didn't feel ready for it. *The officer who gave the order to fire was Captain Everett J. Mundy, and it was his ability to make an instant decision that won the day for the New York Police Department after so many hours of agonizing suspense.* Okay then. Go!

"I guess," the FBI man said.

"I don't want any goddamned guesses, Siegel."

"Okay. Yep. I could drop him right now. He's standing with the phone in his hand near a shaded lamp; he's not dead clear because I'm looking at him through the curtains, but as a solid profile he's a perfect target, square on to the window."

The sweat was running down Mundy's flanks under his shirt. "Where's Tina?"

Listening to Bobbie talking, halfway across the room from Mundy, Nick Valenti heard his muted voice and turned his head. What the fuck was Mundy cooking up now? There was bright sweat on his face and he was talking into the phone like he was trying to eat it.

"I think she's standing by the doorway to the music room," Mundy heard the voice on the line. "They're in the main—"

"You *think* she's there? For Christ's sake—"

"Well *something's* there, her size; but there's not enough light from the lamp that's showing up Dotson to be absolutely sure."

Mundy had his eyes closed and his mouth in a tight line as he crouched over the phone. Bobbie was still talking and Joe's voice was still coming over the amplifier but Lieutenant McNeil and Lindquist had caught the urgent sound in Mundy's voice and were turning their heads to watch him. Nick was trying to make up his mind whether to do anything: that son of a bitch was blowing a fuse over there. *Who'd called him, anyway?*

"Could she be anywhere near him, Siegel? Could she catch any flak? What about ricochet?" The sweat had started running into his eyes and they were stinging. *Holy Mother of God, Joe Dotson right in the fucking sights and Siegel up there with a deer slayer that could put a .44 Magnum steel-jacketed ball right through that bastard's body and through the wall behind him without even slowing up. He just had to say the word . . . just say the word . . .*

"There's just the wall behind him," Siegel told him, his own tension vibrant in his voice, "and it's at an angle of maybe forty-five degrees. There's nothing this side of the target to provide a ricochet. I mean I'll be going straight through the glass and then through him."

Mundy was seeing the engineer's plans in his mind: the telephone in the big salon was twenty feet deep from the east windows, and the archway to the music room where Siegel thought she was standing was closer to the windows, ten feet deep at the center line, with the four-foot archway putting her between eight and twelve feet from the windows. It'd be a ball going through the glass, so there'd be fragments and they'd still be traveling fast when they reached her, and they'd still be spreading out . . . *okay, so she gets a few bits of glass buried in her face, isn't that better than—? But she could be blinded, sure, we'd have to take—*

"Captain Mundy?" Siegel's voice came.

"I'm here."

"The view I'm getting of the room tells me that if that's not her standing by the archway, she isn't in there at all. There's the wall right behind him, and no other shapes anywhere near, no shapes that could be her, okay. Do we go?"

A chair scraped on the uncarpeted floor as Nick Valenti got up and loped across to where the commissioner was sitting on one of the crates.

"Sir?"

Dakers squinted up at him against the glare of the tubes. "Well?"

"Do you think Captain Mundy's got some excitement for us?"

The commissioner quizzed him with his red-rimmed eyes, hearing in Valenti's voice precisely what was going on. The negotiator had tried to make his question sound hopeful and respectful at the same time, but what he'd really been saying was, *Will you stop that trigger-happy son of a bitch from doing whatever it is he's doing?*

Mundy heard the FBI sharpshooter's impatient voice again on the line. "Do we go?"

"Hold it," Mundy said. If the shape Siegel was seeing by the archway was *not* Tina St. Clair, she could be anywhere at all—and that included on the other side of the wall behind Dotson. There was a corridor there, leading from the pool area to the rooms on the west side of the apartment, and that .44 Magnum ball would go through Dotson and the wall too if it didn't hit bone and slow up or deflect. It was a risk.

"You still there, Mundy?"

"Yes. Listen, we have to be absolutely sure whether—"

"*She moved,*" Siegel's voice came sharply. "Okay, it's her, by the archway, and now she's moved and she's leaning her back to the wall, okay? Okay, we go?"

The pores of Mundy's skin opened again and the sweat began trickling down his face as he hugged the phone and fought for patience while the equations went through his mind: Siegel would make a clean kill, no question; the target was solid and the range was close for the armament and the window glass would do nothing to change the course of the bullet by even a thousandth of a degree at this angle of impact: close to ninety. The flying fragments couldn't kill the woman by the archway but they'd leave multiple cuts all over her left side because her dress wouldn't do much to protect her; that was okay; the bleeding wouldn't be severe and the instant Dotson was down they'd lower the window cleaner's stage and smash their way in and give her first aid. But the glass could blind her, in one eye or both. That was different; it was something she'd have to live with for the rest of her life, and something that he'd have to live with as long as anyone remembered who'd given the order to fire.

He could hear Siegel's voice on the line, talking half to himself. "I've got him right here in the fucking sights, you know that? I'm right over the heart area, a beautiful setup, you know? Just one shot. Just one clean, comfortable shot."

"Siegel," Mundy said.

"We go?"

But Mundy had lifted his head a fraction and found himself looking straight into the cold blue-eyed stare of Commissioner Dakers. *Yes*, he heard his own voice saying inside his head, *we go, Siegel, we go.* And in the silence of his mind he heard the boom of the Ithaca deer slayer and the distant pop as the ball went through the glass and the girl's scream as she saw Dotson going down with his chest blooming like a chrysanthemum, like a crimson fucking chrysanthemum . . . *We go, Siegel . . . We go . . .*

Dakers was still watching him, from three feet away. A good man, Dakers, once a good cop on the beat and now the top cop in the whole city. A just man, they said, and also a man without mercy if you made a mistake.

I was there, Mundy. I was right there with you, and all you had to do was ask me to make the decision. You knew there was the certainty she'd be hit by the glass, and the possibility it would do more damage than you could estimate. But you just went ahead and gave the order to fire.

"Mundy. He's right in my sights, for Christ's sake."

"Hold it, Siegel." He passed the phone to Dakers and got out of his chair and wiped at the sweat on his face and saw Valenti watching him and thought *you bastard . . . you interfering bastard . . . I could have finished this whole thing, God damn you . . .* Valenti hadn't been here before; he'd been over there sitting on a crate, and he'd come over here and he'd brought Dakers with him.

As Dakers took the phone he heard the voice of the FBI man. "Do we go, for Christ's sake?"

"This is Commissioner Dakers. What is the situation?"

"Oh. Sure. Okay, sir. I've got Dotson right in my sights."

Dakers went on listening as Siegel gave him the details; then he asked him: "How close to the woman would the bullet pass?"

"I'd make it two feet, sir. No less than two feet."

"That's too close, because of the glass fragments. Keep up your observation and let me know if she moves away. You don't fire without my personal orders. Is that clear?"

"Yes, sir."

Dakers looked around for Captain Mundy and gave him the phone back. "Keep in contact with him. He doesn't fire except on my personal orders." He left Mundy to it and went across to where Eugene St. Clair was sitting with his back against the wall and his hands folded neatly on his lap. His eyes were closed as the commissioner came up, but he raised his head at once.

"They can see your daughter from the roof," Dakers told him, "and she looks perfectly okay. You can go on up and take a look through the binoculars, if you like. After that, I'd get some sleep. Everything's under control, don't worry."

Under the drooping lids the man's eyes were feverishly bright, and Dakers couldn't tell whether he'd believed Tina was dead by now, and was reacting to the good news, or whether he'd believed she was still "perfectly okay" and had thought Dakers was bringing bad news. He was living with his nerves on a roller coaster.

"They can see her?" was all he said. "Thank you, then I'll go up there."

Dan Warner was tilting his chair back and forth as he watched Bobbie Gifford, ready to guide her if Dotson said something she didn't know how to handle.

"It's been a long time," she was saying. "It has to be three months since I saw you, Joe."

"I guess. I lose track of time." His voice, coming over the amplifier, was taking on a new note, more personal, more sentimental; and Dakers, coming back to stand near the chief, began listening carefully. "But I miss you, Bobbie. Really."

"I miss you too, Joe." For a minute she forgot what she'd come here to do; she was listening to Joe's quiet voice like she'd listened so often before, and could picture him more and more clearly. The crazy thing was, he'd been almost perfect, because it didn't matter how women said they wanted a man who could drive his hotrod faster than anyone else or take them to the ritziest places to eat or screw them fifteen times a night without even stopping to breathe; what a woman wanted, what a real woman wanted, was someone strong and gentle and easy to be with, someone who told her she looked prettier than Candy Bergen even when she didn't have time to change out of her oldest clothes or put on any makeup or wash her hair. And that was what Joe had been like. Except for that time when he'd picked her up and swung her in his arms and she'd suddenly— Oh, Jesus Christ, if only he hadn't started to act so scary . . .

"Where are you calling me from, Bobbie?"

"Uh? Right across the street. Gee," she said with a sudden catch in her breath, "I could almost yell from here, and you'd hear me!" The idea had gotten her scared again, because she'd told them okay, if he wants to meet me somewhere then it isn't going to be anywhere on our own, I'll want you guys just crawling around in my hair, okay? And I'm not meeting him anywhere *high*, is that understood? No balconies! She didn't think they knew what the fuck she was talking about but that was how it'd have to be: she wasn't meeting Joe Dotson alone.

"You could wave," he said.

"Huh?"

"I might not hear you," Joe said, "if you yelled. But I'd see you if you waved. I bet you look real pretty tonight."

Commissioner Dakers looked around for McNeil. "I want you to go up to the roof and stay close to the sharpshooters there. You'll liaise with Captain Mundy on the spare line, and I shall be here supervising any action."

"Sir."

"There's a chance Dotson might move to a window, if the girl here goes onto the roof and waves to him. I might decide to open fire if Tina's at a safe distance. You're to observe the sharpshooters, so that if anyone makes a mistake you'll be able to report." He went back to watch Bobbie Gifford.

As McNeil reached the roof and picked his way over the telephone cables to the parapet, Ben Siegel didn't move either his body or the gun. Prone on his stomach, with the long blue barrel resting comfortably in the niche he'd chopped out of the brick with his hunting knife, and the man-shaped target fixed motionless at the cross hairs of the telescopic lens, he was going into that strange timeless place where the world closes in and he was like in a capsule, alone with his gun, alone with his gun and the man in the lens, his breathing regular, his muscles relaxed, the index finger of his right hand embracing the trigger and feeling the tension of the first spring, playing with it, sometimes touching the hard resistance of the second spring, the one that his hooked finger would pull against and fire the charge and send the ball spinning through space toward the man standing there in the cross hairs, the man who would have time to hear the bursting of the window glass but not enough time to understand what it meant, that it

218

meant the target was now under penetration and receiving the ball as planned.

It wouldn't be the first time that Siegel had done it, and that was why he was familiar with this feeling of isolation, of total command of his environment: not the environment that surrounded his prone body on the cold and windy rooftop, but the environment that framed the target over there, extending only from rim to rim of the lens in absolute underwater silence while time stopped, and waited for him, and for the massive explosion that would hurl the ball and kick the gun and fill his stomach with the hot fires of satisfaction that he could find nowhere else in his life, only here, only now.

Someone behind him picked up the phone and spoke.

"Captain Mundy? McNeil here. I'm liaising."

Below in the command post, Mundy acknowledged.

"I don't know about that," Bobbie Gifford said into her telephone. "I was dancing all night. I wish it'd been with you."

There was a silence from the amplifier and Dan Warner half-turned his head toward it, still watching the girl. They had everything ready, if Dotson agreed to meet her: rendezvous, coverage, backups, firepower, an ambulance.

"You wish you'd been dancing with me?"

"Well, sure," she said. "I still love you, Joe."

And this is it, thought Nick Valenti as he watched the bright curls of the girl under the glare of the light tubes, this is how we're finally going to do it. We're going to follow the script, and the script is real life, where these two people once loved each other and lived with each other and danced all night together. We're going to show Mundy and these goddamned popgun cowboys up there on the roof that we don't have to kill people when they don't understand us; we have to try to understand them first, and find out what's wrong; it's a two-way thing, give and

take, and the only really difficult thing you have to do is
not scare anybody, and that's only difficult because everybody scares so easy.

This was his creed. It had been his creed since the night
of the kid on the bridge, when he'd stood there in his
rookie uniform with a gun on his hip and talked that black
man down from his desperate high, weaving a kind of
thread between them, word after word until it got stronger,
until it was a rope between them, for hauling that little kid
away from the deep black water under the bridge. This
was the way you had to do it. When people's nerves were
raw with caffeine and adrenaline and fatigue and frustration,
and all they could think of doing was reaching for a gun,
this was the way you had to show them. You had to go
into the human heart not with a bullet, but with love.

"What did you say, Bobbie?" he heard Joe's voice.

"I said I still love you." She hitched the phone higher
to get a better grip on it, embarrassed to have to say things
like this in front of all these people. Because in a way it
was true: she still loved the guy she'd known as Joe
Dotson, before he took sick in his mind. She even loved
him, in a strange kind of way, for that, and wanted to
protect him from his sickness, from himself. And she
knew something quite suddenly that she'd maybe known
all along, but not so clearly as she did now. A lot of what
she'd felt for Joe, a lot of the love she'd felt, was like she
was his mother. Not quite that, though; not really or
exactly that. It was like he was a child, sometimes.

"Would you want to see me again, Bobbie?"

Her stomach did a loop and she felt dizzy and heard a
chair scrape somewhere near her and one of the guys
saying something to somebody else—there was a lot of
activity in the room, like a wind had blown the door down
and got everyone jumping. Dan, the guy with the sharp
face and the bright black Indian-looking eyes, was watch-

ing her with a smile beginning, nodding to her slowly to mean *yes, yes, yes,* while her stomach did another couple of loops and she heard herself saying:

"Sure, Joe. Of course I'd like to see you again." The breath broke out of her chest in a little kind of laugh she couldn't stop, and she didn't know if it was because she was maybe going to see Joe again after all this time or because the idea just scared her to death. "You name it," she said on the tail end of the laugh, "where and when."

They all waited, watching the square gray amplifier. Commissioner Dakers quietly padded across the uncarpeted floor to the telephone at the end of the room, picking it up and hugging it to his chest and speaking in a whisper.

"I want Mobile."

"This is Mobile."

"Dakers. I want to know if the Gifford setup is ready to go."

"It's ready to go, sir."

"Very good." He cradled the phone and stood watching the amplifier. The operation would take time, and there were calculated risks involved. Dotson wouldn't leave that building unless the streets were cleared, unless he felt there wasn't a police officer within a mile of Park Tower. That would be done. The crowds down there would be moved away and cordons would be set up at a greater distance, where Dotson wouldn't see them. Inside the evacuated area there would be twenty-two officers in plain clothes, all of them from the Detective Bureau, all of them highly trained for this kind of procedure, and all of them instructed that their main task was to protect and secure the life and safety of the girl, Bobbie Gifford. Second, they were to try to take Dotson, if possible alive.

It would depend on how accurate they'd been in their theorizing: McNeil, Dr. Weinberg and the others who had put together the briefing. It would also depend on how the girl handled it. Right now she was doing fine.

"It'd really be something, Joe. I mean, to see you again."

The silences before his answers were growing longer. He was having to think. Dakers beckoned to Detective Shapiro, and whispered to him. "Go up and tell Lieutenant McNeil to pick up the hotline."

Joe's voice came over the amplifier. "I don't see how we can make it, Bobbie."

"Why not?"

"All those cops."

"But they'd clear off, Joe. They'd leave us alone. They told me. They want us to talk."

"They don't know anything. They don't know what the hell they're doing." There was a hollowness coming into his voice, and everyone became alert to it, especially Nick. Dotson had kidded them along before, over the Acapulco deal, just to show them he wasn't stupid. He could be doing the same thing again; but this new note in his voice sounded like genuine emotion. "They'd never leave us alone, Bobbie."

She took a deep breath, and watched Dan Warner to see if he wanted her to say anything different from what they'd told her. "Listen, Joe, they brought me here specially for us to meet each other and talk. You know that. They put those messages up and everything."

"Okay. Why do they want us to talk? What's in it for them?"

"They think I can help you. And I know I can."

The sound of Joe's breathing came over the amplifier now. At first it sounded as if he were whispering something to Tina St. Clair; then they realized there weren't any words, it was just his breathing; and Nick Valenti was the first to know that Joe wasn't trying to kid anybody along

222

this time; Bobbie was getting to him, stirring his memories, taking his mind away from the situation he was in right now and leading him back to when he'd been with this bright kid and in love with her, deeply in love.

"I don't know, Bobbie. I don't know if you can help me. I don't think anyone can. Not now. I—I did some—things, I mean I did some bad things, you know?"

"But you didn't mean to, Joe. That was just something that got into you."

"Okay, sure, I know that. I—I'm not crazy." Then they heard his voice break and there was just his breathing as he tried to keep control, and she waited; they all waited, looking quickly at each other and back to the amplifier, back to the little bright-haired doll who'd forgotten they were there now, while his breath came fluttering in the amplifier like the sound of a trapped bird.

"But you need help, Joe. And I can help you, if you'll let me." She didn't like the way he was breathing so hard like this; he'd broken down a couple of times when they'd been together, cried his heart out while she'd held him and stroked his hair and said everything was going to be okay, over and over, everything was going to be okay, the other way around than like it usually was, with the little woman doing the crying and her man trying to pull her out of it, Jesus, life was funny when you looked back on things, and her time with Joe was—oh, Jesus, her time with Joe. He needed help. "I can help you, Joe. They'll get their ass out of here and we can meet and talk and I'll help you, I know I can."

They waited again. This time it was almost a full minute.

"Bobbie?"

"Yeah?"

"There's something—there's something wrong with me. You know?"

"I guess there's something wrong with most of us. Did you ever think about how crazy everyone is?"

He gave what sounded like a laugh, and then it turned into something like a sob as he got control and went on after a while—"I mean something badly wrong, Bobbie. I mean with me. It's something I can't— It's, oh my God, I don't know, I just need somebody to—you know—somebody to help me work out what's wrong with me."

She closed her eyes, rocking herself on the edge of the bunk, like a mother rocking a child, the phone tight in her hand like she was gripping his wrist, Joe's wrist, to make him understand. "Joe, listen to me. You give me the word, and I'll get the fuzz out of here. They'd do it for me. They told me they would. Then we can talk, and I'll help you, Joe. I helped you before, remember, when you had these—when you felt—you know."

Perched on a decorator's crate at the far end of the room, where he'd established himself to keep clear of the police activity, Tom Lindquist watched the girl at the telephone and thought: Now how in hell can a kid like that—what is she, seventeen, eighteen?—offer to talk to a homicidal maniac without any police protection? How close did she herself come to being found strangled or shot to death while she was living with that man?

"It's just the police," Joe's voice came. "They're gunning for me. They—"

"I just told you, Joe, they'll keep away, like they—"

"Okay, but I don't trust them. I did these things—and they'd have to put me in prison, there'd be a trial and everything and I—"

"Joe, whatever you did, you didn't mean to do it. I can explain that to them all. I can prove it. The most they'll do is give you treatment in one of those—you know—one of those places where they can help you."

Dan Warner had raised both hands with their palms flat

and their fingers spread to catch her attention but it was too late; she'd seen him now but she was just looking confused and didn't seem to know what she'd said wrong.

"I've been to one of those places," Joe said bitterly. "How much did they help me there?"

"But Joe, what I mean is you won't ever have to go to prison, see, the only place you'd have to go would be—"

"I'm not going there again. Not ever again." There was a sharp ring to his voice and the amplifier vibrated. Warner was suddenly standing over Bobbie, shaking his head, trying to wipe out with his spread hands the things she'd said and the things she was going to say, and finally she began nodding quickly, she'd got it now, okay, she'd got it.

"You don't have to go there, Joe, I just meant that was the—the, you know, the worst that—"

"They try and kill you in those places." As she listened to the bitterness in his voice she closed her eyes and thought: Oh Jesus Christ I blew it, I went and fucking blew it and now I'll never get to see him or help him or—

"They give you drugs and electric shocks and treat you like you're some kind of zombie that's wandered in there out of—out of some kind of a horror movie or somewhere or—well, I'm never going in there again, you hear me? *I'm never going in there again. They can—*"

"But Joe, listen. I won't let them—"

"You can't stop them. That's why you ran out on me. You couldn't stop them. You couldn't help me. You can't help me now. *Nobody can.* You understand that? *Nobody can.*" Then the shrilling of his voice stopped and there was just the sound of his sobbing in the room, a sound not quite human, thought Lindquist as the hairs on his neck began rising, while the girl rocked on the bunk with fright and loss in her wide eyes as she clutched the phone with

225

her knuckles white in case anyone tried to take it away from her.

"Joe darling, please listen to me, please listen. I won't let them do anything to you—I'm the only one who can help you and they'll see that, Joe, I'll make them see it, and then we'll—we'll talk it through and everything will be—okay again, Joe, because I love you and I'll do anything for you . . . anything . . . anything, Joe . . ."

She was crying quietly now, hunched over the phone so they couldn't see it anymore, as if she were hiding it from them, keeping it safe. Either she didn't know what else to say, or she knew there was nothing he'd listen to now. When he spoke again his voice was hardly recognizable, and Nick Valenti knew the tone: he'd heard it before. Joe wasn't speaking to Bobbie anymore; he was speaking to the whole world, the world of people who didn't understand him.

"I wanted to take you away with me, but you didn't give me a chance. So now I'm taking Tina."

19

WHEN SHE WOKE AND SAW the light in the room she knew this was the last day of her life.

It was like the first snow of winter: you wake one morning and see at once that the light is different; there are no shadows on the ceiling because the snow on the ground outside is reflecting the light upward; and you know what it is, and that something has happened in the night while you were sleeping and that when you go to the window you'll see the world has changed.

She didn't know where the knowledge was coming from, that this was her last day; but she knew that the mind was infinitely more intelligent, and on an infinitely more subtle level, than it was normally called upon to be in daily life. It was only when you could ignore the time, and the Dow Jones average, and the need for new gloves and the eleven-o'clock news, that you could free the mind from the blinding and deafening trivia of conscious thought to let in the cool clear light of the true reality you'd spent your whole life hiding from. She had learned about this from a man with a withered arm and sightless eyes, a guru who had lived in a hut in the hills above Delhi when she'd known him, cared for by small children sent there by the people from the village nearby, because he said that only children were inteilligent enough to understand his reasoning, until their limitless imagination—their window onto the

227

cosmos, as he termed it in Hindi—became clouded and curtained by the logical conditioning of education and commerce. In the weeks she'd spent with him she had experienced, sometimes for minutes on end, a feeling she could only describe as wholeness, a coming together of the fragments of her experience into a luminous and thrumming awareness of what everything was about, a revelation so dazzling that she'd had to turn away from it each time, in fear of the unfamiliar.

"You'll never be able to keep it," he'd told her with the gentlest smile she'd seen on any man, "because you won't really want it. It doesn't go anywhere, you see; it doesn't do anything; it doesn't work when you try to wind it up. You would need the mind of a child again to understand it." His withered arm swung idly, like an elephant's trunk, as he stood up to say good-bye, turning his head to look straight at her with his sightless eyes, knowing exactly where she was. "But never mind. You know it's there now, and you can at least keep that small light burning on your way through your life."

It had almost gone out, of course. You can't, after a lunch at the Four Seasons and with the limousine jammed in the traffic because of the transport strike and the list of afternoon appointments running right off the page, see the shimmer of Nirvana. But today she felt the infinitesimal vibrations of a knowledge beyond the material, and knew she was close to her death. Lying perfectly still in the arms of the man who was to bring it, she watched the play of light that streamed across the city from the eastern heights to flood into the room and herald for her this one last day.

Joe was asleep, his eyes moving restlessly under their lids as he dreamed. Of what? It frightened her to think. They had come into the Louis XV bedroom to sleep this time, in the enormous bed with the brocaded canopy and gilded posts, waking to make love again in the dark oblivion of some unknown hour and then sleeping, she in his arms as she still was, the scent of his man's body sharp on the air and the sound of his breathing rhythmic and at peace.

Five minutes later she was standing over him with the knife.

He'd wakened momentarily as she'd freed herself and got out of the bed. "Are you getting up, Tina?"

"No. Just going to the bathroom."

She'd drawn the curtains to shut out the brightness of the eastern light, and gone to the bathroom on the far side of the dressing rooms, then out through the passage to the nearest kitchen, walking like an automaton, her skin cold not because she was naked but because there were deeds to be done, an ending to be made to this endless usurpation of her sovereignty. She had a right to live, and a right to die when the time came, not when he chose. This wasn't the vibration of mystic revelation she was feeling throughout her body, it was the animal fear of death, of dying; her flesh crawled with it, her bones ached; her whole body was backed blindly against the wall of the morning, seeing in its light the hordes of destruction racing toward her.

Too bad. She'd see them damned first.

It was a carving knife with a handle made from a deer's antler and a long blade curving to the point, and now she was standing over him with it, the breath locked in her chest and her eyes wide open as she stared down at his naked throat and brought the knife lower, lower, until it was only inches from the smooth tan skin.

How hard? How fast? How deep? Other questions, furiously clamoring: where must the blade go in, to give him no time to wake and fight back before the loss of blood weakened him? Was it the airway you had to hit, so that blood got into the lungs? How long would that take—too long? Was it possible to miss, or to find the muscle was hard enough to need great force to penetrate it?

This was a madman. He'd wake at the first touch of the blade and strike out blindly, strong enough to knock it away before it went in deep, fast enough to save himself while his eyes focused on her and knew what she was trying to do, knew who the enemy was and what had to be done.

The blade caught the light from the side of the heavy silk curtains, its shadow lying across his sleeping face with the point touching his mouth, the mouth that had kissed her so generously and with such tenderness in the night when their bodies had been locked together in the act of love. Her hands were wrapped around the handle, her fingers bone-white, the trembling of her wrists sending a shiver into the long bright blade.

It would have to be done right. It would have to be a quick, plunging stroke with all her strength behind it, and she must do it again and again to make sure of things. But there was no certainty: it would be a gamble. His own maniacal strength was far greater than hers, and even if she got close to the windpipe or the carotid artery he'd wake and fight back, seizing the knife by the blade and turning it away, seizing it next by the handle and turning it against her, so that in the frenzy of trying to survive they'd cover these damask sheets, stained with their lovemaking, with the mingling blood of their death-making—pints of it, quarts of it, dear God in heaven, a whole ocean of it running red in the morning light and splashing across the silk brocade and spilling onto the floor, so that when they came they'd say, as she'd heard them say before in her mind, *Oh my God, they're both* . . . before they went and threw up.

She was trembling badly now, and the shadow of the

230

knife was fluttering against his face, so that she felt he'd almost feel it, and wake.

Tina, you have to do it. You have to do this. It's you or him and you know that.

Yes, I know that.

This is your last chance.

Yes, I know.

Then take it. Do it.

I can't.

You must.

But the shadow of the blade was shaking now and she knew that if she tried to drive it downward she'd make a mess of it and he'd wake up and they'd have to go into the whole frightening business, an orgy of bloodletting straight out of *Macbeth,* and then . . . and then . . . there'd be death, anyway, for her. So what was the difference? She'd only be hurrying things along.

A false argument, she knew that. The truth wasn't in logic; it was in the sudden warmth against her hands as the tears began falling, and her fingers unclenched on the hard bone handle, and his sleeping face grew blurred as the tears kept on coming: tears of grief for a death not dealt, or tears of rage for the weakness in her, it didn't matter. Before the real sobbing could start, she stepped back from the bed and turned and ran on her bare feet through the dressing rooms and the corridor and across the marbled terraces to the swimming pool, where she let the knife fall and walked down the shallow steps and gave her body to the water, letting it swirl over her skin while she lay in the shallows, surprised not to see the clear wavelets tinged with red.

When the sobbing was over with—it had been the relief from shock, she supposed, more than anything else—she climbed the pink marble steps and dried herself in the nearest dressing room, and then went along the terrace to the coral-handled telephone in its lapis-lazuli shell and lifted it, dialing Emergency.

In the command building eight men sat talking at the long table the furniture store had shipped here yesterday. They were Police Commissioner Dakers, Chief of Detectives Dan Warner, Captain Mundy, Captain Art Steziak of Emergency Services, Lieutenant McNeil, Lieutenant Nick Valenti, Eugene St. Clair and Tom Lindquist.

It would have looked like a formal board meeting at first glance, except that few of these men had slept more than an hour or two in the last twenty-four, and that the table was littered with the remnants of the sandwiches and fresh milk that had been brought here for them a short while ago, and with the ashtrays and cigarette packs and scratch pads that had been here since yesterday. Three telephones were at the end of the table where Dakers and Valenti sat. If the one in the middle—the hotline—began ringing, it would be for Valenti, the chief hostage negotiator, to pick it up.

A few minutes ago, when the first light of day had shown in the uncurtained windows, reflected from the Park Tower building opposite, they had switched off the tubular lighting; three of them were complaining of migraine, probably brought on—according to McNeil—by the limited-spectrum rays. Tom Lindquist could believe him, but was just the same taking regular doses of the Neosynephrine he carried around with him to keep his sinuses clear.

"We have to reach two decisions," Commissioner Dakers told the others at the long table. "We'll take the question of the gun first." He looked directly at Nick Valenti, who had just been called down from the roof. "Mr. Lindquist has agreed to reveal the combination of the safe in his apartment, and its location, if we get a chance of talking to

Tina St. Clair. He's offered to remain with us here until the situation has been resolved." He looked away from Nick to take in the rest of the company. "We've discussed the possibility that even if Tina secured the gun and faced Dotson with it, she might not feel able to shoot him if he closed in on her. A sane man wouldn't risk walking into a loaded gun, but Dotson is not sane. And the risk is clear enough: we could be putting the gun into his hands. I'd like to hear comments, gentlemen."

Mundy spoke at once. "I don't think he needs a gun, sir." He sounded impatient, and McNeil noted that the man's increasing fatigue was affecting him less than his increasing frustration. "She's told us that Dotson is very strong, so if he wanted to finish matters over there he'd simply use his hands or a knife or what the hell."

McNeil glanced across at the banker, and saw the heavy lids close for a moment. Even if Tina walked out of that building right now, free and unhurt, this man would never be the same again.

"But the gun would give Dotson ideas," Nick said, looking straight at Mundy. If anyone were going to be an accessory to Tina St. Clair's death it'd be this goddamned hotshot. All he wanted was action, even if Tina herself had to get it for him. "One of the things I've learned about Dotson is that he likes playing the clown—remember the Acapulco gag? If we put that gun in his hands he could have himself a ball. He could drive Tina out of her mind with it, like I've seen it done a dozen times in a hostage situation: the accumulated strain of having a gun held to your head can blow your reason away. Or he could simply go trigger-happy and see clay pipes wherever he looked, and those goons up there on the rooftop could start returning his fire—which is okay, they might hit him. Or of course they might hit Tina St. Clair." He didn't look away from Mundy. "I mean a gun is a toy, and it's made for kids who haven't yet learned to talk."

Dakers dropped some ash into the tray with studied care.

"If that's so," Mundy said with his chin tucked in and his eyes on Valenti, "maybe we should question the fact that the entire police department has carried guns ever since—"

"We'll confine ourselves to the immediate issue," Dakers cut in sharply. "McNeil, I want to hear from you."

"I'd suggest a compromise, sir. We could tell Tina how to get hold of that gun, but warn her that if she's not prepared to face Dotson with it—and shoot him dead if she has to—she should leave it just where it is."

Chief Warner swung his head. "You think that with the strain she's under she's capable of deciding precisely what she's going to do in some future situation that's potentially dangerous, potentially lethal?"

"No, Chief, I don't. Not necessarily. But what's really on our minds is that *somehow* she must be given the chance of saving her life."

"Or the chance," Lindquist put in quietly, "of at least knowing she could if she chose to. How are we going to feel afterward, if anything happens to her, and we didn't tell her the gun was there?"

"We're going to feel about the same," Nick told him, "as if we did tell her, and he shoots her with it."

There was silence for a time as the cigarette smoke clouded upwards against the wan light at the windows. Dakers leaned forward, interlacing his nicotine-stained fingers. "If she could hide somewhere with it. Just keep it with her, as a last resort . . ."

"If she could hide anyplace, sir," Nick told him, "with or without the gun, we'd be going into a shut-ended phase. He'd look for her, and if he couldn't find her, he'd be liable to set off the explosive and blow the top of the building up. Remember, his one aim is to take her away with him, as he puts it."

"I agree with that," McNeil said. "And if she managed to hide and use a phone and tell us to go in and get Dotson, he'd do the same thing, the moment he heard us coming."

Valenti nodded. "He has three aces. He has the explosive; he has Tina; and he's ready to die. We've nothing to match that kind of hand."

Again there was silence, and again Dakers broke it. "Those points are well made, but let's confine ourselves to the question of the gun." He squinted through the smoke at the man in the dark crumpled suit. St. Clair was sitting with his back straight against the chair and his hands resting squarely on the polished mahogany table, his hooded eyes undulled as yet by the fatigue but his face gray under the growing stubble. "Mr. St. Clair, I'd like your thoughts if you'd care to express them."

The banker looked at him and away again, simply to acknowledge the invitation; then there was silence for a full minute as he considered. But at the end of his analysis of all the options there remained the dilemma, and the two opposite scenes, each unthinkable: Tina helpless in the bare hands of a maniac, with no means of saving herself; and Tina going down under a rain of bullets from the gun he'd seized from her. In the background of his thoughts he could hear the broken voice of Elizabeth: *But why didn't you tell her the gun was there? She could have saved herself.* Or if matters went the other way: *Whatever made you put a loaded gun within reach of such a man?*

Captain Mundy's chair creaked as he shifted his weight on it. On the other side of the table Lindquist ran his fingers through his pale ruff of hair. *The real answer is not to have told them the gun was there. Too late now.*

St. Clair spoke at last. "My daughter refused to coax that man to a window and see him shot. Surely she'd find it even more abhorrent to shoot him herself?"

"Less, sir, I believe." McNeil had been waiting for this point to come up. "She couldn't bring herself to deceive him, to set him up in a death trap. But facing him with a gun in her own hand, she'd be in a position to say: 'If you move one inch, I'll shoot. If you keep still, you can stay alive.' That's a straightforward deal, and she'd have nothing to reproach herself with if *he made her* shoot him. And I think we should point this out to her on the phone."

Mundy swung his chair away impatiently and went across to the water fountain. "It's nice to think we're going to have a long conversation with her. But she could be dead before the phone even rings."

"Until it does"—Nick looked round at him—"we have the time to reach a decision."

Mundy came and stood over him, bright-eyed with tension.

"*If* it rings. But it doesn't *have* to. That guy over there has probably killed five people in his life so far and whenever a full moon comes around what's left of his mind goes clean out of whack and turns him into a homicidal maniac—and it comes around again tonight. So this is the last day we've got. Are we going to spend it sitting on our hands rapping?"

Nick got to his feet and stood facing him, hunched in his windbreaker. "If she calls us, we have a chance of getting Dotson on the line. Then we can start work on him."

"This isn't a hostage-negotiation setup anymore, Valenti, and you know that. Either we sit here discussing the precise color of bullshit while the time runs out, or we can—"

"Captain Mundy." The commissioner didn't raise his voice. "Lieutenant Valenti. Sit down, both of you."

Mundy jerked his head to look at Dakers, and McNeil saw that for a moment he'd forgotten the commissioner or anyone else was here: he could see only Valenti. Then the bright stare went out of his eyes and he moved away from the lieutenant and found his chair.

"Sir." Valenti sat down again, fishing in his pockets for a cigarette.

"We are under increasing strain," Dakers said with a chill in his tone, "and I'm ready to replace both of you in this operation the moment you show any further sign of losing your control. Do you understand?"

"Yes, sir." Mundy didn't look up at him.

"Sir." Valenti found the pack and lit up.

"Mr. St. Clair," Dakers said in a gentler tone, "now that you've heard these different opinions, do you still feel your daughter would balk at shooting Dotson, even if we persuaded her she has every justification, in self-defense?"

Voicing his despair for the first time, Eugene lifted his hands from the table and dropped them again. "How can I know? How can I possibly know?" In a moment he went on: "Perhaps she would reach her decision when she knew there was a gun there. If she then took it, I think she'd use it."

Dakers got out of his chair and went to the window, looking across the street to the penthouse opposite. As Dan Warner had said, it was a crapshoot; they had to bet on blind numbers and in the dark. But just the same they had to bet. Or he had to.

He turned around and went back to his chair. "Thank you for your comments, gentlemen. If we have the chance to talk to Tina St. Clair again, I shall tell her the gun is there if she wants it."

Everyone moved, getting a cigarette, stretching their

237

legs, going to the coffee machine; Detective Shapiro, officially the physical liaison agent between the units, in fact the general handyman and gofer, began clearing the mess of sandwich papers and empty milk cartons from the table as Commissioner Dakers looked at the pasty-faced man with the colorless eyes sitting at the far end of the table in a worn and faded track suit. Captain Steziak, chief of the Emergency Services Divsion in the field, hadn't spoken a word since Dakers had called him in here; there was no ashtray in front of him, no coffee cup; he was sitting with his narrow, ferretlike head tilted downward slightly as he gazed in front of him; only McNeil knew that the man was in meditation, his brain waves slowed to the alpha rhythm and his mind in a state of deep relaxation. McNeil knew this because he'd taught him how to do it.

"Captain Steziak?" Dakers said as he sat down again.

There was a second's delay before the pale head turned and the eyes focused.

"Sir?"

"We have to reach a second decision. Tell us what you think your chances are of going in there and bringing Miss St. Clair out safely."

Art Steziak angled his chair to face the commissioner. "They've finished the tests with the window glass. It took seven minutes to cut through the double pane and lift it out with a vacuum sucker. I've been through the operation several times in my mind, and there's no physical problem. It's now six-twenty-nine. If they dropped me onto the roof thirty minutes from now, I could be inside the apartment by seven-fifteen. It shouldn't take me long to locate and subdue Dotson. Maybe fifteen minutes, depending on where he was. I'd say I could have the hostage out safely by seven-thirty. An hour from now."

There was total silence for a couple of seconds and then everyone began moving again to relieve the tension. None of them could keep still as the thought flashed through their minds: *Tina safe, an hour from now.*

Dakers blew out smoke and said: "For those present who aren't familiar with Captain Steziak's record, I'll say briefly that he's an acknowledged expert on this kind of single-handed operation and there's nobody in my department with a better chance of succeeding. That doesn't mean he's infallible or that something might not go wrong that he'd have no control over."

Two or three of them—Mundy, Lindquist, Chief Warner—were out of their chairs and pacing the room now.

"Sir?"

"McNeil?"

"We can't have it both ways. If we tell Miss St. Clair there's a gun for her to use, we wouldn't be able to send Captain Steziak in unless we were sure the gun hadn't gotten into Dotson's hands."

"In my plans"—Steziak looked across at him—"I don't preclude a shoot-out."

"Okay, but that would reduce the chances for her safety."

"Oh, sure."

The commissioner looked at Chief Warner. "Dan?"

"There's no way he could disarm whatever kind of explosive Dotson has there, before setting out to locate him. There's no window to the lobby on that floor, and he'd need to move the chest away from the front door or the refrigerator away from the other door, and that would take time and make some noise. If the explosive weren't there, I'd say let's send him right now. But it's an added risk, and a big one."

Dakers considered, looking at the top sheet of the penthouse plans, which showed the overall layout. But his practical thinking was being sabotaged by the emotional content of what Steziak had projected. *Tina safe, an hour from now.* Cheering in the streets, the crowds surging forward, the spotlight on Steziak, the hero of the hour; on Mundy, the genius behind the coup; on himself and the whole of his department. And the press going wild . . . *TINA FREE . . . In one bold move, the New York Police Department, under the direct orders of Commissioner William Dakers, took the initiative in this most harrowing of situations and succeeded in . . .* Yes, indeed.

Handshakes, home and bed. That too would be welcome. And Tina, with a life to live after all. And the warm and self-indulgent joy of answering one of these phones and turning to Eugene St. Clair and saying, "Your daughter's safe. They're bringing her out of the building now."

It was temptation, understandable but dangerous. He had to think with his head. "You're confident?" he asked Steziak.

"Totally confident, sir."

"Mundy?"

"I think it's our only chance, sir."

"That isn't the issue."

Mundy was standing near the window, and instinctively moved to the at-ease position, perhaps sensing a historic moment. "I've every possible confidence in the plan I've worked out with Steziak. And in Steziak's ability to pull it off successfully."

Dakers didn't ask for McNeil to comment. He was a psychologist, and if they went in there with a loaded gun the time for psychologizing would be over.

"Valenti?"

Nick was standing by the water fountain, hunched from the strain of waiting, red-eyed from too many packs of cigarettes and the lack of sleep. He took a slow step away from the fountain while he considered, and then said quietly: "I think the greatest danger to Tina St. Clair at this minute is from the New York Police Department."

Everyone froze.

This guy, thought McNeil, this lowly *lieutenant*, is trying to get himself fired from the job. He watched the commissioner's face, but it was expressionless.

"I'm not interested, Valenti, in dramatics."

"Okay, sir. Right now, the situation over there is calm. And that's the only single ace we have in the whole of the deck."

"Very well. How do you suggest we should play it?"

"We shouldn't. We have to keep it. Once it's gone, we're done for." He leaned forward over the table, a humped figure with its hands sticking out across the flat expanse of mahogany like a collapsed mannequin's. "The minute we put anyone in there with a gun, the situation changes radically. I don't think Dotson took a gun in there with him, or he would have made threats with it or shot off a few rounds to let us know the score." His face turned slowly to look directly at Dakers as he said reflectively, "You know, sir, I have *never* been in a hostage negotiation where a guy with a gun hasn't either threatened someone with it or fired it. And Dotson hasn't done that, and that's why I don't think he took the dead guard's gun in there with him, either. It's probably in the elevator, the one he went up there in. So we'd be introducing a potentially disastrous element into a presently stable situation."

He leaned back from the table and got out of his chair and shuffled towards the windows, squinting against the sunlight reflected from Park Tower. "Psychotics are often very smart. They can think so fast and act so fast that you're left standing. If Dotson's close enough to Tina when Steziak goes in there, he can snatch up a table knife or put a stranglehold on her from behind, using her as a shield, and order Steziak to drop his gun." In a moment he went on: "Maybe I'd better check on that." He went slowly across to the pale-faced man in the track suit. "If he had a knife at her throat, and told you to drop your gun, what would you do?"

He watched Steziak's colorless eyes go blank as he thought about it. Steziak was a weirdo. He was into ESP and telepathy and God knew what sort of bullshit. But he could think. And he wasn't like that fucking little Napoleon, Field Marshal Mundy. He didn't want action at any cost.

"He'd have to count," Steziak said.

"Okay. He counts. There's the point of the blade sticking into her soft white throat and he gives you three, he gives you five, okay, and he gets to the number, and what do you do?"

"I drop the gun."

Nick wanted to put a hand on the man's arm. He needed friends here, if that girl over there was going to come out of this thing alive. But he kept both his hands stuck into the pockets of his windbreaker. "And you'd have to kick it across the floor where he could reach it."

"If that's what he told me to do."

"You bet your goddamned ass that's what he'd tell you to do. He's bright." He turned away from Steziak and spoke mainly to the commissioner. "He's bright enough to go up there and get the girl he wants and do it in a way that's had the whole police department of this city tied up in knots for the past thirty-six hours. So if he doesn't have the security guard's gun, we're going to risk him getting Mr. Lindquist's gun; and if the girl doesn't let him have that one, we're going to risk him getting Captain Steziak's gun. At least nobody can say we're not making an effort to increase the danger."

Silence came in, and they went on listening to the echo of his voice in their heads. Lieutenant McNeil took off his glasses and cleaned them with his blue-bordered handkerchief; he'd recognized the contained fury in Valenti's voice, and reflected that if the top brass weren't here, he'd be at Mundy's throat, and everyone else's. McNeil had heard him talk down half a dozen hostage-takers, most of them with loaded firearms, his quiet voice stroking them like you'd stroke a scared kitten, as patient with them as you'd be with a retarded child, until one after another they'd crept out of their fear and their refuge and come to him, and brought him their hostages, alive. Valenti could keep his cool in any situation when there was nobody on his back. Right now he was in a rage.

"No one denies," Mundy came in impatiently, "that we don't have to take chances, somewhere along the line."

Nick didn't bother to turn his head; he spoke over his shoulder. "Right. But what we have to remember is we're taking them for her."

Commissioner Dakers chain-lit a cigarette, picking a piece of the filter from his bottom lip and looking across at the chief of detectives. "Dan, I'd like to hear—" Then he stopped dead as the hotline began ringing and Valenti went over to answer it.

20

"THIS IS TINA ST. CLAIR."

Nick Valenti sank onto his haunches, the phone in his hand.

"We're listening," he said.

"He's asleep."

Nick heard the difference in her voice from last time as it came over the amplifier. He'd heard it before, when a hostage had been ordered by his captor to speak over the phone. She'd lost hope.

"He's not with you? You can simply say yes, and he won't understand."

"What? Oh no, he's asleep right now."

"Where are you, Tina?"

"By the pool."

"Do you have anything urgent to tell us?"

There was a pause. "Not really. But I think I'm going to die soon. Is that urgent?"

Eugene St. Clair moved slightly at the table, putting his face in his hands.

"Has he made threats?" Nick said.

"Not specifically. I just know it in my bones. I think he's just waiting for the right time."

"When do you think that will be?"

"Tonight. When he sees the full moon. He talks about

that, quite often. I called up to ask if there's anything you can do for me."

Commissioner Dakers reached down and took the phone from Nick, handing it to Lindquist and nodding quickly.

"Tina, there's a pad by the phone, and a pencil."

"Yes. Who's that?"

"Tom Lindquist."

"Tom? When did you—?"

"In case we get cut off, write this down. Ready?"

"Yes."

"It's the combination of my safe. Start with zero. Turn right four times to sixty-one. Turn left three times to twenty. Right twice to forty-nine. Left again to eighty-seven. Turn right until the dial hits the stop, then pull the door open. Am I going too—?"

"Left again to what?"

"Eighty-seven."

"Okay. Then turn right till it stops?"

"Yes. Read that back to me."

"All right." When she'd finished she asked: "Where's the safe, Tom?"

"Behind the small statue of the Buddha, in the library. Turn the Buddha to the left, then pull it toward you. It comes off at the base. Push the bronze panel. Push fairly hard, on the right side only. It swings open. Then you'll see the safe, with the dial on it."

"All right. I've got that." Her tone didn't change as she said: "But I don't need any cash, Tom. I'm not going anywhere."

"There's a gun in there."

"A what?"

"A gun. An automatic. It's loaded, but the safety catch is on. The catch is on the left. Push it forward. There are ten shots in the magazine. Remember that. Ten."

The amplifier was silent. They watched it, waiting.

In a moment Dakers nodded to Lindquist and took the phone from him; it was slippery with sweat.

"Tina?"

The silence went on. Then she said: "Yes. But I can't kill him."

"Are you sure?"

"Yes. I tried."

"When?"

"A few minutes ago. That's not Tom, is it?"

"This is Police Commissioner Dakers. We're doing everything possible to protect you, but our hands are tied. Any attempt to break in there would endanger you. This could be your only chance. You can take the gun and face him with it. Then pick up the nearest phone. If you have to jack it in first, don't take your eyes off him, and keep the gun aimed at him. Remember the safety catch and make sure you push it to fire. The moment we get your call we'll go in there for you. If Dotson makes *any* move, you must fire, at once. Warn him first, not to move. Do *not* give him any time to close in on you. Begin firing, and keep on firing into his chest. If he still comes close enough, fire at his head, between the eyes. You have every justification, do you understand?"

Waiting, he suddenly found Eugene St. Clair standing beside him, his hand held out for the phone, his eyes pleading.

"You want to tell her something?" Dakers asked.

"Yes. To kill him."

Dakers hesitated, then gave him the phone.

"I can't do that," her voice came from the amplifier.

Eugene gripped the telephone with his knuckles white. "Tina."

They heard her quick indrawn breath. "Is that—Daddy?"

"Yes, my love. And you must listen to me. You will

246

have to find the courage to shoot that man, if you have to.''

"Daddy"—her voice had become breathless—"are you okay? Are you and Mother okay? It's been so worrying for you."

"Your mother is asleep, close to us here in the building opposite. I gave her some Valium, and—"

"You're as close as that? Oh, Daddy-O . . ."

He closed his eyes against the brightness of the reflected sun, trying to think how to persuade her to kill a man; she sounded so young, and so vulnerable. "We're at the top of the opposite building, Tina, and we won't be leaving here until you're free. You must get the gun from the safe, and hold him off with it. It may be enough; it may be all you need to do, to hold the gun on him and call us. The police will be in there within minutes, as soon as they know he can't harm you."

In a moment she said lovingly, "It's so good to hear your voice, Daddy-O. You give me strength. You always have."

"Then you've nothing to fear, my love."

"But I—I can't kill him. I tested myself, and it was no good. He's—not a bad man, Daddy. He's not much more than a child."

"He shot two men to death in there, because they tried to stop him reaching you; they were trying to protect you, Tina. So what did they die for, if you won't save yourself now?"

"I want to save him too. If I can."

"Then this is how you can do it. If he isn't brought under control, he's liable to take his own life, after taking yours." For an instant he had a flash of disorientation, and wondered what it was he was gripping in his hand so tightly, and why Tina hadn't called simply to ask if she could spend the weekend with them; he stood frozen in a

247

wasteland of unreality, cut off from the known world; then he was back again, facing the unthinkable. "Or he may set off the explosive, and do it that way. But if you bring him under control, you can save him too."

"Daddy, I know what you're saying. And I'll try. I'll get the gun. But I can't shoot him."

"Then he'll know that. He'll see you can't do it, and he'll take the gun away from you. *You have to be prepared to use it, Tina, if you get it from the safe.*"

"My God, you know me better than anyone else in the world," her voice came, anguished now, "and you know I can't even kill a fly."

He loosened his hand on the telephone; he'd been trying to crush it. Something had happened to her in there; the man had hypnotized her in some way; she was like a moth at a flame. "You're under an appalling strain, Tina, and it's natural that you can't think rationally. Just do what I'm asking you to do—for your mother, and for me, if you can't do it for yourself. And for the two brave men who tried to protect you. You've always thought of other people; think of them now."

Seconds went by, and when she spoke again her voice was weary, as it had sounded before she heard him on the line.

"I can't promise anything, Daddy. I can't promise anything."

—— 21 ——

A FEW MINUTES AFTER SIX O'CLOCK in the evening. Nick Valenti picked up one of his telephones and dialed a number in Queens.

"I'd like to talk to Dr. Marcellino."

"He's busy right now. Can I take a message?"

"I know he's busy. I just want to talk to him for a minute, that's all."

He stared across the rooftop in the half-light at something with lettering on it, trying to read what it said. It bothered him that he couldn't read it immediately. Everything bothered him now; it was the not knowing, the never-ending not knowing.

"What name is it?"

"Huh?"

"Who is it speaking?"

"Oh. Valenti. Nick Valenti. The doc's looking after Karen, my—"

"You should have told me, Mr. Valenti."

"Told you what?" Suddenly he realized this was a goddamn son-of-a-bitch conversation, when all he wanted to know was—"Listen, all I want to know is—"

"Nick?" It was a man's voice now. "Marcellino. And this is your fifth call, right? I've been in theater since before noon, Nick, okay?"

"If it's okay with you," Nick said wearily, thinking of

making a little joke. But it wasn't funny, and the frustration came back. "You could've left a message, I guess." He could read the lettering on the can over there now: *Pepsi*, upside down.

"You're damn right I should have left a message, Nick, but there's nothing to tell you, except that she's still okay. She's perfectly okay. But we have to operate, just the classical cesarean—we discussed the possibility, remember?"

Nick felt himself shrinking, drawing in on himself, trying to find shelter. "So you're going to have to do it."

"That's right. And listen, Nick, I've done it a hundred times, okay? A couple of hundred times, so many times I've even forgotten. So there isn't much we have to worry about."

In his job, Nick Valenti knew the significance of words, the weight they carried, even the short, easy ones, sometimes especially the short, easy ones. He said in a moment: "Not 'much' to worry about?"

"Right. You know the score, Nick. With some people I have to kid along, because they can't take it up front; but not with you. That makes it easier for both of us. Any operation is a risk, but Karen is healthy and her present readout is very satisfactory—or we couldn't have her in here tonight. She's down for eight o'clock."

Nick looked at his watch. Two hours from now. Suddenly it was all coming at him very fast, closing the gap. And he couldn't try to take any kind of shelter anymore: it was time to face it head-on. He took a deep breath, and felt bigger, and stronger.

"She'll be okay, Doc, with you in charge of everything."

"Damn right she'll be okay. We're going to see to that." Nick heard relief in the man's tone. It wasn't too often, maybe, that people remembered the doctors needed reassuring too. Jesus, the job they did, the responsibility they took on . . .

"What about the baby?" he asked Marcellino.

The silence began drawing out. "Huh? We have to see. We have to take things easy, take things as they come. There are some complications, as I told you, Nick, but we have ways of dealing with them, lots of different ways. We'll do everything we can. And that's a whole lot."

Nick waited till he could get his voice right; he didn't like his voice to show anything unnecessary. "So it looks like Karen's going to come out okay, but not the kid."

There was another silence, while Marcellino got his voice right too. "That would be putting it at its worst, Nick."

"Sure. I know what's you're saying. Doc, should I be there?"

"Right now?"

"Right now."

"If you can make it, yes. Karen's under the prelim anesthesia, and she doesn't know too much about what's going on. You won't find much real conversation, you know?"

"She's not scared, is she, Doc?"

"Scared? For her it's just like Christmas; the prelim dope does a really beautiful job. But it's up to you, Nick. I know you're not just sitting around out there with nothing to do. A lot of people are depending on you." He gave a short laugh that was meant to sound rueful, but it just sounded weary. "That's a feeling I can recognize myself."

"Sure. Is Maria there?"

"She's been here the whole time."

"She thinks I ought to be there, too, Doc."

"Sure she does. She's a mother."

Nick waited for him to say something more, but he didn't. The silence went on. "I'll see how things are jumping," he said at last, "around eight o'clock." He looked up as Al Groot, his backup negotiator, came onto the roof from the stairway. "I'll see if I can get away, Doc."

"Sure. You do that. Everything here is under control, so you don't have to worry. How is it with the Tina thing, Nick?"

"We have the game plan ready, but it's his move next."

"I wish you luck. You know something, Nick? A lot of the time I'd rather not have my job, but Mother of Jesus, I'd rather have it than yours."

Al Groot, the backup hostage negotiator, peeled a banana and lobbed the skin across to the garbage can below the water tower; it half-missed, straddling the rim like a clothespin.

"You gotta get your potassium," he said to nobody.

People had started doing that, lately: talking to themselves, or to nobody. You didn't get many answers.

Nick put the phone down and leaned back against the leg of the water tower, watching the windows opposite. He liked it better up here on the roof; there was too much brass down there at the command post; and there was Mundy, bloody Mundy.

"You go to mass?" he asked Al Groot. Al had been ordered to take an hour's break at five this afternoon; he'd begun arguing with the sharpshooters about life-and-death decision-making, a heavy subject. He'd said he'd go to St. Pat's, just down the street.

"Sure," he told Nick. "It was beautiful. They offered prayers for her."

"For who?"

Al looked at him. "For Tina."

"They did?"

"Sure. 'Our beloved sister whose life is in peril.' "

"Who conducted?"

"Father Kilcuddy. You want some potassium?"

"No." He sighted past the dish amplifier they'd rigged up this afternoon, after Tina had been told about the gun. There was an amplifier on each of the four roofs facing Park Tower, to pick up the sound of shots inside the penthouse that would otherwise be muffled by the double glazing. If they heard shots, they were going in.

"Did they pray for Joe too?"

"Uh? Kind of. They hoped he'd find charity in his heart."

"Amen. Where's Steziak, d'you know?"

"Waiting for the top brass to make up their minds. He's ready to go."

"They're playing with fire, Al."

"Oh, sure."

"It isn't the way."

"Well it's one way. If she can pull that gun on him, she's got it made; but if she can't, there has to be some other way, before suddenly it's too late."

Nick didn't answer, but went on watching the blob of light in a window on Fifty-sixth. It was the reflection of a light that had gone on in a window of Park Tower fifteen minutes ago; it was the main kitchen of the penthouse. The sharpshooters over there on the rooftop on Fifty-sixth were on alert status, waiting for a chance of Dotson showing up against the window, with Tina in the clear somewhere.

Dakers and Mundy and Steziak were closing in now. If the goons on the roof couldn't pick Dotson off, Tina might try doing it herself; or if not, Steziak could go in. They were pushing things now, and if they weren't more careful they could push things the wrong way, and too far.

He shifted his shoulder blades against the strut of the water tower, thinking of Doc Marcellino again, and of Karen, and Maria, and the kid, his kid, curled up in the warm and the dark and waiting for the world it might never get to see.

"Hey, Nick. Did you call the clinic again?" Al pushed the remains of his sandwich supper into the brown paper bag and lit two cigarettes and handed one to Nick.

"Yes."

"How's Karen?"

"She's fine."

But let us pray for our little beloved brother, or sister, whose life is also in peril.

22

THROUGH THE SLITS IN HIS lids he could see the long bright rippling of the water down the length of the pool, and much nearer, the striped turquoise towel she'd dropped across the carved onyx seat by the dressing tent. The sunlamps were burning, throwing heat and light from panels inside the big glass dome overhead, and when she'd gone into the pool a minute ago her body had looked golden, coloring the blue water as she had slipped into its wavelets, glowing like coral under the surface.

His eyes closed again, and for a while he listened to the musical sound of the water as she moved in it, breaking the surface; then there was only the warmth on his skin, and the half-seen, half-heard images and sounds of faraway places, and the swinging of her hair as she turned again and faced him.

"I just don't understand you, Joe. I was only gone about ten minutes, for Christ's sake."

"I love you," he said.

"Okay, that's—you know, terrific, but I still don't understand. It's like you don't trust me."

Deep green eyes and a freckled face and her hands flying everywhere as she talked, going up to her hair and pulling it back, fluttering in the air like birds while he stood there and loved her so much that he didn't know what he was going to do about it.

"Mary," he said, "I love you so much I—don't know what the time is. You know?"

She started laughing a little, still not understanding, her thick bronze-red eyebrows lifting and wrinkling her forehead, not understanding but ready to give up instead of going on—she never liked fights any more than he did.

"What the time is?" she said, throwing her shoulders around now, with that terrific body-language thing she did so well. "I guess you've got it bad, Joe." She turned away and took the things out of the bag and put some of them in the fridge.

"I thought you might be—you know, meeting a guy," he said ruefully. "If you did that, I—"

"Oh my God, Joe." She swung around at him with her long hair swinging. "I don't want anyone else, don't you know that? You're the most terrific guy I've ever met, didn't I tell you?"

She came and ruffled his hair and afterward they had their supper and she did the dishes and played some rock while he went through the safety drill again in the book on explosives—he was studying down at the Tech because there were jobs going in demolition all over the county, because of the new federal loan—and he helped her take the garbage can down all fifteen flights of stone steps because the elevators had gone out of whack again; and when they'd sat on the balcony for a while to get their breath back he knew suddenly what it was he'd have to do, and after that he didn't remember very much, just the way she'd tried to hang on to the balcony rail at the last minute, the way a cat clings on with its claws when you try to get it down from a tree; she was strong for her size and he'd had to prize her fingers off the rail, like the time when he'd gone up to bring Jack Santano down from the scaffolding; and all the time she was kind of not-quite-screaming, a kind of terrible laughter deep down in her

throat, with his name in it somewhere . . . *Joe . . . don't,
Joe* . . . and then her long red hair went flying out in a
cloud against the lights of the street below and she was
falling, turning slowly in the air till she was on her back
for a moment looking up at him with her eyes wide open
and her mouth in an O that wasn't making any sound—
they never make any noise, Santano had told him soon
after he'd got the job, they never make any noise when
they go down the hole, that's a lot of tarbuck—and then
her head began going down because that was the heaviest
part of her, and he just saw her legs opening inside her
skirt, which made him feel kind of sick because it was
sexy but at the wrong time, and he couldn't look anymore,
so all he could remember now was seeing her while she
was still alive, with the moonlight on her face as she'd
looked up at him, and then her legs like that. What mat-
tered most, afterward, was that she was safe now, and he
was safe. Nobody could ever take her away from him,
ever.

The water lapped at the edge of the pool, and he listened
to it without seeing anything in his mind now, but feeling
a sense of terrible loneliness, and loss, the feeling that
often got into him and slowly turned into a darkness so
deep that he ran screaming through it trying to find himself,
knowing he was in there somewhere and knowing that
until he found himself he'd never get any better, he would
go on doing these terrible things that he didn't want to do,
but had to do.

The water lapped in the silence under the big sunlamps,
and for a minute he knew where he was again; then the
wheels began turning, the huge red wheels with the flags
on the spokes, red and yellow and blue and green, fluttering in the wind as the wheels went faster and Sandy was
laughing to him as they got out of the little cable car at the
top of the tower, laughing and saying—"Hey, Joe, shouldn't

you buy a hot-air balloon or something? You'd save yourself an awful lot of money in the long run, you know
that?"

But she enjoyed it, really, and he liked standing there
with her on the very top level of the Sky Tower and
watching her face and her gray-green eyes and the way her
hair swung like that in the wind so she'd have to draw it
back with her small freckled hand, turning suddenly and
laughing to him because she knew he was watching her
and was really doing it for him, playing with her hair like
a lot of girls with long hair did, not to get it out of the way
but to make you look at it—"Joe, did I ever tell you I find
you a very strange man?"

"Sometimes," he said, but his smile felt suddenly frozen on his face like someone had stuck it there, because it
made him feel so scared, to be thought of as strange. He
didn't like people saying that, simply because it scared the
hell out of him, which was logical enough, it made good
sense, so he couldn't really be—well, so strange that—but
he knew that he was, yes, very strange, and had something—
wrong with him. He was—

"But I like it," Sandy was saying, laughing to him so
delightfully and making him love her so much that he
knew it couldn't go on like this, there'd have to be something bigger between them, their own new world for them
to live in while other people, small people who— "You're
mysterious, Joe, and I like it." She wasn't laughing now;
her voice was softer, and kind of secretive, and she had
her head close to his so nobody could hear, though the
nearest person had to be way down there on the ground
because this was the last car up and they were alone. "I'm
never going to ask what's on your mind, either, because I
hate that in people—what are you thinking about? Like
they never heard of being private—and because if you told
me what you were thinking about, you wouldn't be myste-

rious anymore." Then she began laughing again, softly. "I told Debby at work yesterday that I go out every night with a strange man, and she thinks I'm a nymphomaniac!"

The laughter turned into kissing and they stood there alone in their world, high in the evening sky with the rim of the moon showing across the shoreline fifty miles away; and he loved her so much that he knew it couldn't just stay this way forever: they would have to become eternal lovers, like stars in the firmament, with a heavenly choir always singing somewhere, kind of in the background, because they were very special people and would—would find their destiny together, which was a phrase he'd seen in a book and had always remembered because it was so mind-blowing, just two people hand in hand and rising away from the earth toward the moon to find their destiny.

They went to the Sky Tower again the next Monday. Monday nights were best because not many people were there; and all he could remember now was how light she was as he swung her into the air, with one of her hands grabbing him around the neck until he pulled it away and she went over the rail at the top of the six-hundred-foot tower and seemed to float there against the lights of the shooting gallery a long way below, floating and not moving very much, just getting smaller with her arms out like she was trying to find something to grab at in the thin nothingness of the air, while he stood there shaking and making sounds he didn't understand; all he understood was that he could never lose her now, while she lay there like she was dancing but flat on the ground, never lose her again, while the blood crept across the gray stone and touched the lucky charm and kind of melted over it, *take him away, someone, for God's sake take Joe away*, never lose her again, ever again, ever again.

For a while the lapping of the water broke into his thoughts, and when he opened his eyelid just a little bit he saw her slipping through the amethyst water like a liquid flame, sending diamond drops into the air as her hands broke the surface away; then he closed his eyes and slipped below the waters of his own world, going deeper and deeper into the dream.

It was the dream that had come to him often, since he'd met Tina, coming down from the clouds to look at her through the window. They were standing hand in hand, like children not sure of the way, facing the windows that ran from wall to wall in the long gold room; the filmy curtains were drawn closed but they could see the building opposite, and the buildings on each side, and right across the city toward the east: towers and rooftops and angular castles standing in a black frieze against the big bright circle of the moon.

He looked down at her, and she looked up, smiling to him; her hand was strong in his, squeezing his own; he could feel her fingers trembling.

"Are you excited?" he asked her.

"Yes. Oh . . . yes."

The heavy ornament was in his other hand. It was a bronze sculpture with a thick body, a woman with big breasts and stomach and buttocks but a very small head; it wasn't all that much to look at, but it would do the job.

"I love you," he said.

"And I love you, Joe." She was still smiling up at him as he raised the heavy ornament and hurled it at the window right in front of him. Everything seemed to slow down as it hit the glass and broke through it, making a circular wave, like he'd thrown it into water; but it made a lot of noise, quite an explosion as the glass broke into glittering pieces that separated and flew outwards as the figure of the woman went through it, twisting slowly until the heavy base was at the bottom, so that she seemed to be leaning forward and diving through as the bits went on flashing in the light, their edges dark against the moon but their surfaces catching its yellow fire.

They ran forward, still hand in hand, and leaped through the hole in the window; the entire pane had been smashed away and their feet didn't touch anything as they went through, falling at first the way a bird dips in flight, then rising as the dark wind caught them and carried them higher and higher across the street and the buildings and the heights of the city toward the enormous moon, away and away into the farthest reaches of the night, where no one would ever find them.

That was how it was going to be.

Their earthly bodies would of course fall into the street below, and there'd be a funeral and everything, a big one for her because she was so rich, and just digging a hole for him in that—in that—in that place where they'd kept him once, but that didn't matter because *they* wouldn't really be there—*they* would be flying higher and higher, drawn upward by the moon's celestial light to find their destiny.

That was how it was going to be.

—— 23 ——

THE BROOM HANDLE STARTED TO split.

She could see the white crack widening, where the paint was flaking away. It wasn't strong enough, and if she went on forcing it like this it would snap, and he'd hear it.

He was in the shower.

This was how near she had come to accepting the inevitability of death: ten minutes ago, he'd said he was going to shower and change, and she'd just said fine, she'd go into the kitchen and see what they could have for dinner; and it wasn't until she was standing in front of the refrigerator that she realized this was the one blocking the back door, the door to escape, and to life.

She should have hurried here; it would have saved seconds, and her life might depend on seconds: on how far she could get before he came.

She was shaking all over, but trying not to do anything too fast. Time was very much of the essence, but if she went too fast she could knock something over or break something and make a noise and bring him running. He could be running right now toward the kitchen, but she didn't have to think about that. He too had accepted the inevitability of her death, or believed she wasn't strong enough to move either the box ottoman or the refrigerator. Probably he was right, but she had to find out.

She couldn't hear the shower; the bathroom he was in

was a long way off—ten or fifteen seconds at a fast run along the corridors—and the walls in this place were like in a château; so there wouldn't be a chance to put the broom or whatever back in the closet before he came, when he came, if he came. Suddenly he'd be here.

Time was running out—toward what? Toward a few last hours imprisoned here with a homicidal maniac and a bloody death, or toward years and years of life still ahead of her, with the terror of these two short days fading in her memory like an old photograph? The difference was paralyzing, and that was going to hamper her movements if she couldn't shake it off. What she had to do was simple enough: lever the fridge clear and open the door and go across the lobby into the elevator and press the button for the ground floor and give thanks, all the way down, give thanks for life. But the fact that so much depended on doing these simple things was numbing her mind. It was like walking along a low wall in the garden: you were perfectly surefooted, even when you looked down, because there was the grass and you could jump without hurting yourself; but if you had to walk along a plinth at the top of a building you'd never make it: your legs would turn to jelly and you'd go pitching over, like someone had pushed you.

She got out the vacuum cleaner, which had a metal handle, and began levering with that. She had to believe that this was the wall in the garden, so her hands would grow steady. But the idea of falling was on her mind, because he'd talked about it today. They'd done a lot of talking, today; she'd asked him about himself, and his quiet voice was still in her mind as she worked at the refrigerator.

"I've been in it off and on. I mean I haven't always been in window cleaning." With his slow and attractive smile—"But you don't want to know about things like that."

"Why not?"

They were in the music room, with the pale October sunlight in the windows; motes of dust floated in it, like satellites in a microscopic universe, as she sorted through the sheets of music by the piano.

"Well Jesus," he said, "I mean—window cleaning!"

"If someone like you didn't do it, it'd get darker and darker inside all the buildings, till the sunlight went out. It'd be like the end of the world creeping into the city."

He swung around to look at the windows. "Gee, you make it sound so dramatic!"

"Besides," she said, finding the Grieg album, "it isn't everyone who has the guts to be a human fly."

He came over to the piano and sat on the floor with his legs crossed, looking up at her. "Oh, I don't mind heights. They don't bother me. It's only when I'm high up somewhere that I feel—I mean I can do things that—" She saw the intelligence leaving his eyes, until they had that mindless gaze of the dog, and she had to look away, with a shiver going down her spine. "—I can't really explain it," he went on, and his voice was hushed. "When I'm someplace up high, that's where—that's where it all is. Everything. I mean it's the—answer to everything. You know?"

She watched the motes of dust moving on their cosmic pathways across the strings of the great harp standing against the wall, afraid to look back at him, into his dog's eyes; she looked down, instead, reading the words *The Tragic Overture* and trying to think what they meant.

"Yes," she said.

"But some guys don't like heights. They have to work with it. They have to make themselves go up there." She heard the change of tone as his mind turned from its dark side into the light again.

"That must be scary," she said, and looked at him full

in the eyes, letting out a breath as she saw they were normal again.

"Oh, it's scary all right. There was a guy who—are you okay?"

"Am I—?"

"You looked—"

"I'm fine. I was just thinking, you know, how scary it must be when—"

"Oh, sure, yeah. There was one guy—his name was Jack Santano—and he was one of those who have to make themselves go up there. He needed the job, see. But one day he was up there, forty-two stories above the street—it was over on the Upper West Side—and he suddenly flipped. You know?"

"You mean he—"

"Psyched out. He burned out his marbles, okay? And they sent me up there to bring him down. It was the first time I'd had to do it, and I was pretty scared myself. They knew what had happened to him because one of the other guys could see him clinging there to the scaffolding, white as a sheet and not moving anymore. It's kind of like dying." He gave a shrug suddenly. "Hey, listen, you don't want to hear about things like that. Play me something. You promised you'd play me—"

"I will, in a minute. But I want to hear about how you brought him down. You—you fascinate me, when you talk about yourself."

He stared up at her with his gray eyes wide. "I *fascinate* you? Jesus, do you know what that means to me, Tina?" She was sitting on the piano stool, and he shifted his position, moving forward and kneeling in front of her and laying his head on her thigh. "If you weren't in this world," he said slowly, "I don't know what I'd do. I'd know you were somewhere. There'd be a kind of—you know—a vibration in the air, or a kind of light moving, just on the other side of where I could see, or the echo of your voice, even though I wouldn't hear your voice itself, you know what I'm trying to say?''

She stroked his head, thrusting her fingers through the strong thick hair, moving them gently across the scalp, across the skull that held the madness that she was soon to die of, as if with her fingers alone she could draw it away.

"You're trying to say how much you love me," she said, "and not doing a bad job." But she didn't want to think about it; his love was need: he needed her so much that tonight when the full moon rose he was going to kill her, so that no one else could ever take her away from him. That wasn't so insane, when you thought about it; there was a certain basic logic in play, straight out of Greek drama. "Tell me about Jack—Jack who?"

"Uh?" He lifted his head. "Right. Jack Santano." He sat back on his haunches again, looking up at her like a small boy who'd been asked to recite. "Yeah, he was psyched right out of his skull up there, you know? When I got to him—I went up in what we call a boatswain's chair, it's a kind of one-man stage, a kind of cradle on ropes, see—when I got to him, he was clinging onto that scaffolding like his hands had turned into a vise. I spoke to him, but he didn't even hear—he was way out someplace, scared right out of his mind. You know what? I had to use a screwdriver to prize his fingers off the tubing. The scaffolding was made of iron tubing, like it usually is, and you can really get a good grip on it. It was like he'd, you know, died, and rigor mortis had set in. He didn't speak to me—he didn't even know I was there. He was in what they call a cata—okay—a catatonic fit, like a muscle spasm, a defense mechanism, really: when your mind switches off, your body knows how to survive, how to save itself, by gripping on like hell until someone comes."

Watching his open face, hearing his eagerness to explain,

to make it interesting for her, she wondered why her mind hadn't switched off yet, and if it did, what means her body would choose to survive, to save itself.

"How did you get him down?" she asked him.

"In the boatswain's chair. I just sat him in there and hit the button and went down with him. He's okay now; I see him from time to time; but he doesn't work heights anymore. We get guys like that—they quit. I can see why. Some guys try and brave it out, get over their fear; that's dangerous; some of them go down the hole that way. I've seen it."

"Go down—?"

"That's what we call it—means to fall off the scaffolding or whatever it is you're working on. Someone says, what happened to Bob? And someone else says, oh, he went down the hole. That's awful, I mean we all feel it. They don't scream, you know? They don't make any noise. For a while, when you see them suddenly in the air like that, they look like they're flying, not falling, because usually their arms and legs open out, and then they—they kind of tilt over and—and you're thinking *oh Jesus Christ what have I—what have I—*"

He shut his eyes and sat there rocking on his haunches, gripping his feet with his hands while his face slowly lost its color and she stared at him, suddenly knowing there was something here she ought to understand, something going on in his sick mind that had to do with herself. But she couldn't connect the *what have I* part of it with the rest, unless . . . okay, he'd *killed* Jack Santano, made him fall in some way, and this was the story he'd made up and had to tell people . . . this was the confessional . . .

"Yes, Joe," she said, "what have I—?"

She waited, but he didn't say anything; he went on rocking his body, his eyes clenched shut and his face bloodless, his breath held for seconds on end and then releas-

267

ing with a shudder as he brought Jack down . . . or pushed
Jack down . . . while the dust floated gold in the sunlight
and a page of the music album dipped to the slight movement of air from the conditioner vents and she felt the
pulse beating fast at the side of her neck because she had
to ask him, had to know.

"What happened to him?"

He said nothing.

"What really happened to Jack?"

His eyes came open, and she found herself looking into
desolation. "Jack?" he said. "He's okay. Jack's okay.
But play something for me, will you? You said you'd play
the piano for me . . . and I don't want to talk . . . anymore."

The refrigerator was moving.

It made some noise, but not a lot. Every time it moved,
she pushed the handle of the vacuum cleaner farther into
the gap, heaving on it again.

She didn't know how long she'd been in here; it seemed
like an hour; it was probably five minutes. She'd begun
sweating, though her skin felt deathly cold; once she had
stopped work to get her breath, and lost a second or two of
vital time. What were the equations governing this absurd
struggle with the refrigerator? She had lost time, to recover
strength; but if she had saved that amount of time, would
the necessary amount of strength still be available? If she
could switch off her mind, would her body work these
things out for her, as Joe had said, in the interests of its
survival?

She pushed the handle in deeper and heaved again, and
the huge refrigerator moved another inch. She could see
the whole width of the door now, with its thick white
paneling and the dark blob of the observation lens in the
middle; the handle was this side, otherwise she couldn't
have used a lever: the other side of the fridge was close to

the wall, with no room to maneuver. There was enough space now for her to open the door a few inches but there wasn't any point: she needed a couple of inches more to slip through, and if she opened it now there wouldn't be anything to lever against.

Don't come now, Joe.

If you love me, don't come now. I'm too close now, and there's a chance. Don't take it away at the last minute: I couldn't bear that; I'd go mad, and then there'd be two of us, two raving lunatics running around this rather comfortable apartment tearing their hair and filling the place with wild laughter . . . *dear God don't let him come, don't let him come now and find me here* . . .

White paint flaked off the door as the end of the handle bit into it, flexing badly. There'd be no warning if it flexed too far; it would just fold in two. But there was enough room now for her to force her body between the door and the fridge, and if the handle broke she could try using her body as a lever; there was a lot of wavy tubing at the back and there was heat coming off it—this was the first time she'd seen the back of a refrigerator, a big day for her, she was learning things about refrigerators and Jack Santano and suicide pacts: he'd talked a lot about suicide pacts while they were lying in the shallows of the pool at some time in the long afternoon, with small plates of caviar and a bottle of rosé; it had been quite romantic, except that she always found the idea of suicide rather frightening.

Heave, and go on heaving. Give it all you've got.

The refrigerator shifted another inch and then the handle broke and she fell backwards, losing her balance and hitting the floor with half the handle still in her grip and the cable tugging. It had made a noise but there was nothing she could do about that; she got up with her shoulder burning and forced her body between the fridge and the door and began pushing with her hands, arching

her back as the sweat ran into her eyes and she shut them
and let them stream, pushing and feeling the thing move,
pushing again and pushing with the strength of a trapped
animal.

"It was beautiful," he said.

The water lapped at their bodies.

"Romantic, anyway. I'm not sure about beautiful."

"Well, okay, sure, it's sad for people to die." He
spread some caviar on the thin dry toast. "But I mean it
was what they wanted to do. It said everything in the note.
I can remember most of the words. It said something like,
*We love each other too much ever to be parted, and this is
the way we want to go. Do not feel sad for us.* I read it in
the paper, and took a cutting and kept it on me for a long
time. I was very—you know—I guess you could say moved
by the whole thing, touched by it. Wouldn't you be?"

"Yes, I would." It was all she could think of saying,
because it was really a one-sided conversation: he was
talking about her own death, and maybe his, while she was
meant to be discussing those other people, in another time.

"She was going to die anyway," he said. "She had
leukemia. And he didn't have any of his folks left, or not
close ones, no mother or father. I mean there wasn't
anyone he could hurt. It was just that he couldn't live
without her."

He poured some wine for her, and then for himself,
watching her with the water's reflection flickering across
and across his face, waiting for her to say something.

"If it was what they both wanted to happen, okay." She
put her plate onto the top marble step and concentrated on
the wine; she'd learned not to eat when she was thinking
about dying.

"Right, they both wanted it. I remember the end of the
message they left. It said: *And now we shall forever be*

one, going together into the new world that is waiting for us. I thought that was a beautiful way of saying it.''

"Very poetic."

"Right. Poetic."

"But I—"

In a moment he said: "Yes?"

"Nothing." She sipped her wine, savoring the chill kiss of the glass, feeling the small waves touching at her body, exquisitely aware of life. And she was damned if she was going to talk to him about it again—about her death, about his dealing it. She'd tried that: she'd made what she thought was a breakthrough, getting him to talk about it; but it hadn't done any good. If she told him now that she didn't want to go through a beautiful and poetic suicide pact, he'd just look away and tell her she mustn't think about such things.

He was waiting for her to go on, but not looking at her directly; he was facing away a little with only his eyes turned towards her, watching her at the edge of his vision. It frightened her. His mind, like his eyes, was only half with her, and half with the sick and deathly dream he'd been talking about.

We think he killed five people, one of the police officers had told her over the phone. *He shot two men to death,* her father had said, *because they were trying to protect you.*

It was hard to believe, because he was always so gentle with her. The greater part of what he called his love for her was obsessive need, yet there was kindness too: he wished her no harm. The idea was crazy, but then he himself was crazy; there were two people in him: a man and a child, a child-monster. Not so hard, perhaps, to believe he'd done those things, as she watched the water reflections fanning their light across his secretive eyes. He'd shown no mercy to those others, and he'd show none to her when her time came.

*   *   *

The refrigerator shifted another inch.

Her shoulder had been bruised by her fall, and now it was throbbing as she braced it against the back plate where the wavy tubing was and pushed with her hands flat on the door.

Sweat dripped from her face and soaked into the white silk Jonal she'd put on for the evening: he liked her in white, she'd remembered his saying. Pausing to rest, she listened to her breath sawing in her throat, and thought how animal the sound was, raw and primitive; she could feel the beating of her heart everywhere: her whole body pulsed with urgent life.

Pushing again, forcing her shoulder against the refrigerator until the flesh burned, she moved the thing another inch, and for the first time tried the door, turning the scalloped brass handle and hearing the lock click free. The door swung back, and she tried to squeeze through, pulling her breasts sideways to protect them from the door's sharp edge, forcing her buttocks through the narrow gap and for a moment thinking she could make it; then she got stuck, and couldn't move either way until she reached with one hand for the refrigerator and pulled herself back into the kitchen.

Another inch would do it. She closed the door, though she found this extraordinarily difficult: on the other side was freedom, and life—she'd actually seen part of the service elevator out there, with a man's shoe jammed between the doors to keep them apart. When she braced herself against the back of the refrigerator her arm felt sticky, and slid across the back plate until it lodged against the tubing. With her hands on the door she pushed hard, without making progress; it wasn't till the third push that the fridge shifted again, and quite a lot this time, more than an inch.

She opened the door again and squeezed through, noticing the streaks of blood across the back plate where her arm had been, and ignoring it. She was through the gap now and standing suddenly in the lobby, crying with relief as she lurched across to the elevator.

"Tina!" his voice came from behind her. *"Tina! No!"*

24

"THIS IS NURSE FINLEY."

"I asked to talk to Dr. Marcellino."

"He's busy right now. Can I give him a message?"

"This is Nick Valenti."

"Oh. Hold on a moment, will you?"

Watching the silhouette of the sharpshooter against the glow of the building opposite, Nick decided that if the doc said he had to be there, then he'd be there.

Al Groot was crouched against the foot of the water tower, throwing peanuts into his mouth. "Tell her hi for me, Nick."

"Sure. What time's moonrise?"

"I'll check." He got up and ambled away.

The sharpshooter moved his position, easing the rifle an inch along the parapet, settling his elbows on the hessian pads. Watching him, Nick thought: I'm beginning not to care. I'm beginning not to care whether Mundy convinces Dakers to go in, send Steziak in, or tell this goon to loose off a few hundred rounds just to give the press something to talk about. And that's dangerous, beginning not to care.

"This is Marcellino."

"Nick. I want—"

"Sure. How are things over there, Nick?"

"Nothing's happening."

"Half the people here are glued in front of the TV. They want to see you bringing Tina out safe."

"Sure." He couldn't think of anything else to say.

"Okay," Marcellino told him after a moment, "we'll be taking Karen into the ops room in just a few minutes now. Nothing's changed, Nick. We have high hopes."

"For Karen?" His heart stopped. The night stopped.

"Huh? Karen's going to be fine. No problem."

Nick let out his breath. "High hopes for the kid. For the baby. You mean." He waited again.

"Right." There was the sound of metal clinking in the background, and a woman's voice, and a kind of thump, maybe a door closing. "Tell him I'll be right in there," Marcellino said, but not to him. "Who's scrubbing?" The woman's voice sounded again, and the clinking of metal faded down. "You there, Nick?"

"Yes."

"Okay, why don't you—"

"Should I be there, Doc?"

"Like I said before, it's up to you." There was a brief pause. "She's going to be fine. Karen. I guess there isn't much you can do here, at least for a while. Why don't you call me again in maybe an hour? I have to go now, Nick."

"Sure. Tell Maria I'll be along, okay?"

"I'll do that. And don't worry."

The line clicked, the dial tone came in and he listened to it for a while and then realized what the sound was, and put the phone down onto the cradle, and felt the terrible distance draw out between here and the clinic, until it was the other side of the world.

"You talk to her?"

"What?" Al Groot was crouching beside him. "No."

Al seemed to be waiting for something more than that, but he couldn't think of anything.

"That Marcellino," Al said in a moment, "he's the greatest."

"Right."

Al waited again, and then said: "Moonrise is at seven-fifty-three."

"Moonrise?"

"Yeah. It's at seven-fifty-three. That's official—I don't know where they take the sighting from, though. For him over there, it could be a few minutes either side. There's the Ritz Tower in that direction, and other buildings."

Nick put his palms against his face and drew them slowly down; then his fingertips began playing with the stubble on his jaw. "Seven-fifty-three. Okay."

"You think that's when he's going to do it?"

Nick looked at his watch, then across to the building opposite, at the curtained windows lit only by the glow from the street. "I was talking to McNeil. He thinks that's all Joe's been waiting for. The moonrise."

Al nodded. "You think it's our deadline?"

"For Christ's sake, Al, I don't know anything. I don't know anything. All I know is, in this life nothing's certain."

Police Commissioner Dakers chain-lit another cigarette and squashed out the stub and blew out smoke and looked at Mundy. "What time would that give us?"

"We can't be absolutely precise about it, sir, but from the sightings I've had taken, Steziak should see the top edge of the moon somewhere around eight o'clock, rising above the Findlay Gallery to the north of the Fuller Building. So that gives us a conservative forty minutes from now."

There were only the two of them in the small unfurnished office at the end of the corridor from the command post. Dakers had left Chief of Detectives Warner and the other officers at the post. This was to be his decision, and if there were going to be any blame thrown around afterwards for getting it wrong, he would take it exclusively.

He went to the window. There were no lights on in the penthouse, at least on this side. He could just make out the sharpshooters on the rooftops adjoining, and the reflection of a sign winking rhythmically in a lower window. There was almost no sound rising from the street; the nearest traffic was a block distant in each direction, and the crowds were very quiet now. A short time ago, something like a cheer had gone up and it made his skin crawl because it was just after he had made his decision to send Steziak in; for a moment he'd thought that somehow the news had got out by some kind of telepathy, from the inside of his head to the people down there. When your nerves were under stress, you became paranoid; you could believe in anything. Nobody down there knew the decision he'd made; only five people up here knew it, and they wouldn't talk. If Joe Dotson was given cause, in whatever way, to suspect that Steziak was going into Park Tower a half-hour from now, Steziak could get killed, and so could Tina.

They could get killed anyway. His decision could be proved wrong. Maybe he shouldn't have listened to Dan Warner . . . "The longer this goes on, the more I think we'll finally have to use force." Or to Lieutenant McNeil . . . "I'm afraid of the risk we're taking, sir, in just doing nothing. I'd back Valenti, any day, but Dotson's liable at any time to plunge into a manic state after behaving reasonably for so long under the stress of knowing we're here. Also I have the feeling he's simply waiting till he sees the full moon rising. It's been a feature in all the other deaths." Or of course to Captain Mundy . . . "I see it this way, sir. If we had no way of getting in there, we'd feel totally helpless. But we're not. There is a way in there, and I think we should take it."

Standing at the window, Dakers went over their arguments again, trying to judge how much these talented and experienced officers were being influenced by simple frustration, by their professional credo that to do something was better than to do nothing; but it was impossible to know. Aside from the inevitable background mood of frustration, their arguments hadn't been emotional. Mundy's plan was detailed and logical; Steziak had proved himself more than capable of carrying it out. The only officer at the command post he hadn't asked for advice was Lieutenant Valenti; all attempts at negotiation had failed, and out of respect for the man's feelings he'd given instructions that the chief negotiator would not be informed of his decision.

He turned away from the window. "All right. Send Steziak in. Tell him to shoot to kill if he has to. His objective is to save the hostage."

Nick Valenti was sitting alone under the water tower on the roof when Al Groot, his backup negotiator, came through the staircase door and loped across to him in the starlight. For a couple of minutes he stood against the tower support, looking around him with his hands tucked into his reefer jacket. Cold air moved past his face, smelling of the ocean towards the east. The only people up here, except for Nick, were the three sharpshooters and an FBI liaison officer, ranged along the parapet facing Park Tower.

Closer to where Al was standing, Nick looked suddenly isolated, abandoned, crouched there under his plaid rug and surrounded by his four silent telephones.

"You okay, Nick?"

"Uh? Sure. Why don't you take a break, Al, while things are quiet?"

"Yeah . . . well. You need anything?"

"Nope."

278

"Cigarettes, or anything?"

Nick looked up at him in the faint light. "What's up?"

"Uh?" Al gazed across at the Park Tower building with its dark windows, then dropped slowly to his haunches, pulling out a pack of Kools to give his hands something to do. "Nick, you're not going to like this. The way I hear it, Mundy's going to send Art Steziak in to—" He broke off as the rhythmic throb of a helicopter faded in from the north, across Central Park. They turned their heads to listen.

"Steziak?" Nick said softly.

"We know Mundy, right? All he can think about is—"

"*Without telling me first?*"

Al felt himself backing off as he heard the rage in the man's voice. "I guess there wasn't time, Nick, or—" He broke off again as the sound of the chopper grew loud above the buildings. Nick was on his feet now, and they watched as the Bell Jetranger slowed and hovered, while a single figure began dropping from the belly of the machine on a cable, to land on the roof of Park Tower.

"Without telling me first," Nick said again, and this time his voice was so quiet against the throbbing of the chopper that Al barely heard it.

"Huh?"

Nick didn't answer, but crouched suddenly and picked up the hotline phone.

As the air became still after the gusting downdraft of the rotor blades, Captain Steziak bent to tighten his shoelaces for the last time, then straightened up and swung the short-barreled repeater rifle across his back and settled the strap and ammo belt. At his hip there was holstered a Smith and Wesson .44 Magnum, and that was what he would probably use, if he had to use anything. At his other hip was the wallet containing the glass cutter and grip tape for breaching the window.

At 7:41 he swung himself onto the cleaner's stage, just as Marvin Rico had briefed him, pressed the winch-motor button and felt the slight jerk as the stage began lowering, six hundred and ninety feet above the street.

From the shoreline of the Bronx, ten miles away, the rim of the full moon had just begun showing across the waters of Long Island Sound.

25

SHE COULDN'T KEEP STILL. SHE wasn't trying to run away because there was nowhere to run to, but she kept on swaying to one side and then to the other while he held her wrists to stop her falling down. It worried him. It looked like she was sick or something, her eyes shut tight and the moaning noise she was making all the time.

"Tina," he said, but she kind of threw her head back till her long hair was hanging down behind her, and the moaning noise went on. "Tina, you're okay now. I'm with you now." She was in a beautiful white dress, but there was blood on it, from her arm; she'd hurt herself, maybe when she was moving the—moving the fridge away—the fridge away from the—door but she didn't have to do things like that, she mustn't run away from him now. She didn't know how much he loved her. "Tina, I won't let anything happen to you. I love you. I love you, Tina."

When she opened her eyes she just stared around and then at him, like she didn't know where she was, didn't recognize him. She was so incredibly beautiful, even when she was staring at him this way like she didn't even know him.

"I'm Joe," he said. "I'm Joe."

She gave a kind of shudder, like she suddenly remembered him but it made her scared or something, and that really got through to him, because there was nobody in this whole world who loved her more than he did. Then she was pulling away from him and her wrists slipped right out of his hands and she ran blindly towards the elevator and almost reached it before he dragged her back; then she got free again and ran around the lobby from wall to wall with her eyes shut and her hands reaching out to stop herself hitting the walls, and now she was screaming, throwing her head back and screaming so loud that it scared him—*"Oh, my God, can't anyone help me? Can't anyone help me? I don't want to die!"*

It was terrible, and now she was running down the lobby past the staircase door where the dynamite was stacked, trying to reach the other elevator, the one opposite the front door, and he had to run after her as fast as he could, and he was a good runner, he'd been a good fast runner since he was at grade school, before—before the balcony—before it all happened that—day when—*"Tina,"* he called out to her, *"Tina, you mustn't leave me!"* But she didn't answer; she was running past where the dynamite was stacked, with her long hair flying out and her hands reaching in front of her like that, like her eyes were still shut and she didn't want to hit things—*"Tina,"* he was screaming, *"you mustn't go near the balcony—Tina come back, you mustn't—"*

Then he caught up with her and his arms went around her and her hair was in his face, scented and warm as she swung her head from side to side and tried to fight him off, because she didn't understand how much he loved her, didn't understand that if she left him he'd have to die. "It's okay now, Tina, it's okay. I'm here now."

It sounded almost like she was laughing now instead of screaming, laughing about something, but it was a terrible sound and it scared him, it was like she was losing her reason. He held her tight, but as gently as he could, not to hurt her, because even the thought of hurting her made him feel sick.

"I'm here, Tina," he kept telling her, trying to reassure her, "you're okay now, I'm here." But she went on laughing in that terrible way, and started struggling again, so he just picked her up and carried her back through the doorway into the kitchen, squeezing her through and putting her down and letting her run off while he slammed the door shut and locked it and heaved the fridge against it: it was okay for her to run now, there was nowhere she could go.

When he looked for her he found her lying on the floor in the big gold room, like she'd flung herself down with her face on the carpet and her beautiful white dress kind of swirling all around her, reminding him of a water lily. She was just crying quietly now, and he bent down and stroked her hair, whispering to her, whispering to her all the time, desperate for her to know she was okay now, he was with her and everything was okay again.

But there was this pounding going on inside him, like his heart was filling the whole of his chest, and he was starting to get shivery, like it sometimes happened, with his whole body shaking and his skin going cold. He'd had the feeling before, like when he'd brought the roses here for her that time and those—and those two—those two guys had stopped him from—it had—happened before but he never could get used to it, it wasn't a nice feeling at all, it was like when you were a kid, a very small kid, and got lost in a crowd and although there were lots of people around it was like the whole world had gone away and you couldn't move, you couldn't run after it and catch up, you just had to stay there and see the world going away and getting smaller and smaller . . . it wasn't a nice feeling at all and he hated it, because nobody could help him with it, he was all alone.

But Tina was more important than he was, and he went on whispering to her, saying it was okay now; and after a time she stopped crying, and sometime after that she opened her eyes and turned her head to look up at him; her eyes were red and running with tears but she recognized him now, and he didn't feel alone anymore. She was watching him in a way he understood: she wanted to say things to him, but didn't feel it would do any good because she wouldn't be getting through to him. This wasn't a nice feeling either; it was like he was two people and she wanted to talk to one of them, but the other one wouldn't understand.

"Joe?"

"Poor Tina."

She went on looking at him in that way, like he was a friend, but a stranger, and then said with a funny little smile, "Yes. Poor Tina."

"I'm with you, Tina."

"Yes. You're with me."

"I love you so much."

"I know." She lifted a hand to pull the hair away from her face, and he helped her, putting his fingers through her soft warm hair and combing it back, while the cold on his skin went away, and the shaking stopped. But he knew there was still something wrong with him; when he got this terrible feeling, and it went away, it didn't mean he was completely okay again.

So long as you're okay, Joe.

Tina sat up, letting her head fall back again as she shut her eyes and let out a long slow breath, like she'd just come through a storm or something; then she opened her eyes and looked at him for what seemed a long time, like she was thinking about him very deeply; then she said: "My God, I need a drink, Joe. How about you?"

He got onto his feet at once. He was her slave; he was hers to command. "A drink. Sure."

"Brandy."

"Right." The bar was along one side of the room. "You like the one in the black bottle—right?"

"Remy Martin."

"Right." He found the bottle and got two glasses from underneath the long gold bar; he didn't feel like a drink himself, but to share anything with Tina was—was kind of like being a part of her, tasting the same taste; and it was friendly; having a drink with someone, you know everything's okay, because it's relaxing and you're not bothered about what the time is or anything; you can slow down.

He needed to feel this way, right now. There was going to be moonlight soon, and he could already feel a kind of tugging, like something was trying to pull him off his feet and make him—make him do things—things that he mustn't ever do again, because—the thing was not to think about it. Have a drink, forget it. I'm okay. So long as you're okay, Joe. Sure. Sure I'm okay.

The sweat was running down his sides and he tried not to notice it. Everything would be okay after they'd had a drink together. Then later, when the moon came, they'd look at it for a while, her hand in his; and then he'd smile down at her and ask her if she was excited, and she'd say yes, and he'd tell her they were going where nobody would ever be able to find them.

He picked up the two drinks, and noticed the heavy ornament standing near the end of the bar, the swollen woman with the small head. But that was for later, when the moon came. He brought the drinks over to where Tina was standing with the gun pointing at him.

*   *   *

He stopped, looking down at it.

She held it in front of her, the way she'd seen it done on the firing range, with both hands steadying it and her eye along the sights. She had set the safety catch to fire. Her hands were trembling a little, but that was to be expected.

"Joe," she told him, "stay just like that. Don't move, please."

The cognac was slopping slightly in the glasses, because he'd halted so abruptly. His eyes were inquiring, that was all; if she could judge anything from his expression, he was unsure whether she had a gun or whether he was just imagining it.

"Don't do that," he said, and put the two glasses onto the coffee table carefully.

"Joe. Don't come near me." She was worried by his calm. Maybe he wasn't taking her seriously. He would have to.

She moved toward the telephone, under the gold paneled mirror, keeping the gun aimed at him; but he moved too, coming towards her.

"Tina," he said, "that's dangerous. Give it to me."

He stopped, his eyes on the gun. He was maybe fifteen feet away, but she knew he could move very fast, like a cat. Even from that distance he could reach her before she could reach the phone, but not if she fired.

"The next time you move," she said, "I'm going to shoot." His face was perfectly blank now, and she had no means of knowing whether she was talking to a sane man; he'd switched so often from sanity to madness and back. But he was staring all the time at the gun; he knew what it was, and what it could do. It was heavy, the way she was holding it out in front of her; her arms were beginning to tire. The sweat on her palms was producing a slippery film against the chased steel of the gun, and it didn't feel secure in her grip anymore. So she would have to reach the phone quickly now, while she had complete command and could fire effectively if she had to. She moved again.

He moved too.

"Joe."

He came on another couple of paces and stopped, still watching the gun. It was aimed at his chest, slightly to the left of center. In the upper field of her vision she could see his face. It still didn't have any expression she could read. Wary, perhaps. A little wary.

"Give it to me," he said quietly, and held out his hand. At the movement of his hand she caught her breath and gripped the gun harder, pulling on the first spring of the trigger without meaning to. She was trembling badly now.

"Joe, if I don't get help, you're going to kill me. But I don't want to die. And I don't intend to. I intend to shoot, if you make me. Don't make me."

His face still didn't change; it was almost blank, but not with the look of the mindless dog. The wariness had gone now; he was thinking, reasoning; and that was dangerous.

"Tina, you could hurt yourself. And I can't let anything hurt you. I love you, Tina."

"I know. But if you move any closer I'm going to kill you."

He'd put on a black silk kimono for the evening, from one of the guest wardrobes. He'd been very particular about that, all the time he'd been here; as soon as he'd learned there were things to wear in the guestrooms, he'd taken off Tom's shirt and put it into the laundry room and put on a bathrobe, and tonight the kimono. It had gold dragons embroidered on the front, one on each side, facing each other with their long tongues of fire almost touching, where the V of the material came to a point. She was trying to keep the sights of the gun lined up with the tongue of the dragon on the right, from her viewpoint, over Joe's heart; but her hands were shaking now and it wouldn't be long before she had to shoot, if she couldn't reach the phone.

"Please, Tina. You don't understand guns. I don't want you hurt."

There had been the time, during the hours since she'd talked to her father, when she'd had to work out a few things. Perhaps Joe would never kill her, however long he kept her imprisoned here; perhaps, in the end, he would simply give up, in one of his sane periods, and call the police and ask them to come and get him. And therefore, if she decided to go to the safe and find the gun and hide it where she could get at it quickly if she wanted to, it would end in her killing Joe, and for nothing. And she'd never know. That would be the most appalling thing she'd have to live with, afterwards: never to know whether she had killed this charming man with his sick mind, instead of letting him, in a day or two, simply open the door for her and show her into the elevator with that strange instinctive gallantry that he had.

But then of course there was the other side. It was quite likely that before long the police would break their way in here and find them together with their eyes open and staring and their flesh cold and looking just like all the other bodies the police routinely came upon in the midst of this city's life. And she didn't want that to happen, not because of the usual reasons like the fear of dying and the frustration of being stopped right in the middle of all the things you were busy doing—though those reasons were of course there—but because she didn't want to be found by strangers in the company of a strange sick man who had decided to kill her and leave her untidy, perhaps with her legs spread out as if in a ghastly invitation to sex, or blood all over her, and spittle because of her last long screaming, perhaps with her briefs stained because of the incontinence that sometimes happens with terror (it had actually started, out there in the lobby when she'd heard his voice behind her, but she'd managed to stop it again). Because, then, of the humiliation the whole messy thing would entail. More than anything, she didn't want that.

The gun sights were wavering now across and across the gold dragon, and she tried to steady herself. A vibration was coming into the silence now: it sounded like a helicopter passing over the building. She didn't let it distract her: she must concentrate, totally.

"Stay right there," she said. "Don't move again."

She was halfway to the telephone when he took three or four steps very quickly, light on his feet, and her finger pulled back on the trigger again and for an instant she felt surprise, thinking that with the trigger pulled back this far the gun would have to fire.

He was six feet away now, and she could see the fine gold stitches of the dragon on his kimono and the hairs on his chest in the V of the black silk. She mustn't let him come any closer than this.

"It's your last chance, Joe. Do you understand what I'm saying?"

He didn't answer. She was watching the tongue of the dragon through the gun sights but was more aware of his steady gray eyes. If he were in a mood sane enough, he would know he was close to death. Perhaps that was it: he wanted a way out.

The sweat from her forehead was beginning to run into her left eye, trickling down the bridge of her nose and itching unbearably. The strain on her arms was so bad now that the sights were moving from the tip of the dragon's tongue to its bright gold eye. There was no more pressure left on the trigger spring: as she concentrated on her finger, letting her brain get information, she could feel the hard resistance against the trigger, the resistance of the second spring.

"Joe. I'm going to move now, and pick up the phone. If you move too, I'll shoot you dead. Do you understand what I mean?"

He had to understand what she was saying, or she'd have to live with that, too, afterwards. In the Antarctic, on the expedition, there'd been a baby seal badly injured by the screw of their boat, and it had lain on the ice floe for a long time, with its blood turning the ice pink in a spreading stain until one of the crew, a man with a harelip and a terrific fund of jokes, was able to jump from the boat with his revolver to put the poor thing out of its suffering. She'd realized what the man—his name was Stan something— was going to do, but she was too horrified to turn away in time, and she'd seen him raise the gun and fire into the seal's head. She had seen it's bright black eye, and the expression in it. Seals didn't think with very much sophistication, of course, and she'd probably let her imagination take off as the bang of the gun had sounded, but it had seemed as if the seal were saying, I thought you were going to help me, not do this.

It didn't understand.

"Joe, do you know what I'm saying? If you move, I shall shoot you dead."

He still didn't say anything, but just went on watching the gun with his steady eyes. Perhaps he thought she couldn't do it.

Is that Daddy?

Yes. And you must listen to me. You will have to find the courage to shoot that man, if you have to.

The gun sights wavered across the dragon.

He's not a bad man, Daddy. He's not much more than a child.

He shot two men to death in there. So what did they die for, if you won't save yourself now?

She wished his eyes weren't so steady. If he had his

back to her, it would be almost easy. If the baby seal hadn't been watching Stan, she probably wouldn't even have remembered it.

I want to save him, too.

Then this is how you can do it. If he isn't brought under control, he's liable to take his own life, after taking yours.

She was having to squint with her left eye, because of the sweat; that didn't matter because she was sighting with her right eye, but the sweat was stinging intolerably and she was going to have to take her left hand from the gun to wipe her face.

You know me, Daddy. I can't even kill a fly.

But she didn't have to kill this poor creature; she just had to control him. "Joe. Don't move. If you love me, don't move."

She stepped back toward the telephone but he came after her, standing so close that he could have hit the gun out of her hand. He wasn't looking at the gun anymore, but at her face.

"Tina, there's something wrong with me." His eyes were on hers, questioning, trying to understand. "But you don't have to shoot me for it."

She crumpled without warning, squeezing her eyes shut as the first sob broke and he prized the gun from her loosened fingers, bringing her into his arms as the telephone began ringing.

26

THE RINGING WENT ON, IN the earpiece of the hotline phone in Nick Valenti's hand, over the amplifiers in the command posts and the mobile headquarters van in the Park Tower area, and in the complex of offices and operation rooms at One Police Plaza, four miles away.

There had been fifteen rings. Nick had been counting them. Beside him Al Groot was crouched on his haunches, peeling a wad of gum, feeling angry and embarrassed; it was the first time the Hostage Negotiating Team had failed to resolve a standoff in more than two years; and any minute that bastard Mundy was going to come in loud and clear on the command phone and tell Nick to hang up on the hotline. Steziak would be going in about now, and they wouldn't want anybody rocking the boat.

Nick sat humped under his rug, watching the building opposite. The lighting pattern hadn't changed. There had to be at least one phone jacked in over there, or he wouldn't be getting the ringing tone; but that didn't mean anybody had to answer.

Twenty. Twenty rings. He'd get a blast from Mundy, anytime now, but that was okay. He didn't officially know that Steziak was going in: they should have told him.

The ringing stopped.

"Hello?"

Nick stopped breathing. He hadn't recognized the voice;

292

it could be someone picking up one of the hotline phones by mistake. In a moment he said:

"Hello. Who's that?"

"Joe." The voice sounded very low-key, very subdued. That was why he hadn't recognized it. Joe had sounded pretty chipper, the last time they'd talked. "Didn't you call me?"

"Sure. This is Nick. Remember me?"

Beside him, Al was staring into his face in the half-dark, screwing the chewing-gum wrapper into a pellet. There was nothing Mundy or anyone else could do now. When the hotline was open, that was it—everybody freeze. This call was going out all over the circuit, and in Mobile HQ the tapes had started rolling.

"Yes," Dotson's voice came, "I remember you. We talked before, right?"

"Right. How're you doing over there, Joe?"

There was a long pause. He didn't want to break into it; when they were thinking, you had to let them think; they didn't like being hustled. He sat breathing in the smell of the ocean on the breeze, and Al's spearmint.

"What was that helicopter doing?" Joe's voice came.

"Just passing over, I guess. It's gone now." Nick waited the silence out. It was a long one.

"There's something—" Joe's voice came uncertainly, and stopped again. "I need help."

"I'm right here," Nick said.

Al Groot couldn't hear enough of Dotson's voice because Nick had the phone hard against his ear, so he straightened up and went padding away to the stairhead door, going down two floors to the command post. Commissioner Dakers was still there, with Chief Warner and McNeil and Mr. Lindquist. Dakers was talking on one of the command phones.

"Where's Steziak right now?" He listened for a time

293

and then said: "Okay. Get him direct on his radio. Tell him to hold it. Hold everything until further orders—from me personally, nobody else. Advise Captain Mundy: he's to hold everything. We have Dotson on the hotline." He hung up and turned to listen to the voice coming over the amplifier.

"There's something wrong," Dotson said again.

"Then what we'll do," came Nick Valenti's easy tones, "is put it right. That's what I'm here for. So what's the problem, Joe?"

There was another silence, and they waited. Standing next to Lieutenant McNeil, Al Groot heard him say quietly to no one, "It sounds like he's done it." No one answered, or even understood. What McNeil didn't like was Dotson's subdued tone. He sounded out of his depth, just the way he would sound if he'd killed Tina St. Clair and didn't know what to do next.

"It's not easy to say," Dotson's voice came again. "I mean over the phone."

Valenti gave a pause now. "But you want to talk about it?"

"I guess. I—need, you know, right, to talk to someone."

A second went by. Two seconds. Then they heard Valenti: "So why don't I come on over, Joe?"

Commissioner Dakers turned a blank stare on Chief Warner. McNeil was suddenly picking at a nail. The shock went into Al Groot's nerves and he stood there thinking *Holy shit, it's a breakthrough.*

They were all looking at the gray metal amplifier.

"Why don't you what?" Dotson asked.

"Why don't I come on over. Then we can talk about it."

"Come on over?" Silence came in. "I don't want any people over here."

"No people, Joe. Just me." In the command post they

could hear Valenti swinging quietly into the spiel, not pausing to think now, not giving any impression he was uncertain or cautious or hesitant. "You can trust me, Joe, you know that. You know when you can trust somebody, just by his voice."

Every time Dotson spoke, it was after a pause. He was doing all the thinking, the hesitating.

"But you're the police."

"Right, Joe. I'm their chief negotiator. My job is to listen to people's problems. I've been doing it for—Jesus, I don't remember how long. My job is to help people. You know something? These police guys don't really understand me. I mean they want me to put on the uniform and all that, but they think I'm a kind of freak, because I trust people, and people trust me. And that's not the way they work, these other guys. What I really am, Joe, is just a guy like you. And hey, don't ever tell them what I just told you, okay? They'd fire me, and I need the money." He was laughing gently as he said it.

Al Groot was listening with his whole body absolutely motionless; he wasn't even chewing his gum anymore. All he was listening to was an exercise in hostage negotiation, but with Nick there was an added dimension. He was keeping strictly to the training manual, "going over" to the hostage-taker by minimizing the police involvement, even putting down his buddies for not understanding him; but he was taking the rules across new horizons, asking Joe to share a secret with him, a powerful secret that could get him fired if Joe ever talked. It couldn't be done, maybe, with anyone mentally stable, but the team never had to handle guys like that: the guys they worked with were stressed right out of their heads. They were always guys like Joe.

"I don't know," Joe said in a while. "I don't want you over here with guns and everything."

"Hey, Joe, you know what you just did? You hurt my feelings. I said you could trust me, okay? You know my name—it's Nick, remember?—but I guess you don't know too much about me, so I'll tell you something. When I give my word to anybody, that's it. I mean it's like you got it in big letters cut out of stone, it's something that doesn't break. I come over there to talk to you, and I come bare-handed and even bare-assed if you like." His tone had lightened again.

"I don't know, Nick."

Shit, man, Al Groot thought, *this is beautiful.* Glancing across at the commissioner, he tried to judge what he was thinking, but with Dakers it was seldom possible to do that; right now he was standing there watching the amplifier without any expression, like it was a time bomb.

"It's up to you, Joe, sure. You said you wanted to talk, and we can do that. I'm all yours, you know? You call the tune."

"I know that," Joe said; his tone was firmer now. "I call the tune, right?"

"Right. The only thing is, I've been waiting around for a chance to talk to you for—Jesus, how many days is it now, Joe, can you remember? And I could use some sleep, like say three weeks of it, you know what I mean? And I think if you and I could talk things over between us with nobody else around, I could wrap things up and go home."

More than ten seconds went by.

"I'd like to talk, Nick. But they could tell you to bring a gun with you."

"No way. That's out. If they tried that, I wouldn't go see you. I have your trust, Joe, and that's precious to me."

A long silence began, maybe ten seconds, fifteen. Nick didn't break it. He waited for Joe.

"You wouldn't bring a gun or anything, Nick?"

"I swear to God."

"Then come on over."

Commissioner Dakers turned away from the amplifier and saw Al Groot standing there. "Get Valenti down here right away."

"Yessir."

"What do you think, Dan?"

Chief Warner let out the breath he seemed to have been holding for minutes. "It's a big risk."

"You don't trust Dotson?"

"How far can you trust a homicidal maniac?"

"What do you think, McNeil?"

"I think she could be dead now, sir."

"Why?"

"He's admitting he needs help. I think it's because he's alone now, and out of his depth."

Dakers paced from the wall to the windows and back, looking at nobody now. "We have to go on assuming she's alive."

Valenti was suddenly in the room; he'd been already on his way down from the roof when Groot had met him.

"I think you're taking too much on," Dakers told him right away.

"It's my risk, sir."

"And my responsibility."

"Okay, sir. But if you're going to let me go over there, I've got to go right now. He's waiting. Any delay, and he'll suspect something, and we've had it."

Al Groot could hear the edge on his tone; maybe they all could, but he knew Nick better than the others here. If Dakers wouldn't let him take this final chance, he'd blow just like a volcano.

"He could have a firearm over there," Dakers said.

"We're sure there's some explosive against the staircase door. And he's a psychopathic killer." He looked into Valenti's dark obdurate eyes. "I'm giving you a chance to think twice."

"There's no time, sir. He's waiting."

Dakers stood looking down at him for a minute, taller by almost a foot, and felt dwarfed by the man, by the towering resolve he sensed in him. He was ready to take the risk on his own, but they'd all share the reward if he pulled it off: for this city to defuse a major standoff by peaceful means would bring it inestimable credit.

"All right, Valenti. But go armed."

"No way."

"Dammit, you can conceal a weapon easily enough."

"I've got his trust. He searches me and finds a weapon, he can go wild. So that isn't what scares me. What's starting to scare me is the delay. He knows how long it'll take me to get over there. He'll see me in the street: he's watching for me down there right now. There's a risk, sure, and I'm ready to take it. But the longer I stand here the bigger it's going to get. All I'm asking for is a fair chance."

In a moment Dakers gave a brief nod. "All right. Do what you can. And for God's sake, look after yourself."

Chief Warner had telephoned orders for a plainclothes escort of four men to hustle Valenti across the street, hoping to keep this new move secret; but he told them he had to go alone, since Dotson could be watching from the windows up there. There was no chance, in any case, of getting him to the Park Tower building without his being recognized. Two of the *Newsweek* team keeping vigil behind the ropes of the crowded press area identified the chief hostage negotiator despite his thick stubble and tousled hair, and within seconds the TV crews were flooding the scene with light and swinging their cameras to follow him as he made his way toward Park Tower, a small lone figure crossing the deserted strip of roadway between the cordons, his head down and his hands in the pockets of his plain dark blue windbreaker. A blizzard of flashlight swept over the scene as photographers pressed against the ropes, jostling each other as they tried to keep Valenti in focus.

"Hey, Nick—what's going on?"

"Is she still alive?"

"Gimme a mug shot, Nick!"

"Is Dotson giving up?"

He kept on walking.

Near the Park Tower steps on the NYPD press-liaison officer was trying to raise Mobile HQ for information, but the street was full of voices now and it was difficult to hear anything over his radio. With a dozen microphones thrust into his face he kept on trying, and a few minutes after Valenti disappeared into the Park Tower lobby he was calling out the information just as it came to him.

"The Hostage Negotiating Team has been in contact with Dotson over the hotline. Lieutenant Valenti offered to go across to talk with Dotson personally, and Dotson agreed. We don't know whether this is a real breakthrough, but we have all our fingers crossed. Lieutenant Valenti is going in alone and unarmed, in accordance with his promise to Dotson. The police department will be issuing a copy-printed handout as soon as possible."

Behind the cordon at the intersection of Fifth Avenue and Fifty-sixth Street, reporters were breaking for the nearest telephones, while the three major wire services were hooked up to their offices from their own mobile radio vans parked on the sidewalk outside Van Cleef and Arpel's. Farther across the city, lights were going on in the windows of the newspaper offices as extra staffs on standby were called in for possible story briefings, and already the official news flash was going out to the major capitals of the world: ''NEW YORK POLICE IN NEGOTIATION WITH DOTSON. HOPES RUN HIGH.''

From the doorway of the command building, Al Groot was standing with a group of detectives watching Nick's short figure vanishing into the Park Tower lobby across the street as the last of the photo-flashlight hit the marquee.

''You know something?'' a detective said to Al. ''That guy has to be crazy.''

''Sure. He's beautiful, but he's crazy.'' Al's flecked brown eyes were clouded with worry as he looked across the street. Not even a fucking flak vest. ''He's liable to frisk me,'' Nick had told him, ''and he'd feel it. I don't want to give him any ideas.''

There was a certain amount of logic in that, Al realized. That was the problem with Nick: he wasn't the kind of crazy you could argue with. He thought of everything. The last thing he'd told Al was just before he'd gone down the steps to cross the street. ''Look, if I screw up, do what you can to explain to her that at least I had to try.''

On the fiftieth floor of the building where Al Groot was standing at street level, Chief of Detectives Warner was on the direct command line to Mobile HQ and its communications network. Dakers had briefed him.

''Get me Captain Mundy and Emergency Services.''

When Mundy came on the line, Warner told him: ''Valenti has just gone across to Park Tower. He's going to call us on the hotline as soon as he's contained the situation over there. If we get any indication he's in trouble, I want you to send Steziak in the moment we call you, so have him on immediate standby.''

The moment he hung up he was switched to Lieutenant Farley, the deputy chief of Emergency Services in the field, who was also in command of the FBI sharpshooters on the rooftops surrounding Park Tower. "While Valenti is over there in the penthouse, the only order for anyone to open fire has to come direct from me. Discretionary powers are suspended from this minute until further orders. Even if Dotson is clearly seen at a window and it's seen that he can be hit without harm to the girl, you're to hold your fire. Make certain the FBI contingent understands this; if they start wildcatting they could blow this whole thing away."

The last call he made was to his own deputy chief, who commanded the street and Park Tower posts.

"Steve, has Valenti gone through the lobby yet?"

"He's in the elevator, on his way up. I'm watching the indicator: he's nearing fifty-three right now."

"Okay. I'll be looking for instant reports from you and your unit, in the event you see or hear anything—anything at all. And get the three special-duty ambulances rolled right up to the entrance over there, with their doors to the curbside. Do what you can to keep the media people quiet, and tell Motor Patrol to restrict vehicle movement in the area to the absolute minimum, emergency only—we want no sirens, no lights. The word is, Steve, while that negotiator's in there, everybody freeze."

27

THE ELEVATOR STOPPED.

Looking upwards, Nick saw the indicator light showing fifty-three, and put his finger on the *Close Door* button and for a moment left it there, giving himself time to get control. He didn't know what he was going into, and he didn't want these doors to open automatically and leave him standing here exposed till he was ready. He'd do things in his own time, walk right out there into a hail of shots if that was the way it had to be, but in his own time.

There was nothing on the floor of the elevator. They'd searched everywhere for the security guard's gun down there and hadn't found it. There'd been the possibility that Dotson had taken it into the elevator with him and left it there. It wasn't here.

The daylight tubes above the decorative grille in the elevator ceiling were giving out a slight hum. There wasn't another sound. He felt isolated, and vulnerable, and scared.

Okay, Al. Maybe, just maybe, I shouldn't be here.

But I'm here.

He took his finger off the button, and after a second's delay the doors began sliding back. The world, the world he was going into, and maybe the last one he'd ever see, was revealed to him in the widening gap between the doors, and already, in the first few inches, he could see Joe Dotson there.

He was crouched against the wall beside a stack of explosive with his thumb on the detonator.

So this was the way it was going to be.

Joe wasn't moving. He was just crouched there like he was frozen. His face was pale and his mouth was slightly open and there was nothing in his eyes, nothing at all: they were glass.

It was quite a big stack: a bundle of eight or nine sticks in shiny paper with red warning labels. There'd be something like forty pounds there, yes, like Joe had told them earlier. Enough to blow this whole place apart. That was maybe what Joe was staring at with his glass eyes: the end of the world. But they were pointed at Nick.

Nick could smell the stuff: that familiar fireworks smell. It was what Daisy, the sniffer dog, had smelled when they'd led her up all those stairs and shown her the door at the top. The door was out of sight from the elevator, so Joe must have moved the stuff to where it was now, beside the richly paneled front door of the penthouse, to be ready for when he came.

Now he had come. In the slowing down of time, as his psyche became poised on the brink of extinction, he was able to think: But this guy was ready to talk, so what happened? Nothing had happened. It was just like Commissioner Dakers had said: *We're sure there's some explosive against the staircase door. And he's a psychopathic killer.*

And that's all there is to say. I didn't use my fucking brains, see, so I'm going to get my fucking brains blown all over the fucking city.

His face felt bloodless, tingling, as he stood looking at the man with the glass eyes.

Hi, Nick said, and wondered why there was no sound. Maybe it was because his mouth wouldn't move; his jaws were locked together, clenched like a skeleton's. His mouth was so dry that when he moved his tongue it was like licking sandpaper. He tried again.

"Hi." This time it made a sound, but the sweat began pouring out of him because he'd just scared himself to death. With that guy's thumb on the fucking button, it wouldn't take much to make him press it, just by nervous reflex. All you had to do was say hi.

The guy still didn't push his thumb down. Maybe it wasn't the right word. Maybe you had to say: Holy shit. And *boom*.

He could smell his own sweat as it soaked him. His breathing had changed to a light fluttering, right at the top of the lungs, like even his body knew that if he made too much of a commotion it would disturb the delicate balance of things. And *boom*.

But there was something coming into the glass eyes of the man crouched over all that shit. Some kind of life. It was encouraging.

"Hi, Joe."

Then the doors started closing automatically, and the shock went through his nerves, lifting the hairs on his scalp. He moved one hand to break the beam, and prayed. Joe didn't do anything. Nick kept staring into Joe's face, puzzled.

"Who are you?"

"I'm Nick." Or Napoleon, if you like, so long as you take your thumb off that fucking button. "Remember me? You said you wanted me to come on over here and talk."

He waited. There was a choice of the way he could phrase it: *You don't have to press that thing, Joe*. Or: *Careful you don't go and blow this place into the street*. But whichever way he put it, Joe might think, *Jesus, yes, I was going to press this thing, wasn't I?* And—right—*boom*.

"Talk?" Joe said.

"Sure. We were going to talk. You said you needed some help."

The gray eyes watched him out of the pale face, as the brain behind them began reasoning again. "Oh. That's right. You're Nick." He looked down at the bundle of explosives as if he'd forgotten it was there. Then he looked up at Nick again, his breath catching on something like a laugh. "I didn't mean—you know, this looks—I mean this isn't a very nice way to greet you. Is it?"

His thumb came off the detonator, and Nick stopped dying.

"I guess it's okay," Nick said. "Why not?"

Joe straightened up, and now he looked almost normal, like a man coming out of a sleep. "I don't trust the cops, see. I mean not always. I thought you might come up here with a gun to shoot me with, the minute you saw me."

"I told you, Joe. You can trust me. All the way." He slowly raised the sides of his open windbreaker away from his body. "Want to frisk me?"

"Uh? No. I trust you. You don't look like you've got a gun or anything. I'm sorry."

"You're welcome." There was something lying on the deep midnight-blue carpeting, to one side of the elevator, but he didn't want to look down at it in case it was something Joe didn't want him to see. With that stuff stacked against the wall, he was still walking on eggshells. "You going to ask me in, Joe?"

The gray eyes were watching him with some of the puzzlement lingering in them: he remembered who Nick was, now, but didn't seem quite sure why he'd come.

"Sure, you can come in."

Nick hesitated, then walked out of the elevator onto the deep pile carpeting, as Joe picked up the shoe and dropped it between the doors before they could close.

"Oh," Nick said, "that your shoe?"

"Right. We don't want people up here, do we?"

"Hell, no." They'd had the men from Otis down in the ground-floor lobby, testing all the electrical circuits, wasting their time.

"Go on in, Nick."

"Okay." When he pushed on the deep-paneled front door it swung open, and he went into the enormous gold room, sensing Joe coming behind him and getting the distinct impression he was being pushed into a trap. The lighting was low, and the brightest thing he saw was not here in the room at all: it was the sharp rim of the moon rising above the buildings to the east.

Tina wasn't here.

He heard the door shutting behind him, and the lock clicking home. When he half-turned, Joe was moving the two brass bolts at the top and bottom of the door.

"Keep everybody out, eh, Joe?"

"Right."

Nick waited for him, standing close to the big box ottoman and the heavy vase that were a little way inside the door; they'd heard about those, from Tina.

Tina.

"You all alone, Joe?"

Joe was standing still, just inside the door, waiting for him to move deeper into the room. He was keeping his distance, maybe still trying to think what had made him ask a cop in here. From the impressions Nick was getting—and he was getting them fairly fast, like a million a minute—Joe would have liked him out of here, but felt it might be impolite to tell him to go. How that tied in with a guy who'd apparently shot two men to death in this building a couple of nights ago, Nick wasn't sure; but he'd always trusted his impressions, learning over the years that they weren't often wrong.

"All alone?" Joe repeated. He sounded puzzled.

Then Nick saw the woman, a small figure in white standing against the fluted column of an archway on the far side of the room. Either he'd not seen her in the low lighting, or she'd just come in.

"Oh," he said, "hi."

She came toward them a little way, and stopped; but she was now close enough for him to recognize. He'd never seen her in real life, only her pictures in the magazines and sometimes in the papers and on television; she was smaller than he'd imagined, and very slim, standing straight and perfectly still in a white halter dress, a curl of dark hair over one shoulder. In the magazines and on the screen she always came across as a real pretty chick; but here in this room, this close and in three dimensions, she had the kind of looks—and he was getting his first glimpse into the mind of Joe Dotson—that could drive a guy crazy, if he didn't watch out.

"Good evening," she said clearly.

"I'm Nick Valenti," he said, and took a step toward her, but stopped as she made the slightest movement, a turn of her body away from him. This time the impression was sharp and immediate. This was as close as she wanted him, because of Joe. She'd told them on the phone: *He says he'll never let anyone take me away from him.* Right: he'd be jealous. Paranoiacally, psychopathically. Murderously. They'd left all that stuff outside, stacked against the wall in the lobby; but there was a whole lot more in here, stacked inside Joe Dotson's head and ready to blow if anybody made a wrong move, even said the wrong thing.

"I'm Tina St. Clair," she said formally. "It was nice of you to come."

"My pleasure." He caught the slight movement of her head; she was watching Joe now, somewhere behind him, maybe checking his reaction to what she'd just said.

Nick turned casually to look at him too. He was standing there as still as she was, his big hands hanging beside him, his eyes on Tina. The atmosphere in this place was vibrating with the kind of prestorm electricity that made small sounds carry, and the nerves throb. There were things, too, that Nick hadn't missed: the smashed panels of the huge gold mirror; blood spots on the carpeting; the two balloon glasses on a coffee table, not empty, maybe not touched; and blood streaks on Tina's arm. So much had happened in this room, in this ritzy but isolated apartment at the top of the city, in the past forty-eight hours; some of it they'd heard about on the hotline, but as he stood here getting the psychic and physical aura of this man and this woman, he could feel the anguish, and the passion, and the terror they'd been sharing with each other, shut in with it for hour after hour in the daytime and in the dark, in the sleepless quiet of the night and in the first light of morning. And now they were standing here with a stranger in the room, observing the niceties like nothing had happened, like nothing was going to happen.

Nick felt his eyes growing wet, as he'd felt before when he'd worked his way through to the center of things, the crux of a hostage situation, and understood again the loneliness and the helplessness that some people had to live with, and die of unless you could reach them soon. The first time he'd known this feeling was when he was just a little kid: there'd been a cat up a tree, too scared to climb higher and too scared to come down; and he'd known, as he fetched the ladder, that the thing was going to scratch his eyes out, if he didn't take care, while he was trying to get it down. What he'd learned was that if you let yourself get lonely enough, and helpless enough, the only thing you could finally do was was fight, with your back to the wall—and then *everyone* was your enemy. Everyone.

But Joe had at least let him in here. He'd at least let him fetch the ladder.

"You know something?" Nick said cheerfully. "I could use a drink. How about you?"

"I'm sorry," Tina said, and looked at Joe. "Will you—?"

"Sure. Drink."

As Joe went across to the bar, Nick moved to his left, toward the gold mirror, so that when Joe turned around he'd have his back to the windows facing east. The moon was a full crescent now, broken by the jagged line of the roofs. *I believe,* Dr. Schultz had told them, *that the full moon might have a degree of influence over him, yes. It could turn the scales, in a critical situation.*

I don't know how to handle this, Tina thought as Joe went across to the bar.

This man Nick looked so unimpressive. When he'd walked in, she thought he must be a transient who'd got in here by mistake: a short man with red eyes and stubble and unkempt hair and a crumpled blue windbreaker hanging open on him. Knowing as she did that he was a policeman, here to save her life, she should have felt the urge to run across to him and bury herself in his strong protective arms; but life didn't always turn out as you expected. All she had felt was a sense of letdown, of a sudden increase in hopelessness. He was only one man, and didn't even look like a police officer; and above all, he didn't seem to have a gun. Having come to know something of Joe Dotson, she knew it would take at least two or three men, big men, with heavy-looking guns, to save her.

Why hadn't this man brought a gun with him, and shot Joe dead as the elevator doors had opened? Joe had gone out there to meet him; it would have been easy.

But terrible. She didn't wish it had happened; she was

just surprised that this was the best the New York police force could do, when the place was meant to be surrounded.

"What'll you have?" Joe asked.

"Oh," Nick said, "bourbon. On the rocks."

"Coming up."

Tina heard the different tone in his voice; perhaps it was because he was talking to a man now, and about a drink: he was suddenly in a situation he understood.

"What are you having, Joe?"

"Think I'll pass."

Nick watched him for a moment as he found the bourbon and got the ice from the small paneled refrigerator. "Not going to join me?"

"No."

"How about the lady?" Nick asked him.

She shook her head. Nick moved again, a little closer to where she stood; maybe she had something to tell him; she seemed kind of numbed, which was understandable; but it didn't mean he might not be able to catch some kind of a signal from her, if she had any to give him.

Watching Joe pour the Kentucky over the ice, he made an assessment of his size, and weight, and strength. Five-eleven, two hundred pounds, and muscular: big hands, a strong neck, and quick on his feet when he moved, as he'd shown out there in the lobby. Nick had come here to talk. That was his job, and he'd practiced it and refined it till he was the chief police negotiator in this city, a model for training seminars, an expert: *the* expert. But he wasn't crazy. There was always the chance that the time would come when the talking would have to stop, and he'd have to save himself, and everyone else, in whatever way he could.

He'd only had to do it twice before. A while ago a seventeen-hour barricader had found a piece from somewhere and started firing it at Nick, and he'd just spun around and dived straight over the banisters and smashed through a door and finished up in a garbage dump. The other time he'd seen the guy start fiddling with the bomb and he'd gotten his ass out so fast that he was clear and in the street before the wall had blown out and the guy's hand had landed a foot in front of his face with a gold wedding ring on it. Both times, he'd gotten too close. *Never get too close,* he told the trainees at the seminars.

He was too close right now. In a closed trap. But this wasn't a barricade situation; there was a hostage involved; and when there was a hostage things were different: you had the option of moving right in where they were, or just leaving them to get killed. Watching Joe Dotson now, assessing him as an adversary, he didn't try to kid himself. This guy was stronger, and bigger: much bigger. Nick knew a few sweeps and throws in judo and aikido, but he'd never really trained; he wasn't good enough to subdue a guy this size and weight, without some luck. And if it came to a physical contest, Joe would go berserk; he'd be ten men, not one.

But it didn't have to come to that. He was here to talk, and Joe knew that. He trusted him.

"Do fine," he said, "that'll do fine, Joe." But it was a second or two before Joe stopped tipping the bottle; the glass was already half full and he'd spilled some: his hand wasn't steady. He put down the bourbon with a bang on the gold top of the bar, and forgot to put the cork back; for a moment he stood there looking at the dripping cut-glass tumbler like he didn't know what it was doing in his hand; then he lifted his head slowly and stared at his own face in the paneled mirror; and then he turned his head and looked at Nick; and Nick knew that already the time for talking had stopped.

*　　*　　*

"What do you want?" Joe asked.

"Me?" the man said. "Just the bourbon, I guess." He gave a quick laugh, his eyes flickering.

"Why did you come here?"

"Okay." The man turned away a little, putting his hands into his windbreaker. "I came to talk, remember?"

He was turning back to watch him now, giving him a very straight look that Joe didn't like. He didn't like being watched.

"To talk?" He could feel drips of something on his hand; he must have spilled the drink. He didn't want the drink. He put it down with a sharp sound.

"Right. I'm Nick. You said I should come over here. You said there was something wrong."

"Nick?" A sudden warm feeling came. He remembered Nick: they'd talked on the phone. He'd sounded like a nice guy. Maybe he could help him. "Sure. Right. Nick Valone."

"Valenti. Italian names," his quick laugh came again, "they all sound the same, don't they?"

He was beginning to sound far away, though he was still standing close.

"Nick Valenti. Right." He was beginning to tremble, and tried to stop; he always tried to stop, when it began; but he could never succeed.

"Hey, Joe. Don't I get my drink?"

"What? Sure. I'm sorry."

"That's okay."

He held the tumbler out to him, and he took it, bringing his hand out of the windbreaker and taking the glass, a smile on his small dark face. Nick was a nice guy; he knew about having a drink with someone; it was a friendly thing to do, very relaxing; nothing bad could happen when you were having a drink with someone.

But the trembling was getting bad, now, and all he

could see was the mirror at the far end of the room, near the front door.

"Thanks, Joe. Cheers."

He didn't say anything. It was a small mirror, by itself, not like these big panels, and the moon was in it, just the edge of it, the curved white edge. He felt its pull.

"Where's Tina?"

The man didn't answer, or look anywhere. "Joe," he said, "I'm here to help you."

"Where's—?" The pulling became tremendous and he turned around, so fast that he knocked against something on the bar and it went smashing into all the bottles; but it didn't matter because Tina was there, standing against the moon. He felt calmer now, because she was there. She would always be there.

"Tina?"

"I'm here, Joe," she said, like she knew it was important, saying it in the—in the kind of voice his—his mother used to use when—when she knew he wanted—wanted to feel everything was—was okay.

So long as you're okay, Joe.

"Sure I'm okay," he said.

"That's absolutely right." It was the man behind him. Nick. What was he doing behind him? "You're absolutely okay." He spun around, but Nick was just standing there with the drink in his hand. He was a very nice guy. "But you know something, Joe? You're holding out on me. And I know you trust me, so it can't be that. You trust me, don't you, Joe?"

"Sure. Right. I trust you."

But the trembling was getting very bad now. It was almost a shaking. It wasn't anything new. He'd felt it when he'd been on the—on the balcony with—with Mary and up on the top of—the top of that big high tower with—with Sandy, when she'd gone—

"That's all that matters," the man was saying, "that we trust each other. But you said something was wrong, remember? And that's why I came here, to help. So what's wrong, Joe? You can tell me."

He looked so small, standing there, like he was a long way off; and his voice was so quiet; there didn't seem to be any kind of—kind of contact; no way they could reach one another.

"Tina and I are going away," he said in a rush, like there was suddenly a need to hurry, before something happened. "But there's something wrong with me, Nick. Didn't I tell you? I have something wrong with me." He was shaking now, because the moon was pulling him from behind, and he knew if he turned around and saw it, he'd have to—

"That's absolutely right, Joe. Something wrong with you. But it's nothing we can't fix. That's why I'm here. You mean you don't kind of feel yourself?" He put the drink down on the bar and came towards him, walking slowly all the long way, but not getting any bigger.

"Help me, Nick. For Christ's sake help me."

His teeth were chattering and he felt very cold, and couldn't stop the shaking.

"Sure, Joe, I can help you."

He was right up close now, and a bit bigger. He was putting his arm around him, very gently, and looking up into his face. "I can help you, Joe."

"We're going away together." He shook himself free. "Tina and I are going away. That's why I wanted you here."

"Okay. Like, to go with you? Look after things?"

"No." Shuddering, shuddering, and cold, icy cold. "No. When we go away, you have to be here. Like a priest."

"You want me to fetch a priest here, Joe?"

"No. You're here, now." He looked away from the man and saw the bronze ornament, the woman with the big stomach and the small head. Everything was shaking now, the whole room, shaking and turning as he turned around and said, "Tina."

"I'm here, Joe."

"Are you ready?"

"Yes," she said, in that soft and kindly voice he hadn't heard since—since such a long—long time ago, when he was only—

Someone get a priest, his father was calling, but that was somewhere else, and another time. He picked up the ornament and caught Tina's hand.

"Joe, don't!" someone called as he swung the ornament. It hit the glass like a bomb going off and he pulled her with him and heard her screaming; then she was tugged away from him but he seemed to find her hand again and they jumped, falling at first, then rising as a dark wind caught them and carried them higher and higher across the street and the buildings and the rooftops of the city towards the enormous moon, away and away into the farthest reaches of the night, where no one would ever find them.

The knot of journalists turned their faces upwards as the noise came faintly from the top of the building, a kind of explosive pop; then something came plummeting into the lighted street and smashed onto the roof of a police car, rocking it on its springs.

Glass fragments began falling, glittering in the flat white light of the photo floods as the crews swung their cameras; then the man's figure came into view, the arms spread out as if it were flying. It was small at first, and looked lonely against the tall perspective of the building; for a while it seemed, as it turned slowly in the air, that it was going to fall among the journalists, and some of them started running; but it hit the ground in the deserted area between the police cordons, with nobody near.

As they came through the lobby, Nick was still holding on to Tina's arm; on their way down in the elevator she'd leaned on him for support a couple of times, and he'd been ready for her to pass out; her face was still bloodless, and she hadn't spoken since they'd seen Dotson go through the window.

Walking beside him below the marquee and into the glare of the lights, she said: "I'm all right now."

He kept hold of her arm. "It's been a shock," he told her. "We don't want you to fold up, just when—"

"I'd rather walk on my own."

"Anything you say."

Crossing the open space between the cordons, she saw a lot of policemen and some men in white coats, where an ambulance was backing up. They were all standing around something on the ground. She turned to the man beside her.

"Is that Joe, over there?"

"I guess."

She took a step towards the group of men, but Nick touched her arm. "I can see your father waiting for you, Tina. Look. Your mother's there too."

She turned and looked across the street, and saw them coming down the steps of the building opposite, hurrying towards her.

As she went to meet them, Nick let her go, hearing the media people calling questions to him from behind the cordons. He didn't answer, but went on alone, his hands tucked into his windbreaker and his head down, heavy with sleep.

About the Author

Elleston Trevor is the author of many extremely successful war and suspense novels, including *The Flight of the Phoenix*, now a film classic, and most recently *The Damocles Sword*. Under his pseudonym Adam Hall he is the creator of Quiller, and is recognized as one of today's foremost espionage writers. He has recently published the tenth Quiller story, *The Peking Target*; each of its forerunners has been a world-wide bestseller.

An Englishman, Mr. Trevor lived for many years in the South of France, and now makes his home in the Arizona desert.

The Best in Fiction from SIGNET

More Bestsellers from SIGNET

Buy them at your local

bookstore or use coupon

on next page for ordering.

Exciting Reading from SIGNET